Totally Bound Publishing books by Beck Robertson:

Blood Hunger

BLOOD HUNGER

BECK ROBERTSON

Blood Hunger
ISBN # 978-1-78430-990-9
©Copyright Beck Robertson 2016
Cover Art by Posh Gosh ©Copyright January 2016
Interior text design by Claire Siemaszkiewicz
Totally Bound Publishing

Published in 2016 by Totally Bound Publishing, Newland House, The Point, Weaver Road, Lincoln, LN6 3QN, United Kingdom.

Totally Bound Publishing is a subsidiary of Totally Entwined Group Limited.

BLOOD HUNGER

Dedication

To my darling husband. Thank you for your eternal love and support.

Chapter One

Lola was hungry for fresh blood tonight. Pushing her way through the shadowy darkness of the club – the only light the occasional interjection from the neon strobes pulsing overhead – she made her way through the mass of seething bodies on the dance floor and headed for the bar.

"Hey, Lola, you want your usual?"

Max, the handsome bartender, grinned at her as she approached, and she nodded, flashing him a brief smile before turning around to scan the faces looming out from the semidarkness of the club. Club Vain was stuffed to the rafters tonight, the guest DJ proving popular with the regular crowd, which was good news for her at least – plenty of fresh meat to pick from. Lola licked her lips hungrily as she looked around.

"Scanning for fresh victims, eh?" Max smirked as he noticed her eagerly eyeing the bodies writhing and grinding against one another on the packed dance floor.

"Eh, maybe," she replied, shrugging. "If the right one takes my fancy, that is."

"Just because you're a vampire doesn't mean a girl can't be selective, right?" Max pushed her Bloody Mary toward her. She took it, sipping gratefully before tossing him a note.

"Mmhmm, you know it," she said, taking another big sip of the spicy drink Max knew was her signature beverage. The irony of her drink choice didn't escape her, but hot damn, Max sure knew how to mix a great Bloody Mary.

"Your change, Ms. Devereaux," he said, putting on the mock English butler voice she knew he loved to use.

"Consider it a tip, handsome." She grinned, turning around again to face the dance floor. Max was gay but she still enjoyed the flirty banter the two of them shared. They'd hit it off ever since she'd met the dark-haired vamp on his very first day tending the bar at Vain, and they'd been fast friends ever since.

Lola didn't have too many real friends in little old Burley Falls, that was for sure. Even though the small town had more than its fair share of sanguinarians, Max was one of the only bloodsuckers she'd found that she could actually tolerate.

As for Club Vain… Well, it was a veritable stomping ground for vampires looking for new prey, unbeknownst to the blissfully ignorant clubbers flocking there for the music, a drink or three and perhaps the chance to go home with someone who piqued their interest.

Her attention turned back to the bodies on the dance floor as her eyes made a quick appraisement. The hot, brooding-looking guy to her right was *definitely* a vampire, which was a pity, since she could picture raking her nails down those biceps. But even if she hadn't been looking to feed, she didn't fuck vampires, no matter how hot they were. It was a hard and fast rule of hers.

Yeah, he was a vamp, and so, she guessed, were the two dark-haired girls lurking at the end of the bar, observing everyone who walked past. She'd wager they were looking to feed tonight too.

She watched as a willowy blonde girl stumbled into her line of vision, laughing and tripping over her cream Manolos as she pulled an attractive, muscled-up blond guy by the hand behind her. The pair of them looked like Barbie and Ken. Trailing the pair was a handsome, athletic dark-haired dude and two other women, a redhead and a rather voluptuous-looking brunette, whose clothing seemed to defy gravity in its superhuman efforts to rein in her more than ample curves.

Lola's eyes quickly dismissed the blond guy and his female partner. They were far too glossy-looking to make a truly interesting feed – or a memorable lay. She preferred her targets to have a little more mystery. It was just more fun that way. Speaking of mystery, you could discount the brunette girl. *She* clearly had absolutely no secrets left to hide, and if there were any, Lola didn't want to know what they were. But the dark-haired guy? Now *he* could be interesting. *I wouldn't mind grinding on his –*

Just then, he turned around, interrupting her train of thought as she caught a glimpse of his chiseled face. Her breath snagged in her throat temporarily, as her brain registered his darkly handsome features. He was seriously attractive, *and* he had that intense look about him she really dug in a guy to boot.

And as for those biceps? *Whoa.* Boy, they sure would make real nice handles when she was riding the hell out of him back at her apartment later. Lola licked her lips again as her eyes drank him in predatorily. *Oh yes, he will do. He will do very nicely.* Now all she had to do was get Ms. No Clothes to back the hell off him. She'd noticed the girl's stare of hungry longing, and she recognized the naked lust in the sly glances the brunette kept shooting him. So little Ms. No Clothes wanted him too, did she?

She'd wager the girl's interest wasn't for the same reasons as her own—at least not all of them anyway. After all, a vamp always had to have a little fun, and if you picked 'em right, it was far too tempting not to have a little play with the prey before you sucked 'em dry, so to speak.

Draining her glass, Lola slid it back across the bar to Max, who caught it, raising his eyebrow at her.

"Found someone already—" he started, but she was off before he could finish the sentence, striding out on to the dance floor confidently. Sashaying through the crowd, she was well aware of the admiring glances she received—her spike-heeled stiletto boots, black metallic corset and tight black latex pants giving off a slight dominatrix vibe, not that she minded looking like she liked to take charge one little bit. Being in control of hot guys in the bedroom suited her just fine.

The music pulsed through the floor as she started to dance, keeping Mr. Handsome firmly in her line of sight. Grinding her body, she moved strategically so she was almost dancing next to him, but he still seemed frustratingly oblivious to her presence. Ms. No Clothes appeared to be doing a good job of distracting him with her rather obvious charms. *Not for long though.* Moving closer, Lola jostled him deliberately with her elbow, forcing him to spill some of the contents of the beer bottle he was clutching down the front of his white T-shirt.

"Oh God, I'm sorry," she gasped, straining her voice as she leaned into him, in order to be heard over the heady thump of the club's bassy music. She caught the scent of him. *Damn, the boy smells so good.* She needed to have that lean, toned body between her thighs — that perfectly chiseled face bending to pleasure her. Desire flared in her stomach as she flashed him a smile, *the* smile that no man she'd met yet had ever been able to resist.

"Hey, that's okay." He smiled back, catching her by the arm to reassure her as he flicked the droplets of beer off his shirt with the hand holding the now-nearly-empty beer bottle.

His brown eyes twinkled with obvious interest, moving from her face to run appreciatively down over her body then back up again. He obviously liked what he saw because his stare seemed to linger just a little longer than necessary. Still smiling, she made as if to turn away, mentally counting in her head — *one, two* —

"Hey, don't go."

Result. Guys, they were all so predictable. Turning back around to face him, she fixed him with a quizzical look. He fumbled, searching for something to say, but seeming to fail to find the right words.

"It's just… I wondered if you'd like a drink?"

She grinned, allowing her eyes to flick over his muscular torso, emphasized by the wetness of the spillage on his shirt. *Oh, I'll make him wet all right. Just wait until I get him alone.* She noticed he had a slight drawl to his accent — Texan, if she had to guess. *Damn, can this guy really get any hotter?*

"Shouldn't it be me doing the offering, since I was the one who made you spill your drink?" She arched a perfectly groomed eyebrow.

"Uh, well, I guess, I mean...um... Well, but you're a lady an' all..." He stopped, noticing her mocking expression.

Mmm... She loved a shy guy. They were *always* the best in bed. "A lady? What's that supposed to mean?"

He looked embarrassed. "Hey, I didn't mean anything by it. Don't take it the wrong way. I just don't usually get too many strange women offering to buy me drinks, least not in here — especially ones who look as good as you."

She tried to suppress a grin at his words. He stood there, fidgeting with the top of his beer bottle, looking more than a little uncomfortable, which only made him seem all the more endearing.

"What are you laughing at?" He looked at her, confused.

"*Strange* women?" Even in the semidarkness of the club, she could tell he was flushing a bright, beet red.

"That came out wrong, I never meant *you* were strange. It wasn't —"

"Hey, relax. It's okay," she said, smiling, stopping him midsentence as she placed her palm on *that* chest. She'd put him out of his misery now. He was far too sweet to torture — for the moment, at least. Who knew what she might do to that perfectly constructed, athletic body later?

"I find your chivalry rather charming, actually. Most of the guys in here could probably use a lesson or two in manners from you." She tapped his chest with a fingernail playfully, enjoying his obvious arousal at her proximity.

"Huh? Umm, why's that?" His handsome features scrunched up into that adorable confused expression.

"Oh, just most of them expect to get a girl to go home with them without spending a dime or bothering to get to know her. Then when they get her there, she gets a few minutes of sweaty huffing before they roll off and go to sleep. But somehow I think *you'd* be different." She placed a hand on his biceps predatorily, squeezing ever so slightly. *My God, the boy is solid.* This was shaping up to be one interesting evening.

"Uh...I dunno what to say," he said, looking completely embarrassed.

"Then don't say anything. You don't need to. You're pretty enough just to stand there, looking hot."

"Wow, you're so..."

"Forward?" She grinned.

"Uh, well, I guess that's one way of putting it."

"Yeah, I know. Right? All my friends say that. But *I* say, you gotta grab what you want, right?" She fixed her violet gaze on his big brown puppy dog eyes, looking at him with a hungry stare and licking her glossy lips. Moving closer, she gave his biceps another squeeze before blatantly letting her gaze fall to his crotch bulge.

"Hah, yeah, I guess," he said, biting down on his lower lip as he eyed her. By the bulge in his pants, she could tell he was aroused and by the look of things, he wasn't going to disappoint her once she had him naked.

But he really wasn't sure what to make of her, was he? She was probably the first girl who had ever come on to him like that and she might well be the last. He looked so clean cut and athletic. All he was probably used to was prissy prom queens and preppy little madams. Well, he was about to be in for quite the shock. Licking her lips again, she ran her fingertips across the front of his tight, white T-shirt, enjoying the feel of his solidly masculine chest beneath the pressure of her palm.

"And in answer to your question," she purred, leaning in to whisper in his ear, "the answer is yes."

"Umm…what question?" He furrowed his brow in bemusement.

"You asked if you could buy me a drink?"

"Ah yeah, that."

"Mmmhmm, that. So you wanna take me to the bar or you gonna leave a girl helpless on the dance floor in need of refreshment?" Grinning, he shook his head, looking amused as he turned to make his way to the bar, the look on his face telling her the very last thing he considered her to be was helpless.

At the bar, Max shot her a knowing look as she stood by her latest catch, waiting to be served.

"And what can I do for you two?" Max looked at Mr. Handsome pointedly then back at Lola again, raising an eyebrow. She tried to suppress the Cheshire Cat grin rapidly creeping over her face. The expression Max wore was one of obvious envy at her choice of arm candy tonight.

"Uh, so what are you drinking?" Her new love interest turned to her inquiringly.

"I'll have a Bloody—"

Max interjected, stopping her midflow. "Lola, babe, I think you should try my new cocktail. It's inspired by you, actually."

"Oh yeah? What's it called?"

"The Man-eater," Max said, grinning at her with satisfaction.

She couldn't help but smirk in return. The title *was* pretty apt. She was legendary when she set her sights on a guy she liked the look of, which was fairly frequently. And what Lola wanted, Lola always got—without exception.

With her strikingly pale complexion, large violet eyes, cheekbones that could cut glass, and generous, sensual mouth, not to mention her knock 'em dead curves, no sane heterosexual guy stood a chance. This one would be no different.

"All right then, I'll try it, but only if *you* try it too," she said, turning to look at her conquest.

"Me? I kinda don't really drink cocktails, though…" He sounded unsure, like he wanted to say no but didn't want to refuse her.

She grinned. "No? Don't like the taste of a man eater, huh?"

"Haha. Oh my God, you're too much. Is she like this all the damn time?" He looked at Max for confirmation.

Max nodded, grinning broadly. "All the damn time."

"Yep." She grinned. "Better get used to it. So ya gonna taste me, stud?" Extending her tongue, she leaned in to lick the tip of his earlobe ever so lightly. He shivered as though she'd just electrocuted him. *Mmm, he tastes good.* She couldn't wait to ride the hell out of this one then drain him real slow.

"Hot damn, that felt kinda nice and weird at the same time," he said, rubbing where her tongue had been mere moments before.

"Oh, that's definitely a good description of Lola," Max said, laughing, "kinda nice and weird at the same time. Hmmm, come to think of it, maybe I should make *that* a cocktail—Nice and Weird. It has a ring to it. Dontcha think?"

"Hah. Well, we'll leave you to drink the nice and weird, and *we'll* take two Man-eaters," she said, smirking, not giving her handsome stranger another chance to refuse. Max grinned, turning away to mix their drinks as she focused her attention back to her lust interest for the night. Focusing on him certainly wasn't hard. The boy was damn attractive—those arms, those eyes, that chest. A girl had to stop her thoughts from running away or he'd be tied up on her bed before she knew it. Not that she had any intention of restraining herself when it came to this one, although when it came to restraining him? Well, that might be a different story.

"So you're Lola?" he said, smiling. "I'm Dillon, by the way," he added, extending his hand to her. She flicked a quick glance downward at the proffered hand. *Mmmm, big and strong, and nice, thick fingers, hopefully a good portent of things to come hopefully*

"Yep, Lola, that's little ole me," she said, shrugging casually and grinning as she squeezed his hand.

"A sexy name for a sexy gal." He grinned back at her. Rolling her eyes, she shook her head at him.

"Hey, what did I say?"

"You know what? If you weren't so damn attractive, I might just have to call you out as a giant cheeseball for making that comment."

"I was just being honest." He shrugged, holding his palms up in a gesture of mock surrender. "Can't blame a guy for appreciating a beautiful woman, can you?"

"You have to admit that *was* a little corny," she said, digging him in the ribs.

"Maybe just a little bit corny," he said, holding his thumb and forefinger close together.

"Hope that wasn't some kind of preview of what you're smuggling in your pants," she joked as Max pushed two tall glasses containing a lethal-looking green liquid at them.

"*Those* are our drinks?" She eyed the glasses skeptically. They looked like nothing anyone would want to imbibe, the liquid in them resembling murky pond water. Max pulled a face, pretending to be offended.

"Hey, don't knock it. That little baby is my greatest artistic creation yet. And I used almost a quart of Absinthe in there, to boot," he said, winking as she shook her head. Dubiously she accepted the concoction and sucked on the neon-yellow straw sticking out of the pond weed–colored mixture.

She started slightly as the liquid hit the back of her throat. It was a strange taste, potent with a sweetly sour twist, but it wasn't entirely unpleasant. She could taste the absinthe but there was something else familiar she couldn't quite place as well.

Dillon took a hefty slurp from his glass, and she noticed with amusement how he'd purposefully taken his straw out of the glass and laid it on the countertop first. *Mmmm, Southern boys. You gotta love all that raw-ass, old school masculinity.*

"Mmm, Max, this isn't actually that bad, you know? What else is in this thing?"

"Pleases Queen Lola, does it? Sorry. I can't tell you all my secret ingredients. How am I ever gonna be a legendary bartender if I give all my best mixes away?"

"Pfff, I'll just guess it anyway," she said, waving him away with a flick of her slender wrist, the silver-studded bracelets she wore winking under the pulsing club lights.

"It's sorta sweet. Kinda reminds me of my ma's cooking." Dillon cut in, his brown eyes creasing up as if he were trying to remember something. Out of the corner of her eye, she caught Max eyeing up Dillon's biceps as Dillon raised his arm to take another slug of the mystery concoction. *Oh, hands off, sister. This one's all mine.*

"Hrrm, it's kinda like baked gingerbread," she said, screwing up her face as she took another sip.

"Close," Max said cryptically, eyeing them both with a pleased expression, the sort a parent would sport when watching a child take their first tentative steps.

"Cinnamon?" Dillon looked at Max questioningly.

"Mmhmm." Max nodded, looking slightly dazed and quite unable to come back with a suitably sarcastic quip as Dillon's big brown puppy eyes fixated on him. That was most unlike him. He was usually as acerbic as paint thinner, unless there was a hot guy involved, of course, then he was as sweet as vanilla ice—

That was it. It had to be.

"Vanilla," she announced triumphantly, looking at Max for assent. "It's vanilla and cinnamon."

"Duh." Max pulled a face, chucking his towel at her. Swerving, she caught it, the material still slightly damp from the glasses it had been used to dry.

"Bet you can't guess what else though?" Max grinned as he turned away, busying himself tidying glasses behind the bar.

"Ugh." She tossed the towel at his back, exasperated. "Come on, Dillon," she added, threading her arm through his. "Let's leave Max to washing his glasses and dreaming of going home with a guy as hot as you, while *I* actually do," she said, deliberately within earshot of Max.

"Bitch," she heard Max mutter under his breath as she grinned to herself. It was always like this between them. Their playful back and forth-ing had been going on since she'd met him.

The strobe lights blinked around them as they pushed their way through the crush of Vain's finest Friday night crowd. The irony of the club's name didn't escape her. A fair few of the regulars that frequented the place were definitely a little on the self-obsessed side. And other's indulgences ran darker still.

Looking around her, she noted several familiar faces as they threaded their way through the dance floor. There was Cynthia, lurking at the side, her sharp blue hunter's eyes fixated on a slender blonde girl with pigtails, who seemed quite unaware of the female vamp's gaze as she danced blissfully to the trance beat pumping through the club's sound system.

And there over to her left was Brandon, his dark eyes brooding as he pensively scanned the gathered crowd for potential. He was picky, though, hence why he usually always sported that haunted, slightly underfed look. It wasn't entirely unattractive admittedly, but she preferred her men a little more athletic looking, like the sweet piece of candy she'd managed to hook tonight.

Speaking of underfed, though, her own thirst definitely needed tending to. She'd not been up to par for several days now. It had been way too long since she'd fed, and she was feeling decidedly the worse for wear. The curse may have made her an immortal, but it sure was a bitch if you didn't feed it regularly.

Thankfully though, she'd landed on her feet with this one. Now all she had to do was maneuver them both out of here and back to her apartment for a hot round or two before a sweet blood dessert, which shouldn't be too hard from the appreciative way Dillon kept eyeing her.

"Where are we going?" He turned to look at her as he asked the question, a puzzled expression on his handsome face, and she grinned to herself. By the time she'd finished with him, he'd be wondering if it was all a dream, and *she'd* be nicely satisfied — and in more than one way, as well. At least, she hoped things would pan out that way.

"Back to mine," she whispered, leaning in and nibbling the underside of his earlobe, enjoying how he seemed to shiver as soon as her lips touched his flesh. "There *might* be more of that once we get home," she said, winking at him.

"Jeez, you're one hell of a woman, Lola," he groaned, looking decidedly flustered, the bulge in his pants growing and stretching out the fabric.

Boy, she couldn't wait to get *that* sweet little package unwrapped. Well, not so little, judging by the look of it. She moved to run her fingers over the thick cord of his biceps —

"Hey, slut." The familiar cocky, arrogant tone was followed by a hand crudely grabbing her ass and internally, she cringed.

Drago. Great, that's all I need. Wheeling around, she rolled her eyes as she met the gaze of the attractive but haughty-looking blond guy regarding her with a supercilious stare. His arrogance was palpable, but then Drago was used to women flinging themselves at him, an inevitable side effect of being ridiculously good looking, rich and well connected.

Personally she'd never really found him attractive, though it was his attitude, not his looks, that was the main turn off. And that fact seemed to eat away at Drago — the knowledge his good looks, privilege and power couldn't win him the one thing he desired the most, the toy he hadn't played with yet. Her.

Yep, Drago was a spoiled brat of the first order, but that wasn't the worst thing about him. Drago was a vamp and he had a nasty streak in him that gave her the heebie-jeebies whenever she thought about it. That might sound a bit rich coming from a fellow vampire, but then Drago's dark side went a lot deeper than most vamps, herself included. He preyed on people just for the hell of it, even when he didn't need to feed. She knew he got off on the power trip.

"Hey, Drago," she said, raising her eyebrows as she pursed her lips together warily.

"Nice outfit. Looking good, Miss Devereaux," he said, grinning like a cat and raking his eyes over her predatorily.

"Thanks. I just threw this on before I came out," she said, gesturing down to herself and shrugging.

"So who's your new boy toy?" Drago's lip curled slightly, as if he found something amusing.

"Uh, this is Dillon. Dillon, meet Drago," she said, smiling tightly at Dillon. God, she hoped Drago wasn't going to start trouble tonight. Everything had been going well so far.

"Pleased to meet ya, buddy," Dillon drawled, extending his palm enthusiastically.

Drago arched his eyebrow but didn't take the offered hand. "A cowboy? Really, Lola? I thought you might have outgrown your little hick fetish after that last disaster. What was his name? Brad? Chad? Chip? I lose count. There's been so many."

"Drago, leave it alone," she said, her tone warning.

A cruel smile curved over Drago's icy good looks. "Of course, this one's certainly a fine specimen of man," he said, smirking.

"Sorry, buddy, I don't swing that way," Dillon muttered darkly. He obviously wasn't warming to Drago. Lola tried to stifle a giggle.

"Yeah, he's a cutie," she said, smiling at Dillon and hoping to diffuse the situation.

"Ah, young love. How *touching*. I must say I'm a bit worried for him, though," Drago sneered, his tone making it sound as if Dillon were a pet or a piece of furniture.

"Yeah, why's that?" Internally she braced herself for whatever acid-tongued remark Drago would see fit to dish out. She knew there would be one. He never could stand to see anyone happy, especially if that 'anyone' had previously turned him down.

"Oh, I thought that would have been obvious. You get around a bit, don't you?" Drago flashed a sly look at Dillon, whose face had taken on a most peculiar expression. From where Lola was standing, he looked fit to explode.

"She's a bit of a tramp," Drago added, leaning in and winking at Dillon conspiratorially, as if he'd just imparted an incredible piece of information. "Though I hear she's a good fuc—"

Dillon's fist caught him hard on the underside of Drago's chiseled jaw and he reeled backward, clutching his chin, his eyes agape in disbelief.

"You hit me," he gasped, staring from Dillon to her then back again, looking quite unable to believe what had just occurred.

"I don't like no one talking about a lady that way," Dillon said, shaking his head as he glared at a stunned Drago.

Mentally she cheered. Drago'd had *that* coming for a long, long, time but no one had yet had the guts to put him in his place. Her face ached to break into a huge grin but she knew Drago would never forgive her if she did.

Since she'd been cursed, there wasn't much she feared. Knowing you were immortal tended to boost your confidence that way, but Drago was a different story. After all, he was a vampire too, and an incredibly influential one at that. And even if he wasn't immortal, he was way too well connected in Burley Falls to risk getting on his bad side. His father was the Chief Commissioner of the local police force and the Graythorne family was the oldest and wealthiest family in the whole of the Falls—and that was just for starters. She shuddered as she thought about the sinister entourage of desperate-to-please lackeys that Drago kept around him.

"Come on, Dillon. Let's get out of here," she said, grabbing him by the arm and trying to tear him away before Drago said something that earned him another swipe. Somehow she didn't fear for Dillon's safety if it came down to a fist fight—not that fighting was really Drago's style. He much preferred sniping and backstabbing. He didn't really like to get his privileged hands soiled, not unless he knew for sure his victim couldn't fight back. No, Drago had plenty of cronies who were only too happy to do his dirty work for him.

"Yeah, let's blow this joint," Dillon muttered, turning to go. As they walked toward the exit, she heard Drago's nasal tones behind them, rising shrilly above the thumping bass.

"You and your boy toy are going to regret this little exchange," Drago threatened, his voice a reedy whine.

"Keep walking and just ignore him," she whispered, feeling Dillon's body tense up, readying to wheel back around and confront Drago. Tracing a finger along his taut jawline, she allowed her fingertip to creep upward over his lips as she leaned in to plant a kiss lightly on the side of his face.

"My hero," she whispered, enjoying the immediate effect she had on him as his body seemed to relax again.

"Now, let's get you home and see what else you're made of," she added, grinning as they strode arm in arm toward the club's exit.

Chapter Two

She lived just a few blocks from the club, so getting home was never an issue. Kind of made it easier to feed too. A girl could just leave, visit Vain, select a tasty looking victim and bring him back to have a little fun — no worries, no guilt. Well, maybe a *little* guilt, but she had learned to live with that by now. Okay, maybe a lot of guilt sometimes, especially when she had to drain them so much they could barely walk. She tried not to — she really did — but when the hunger took over…

It hadn't always been this way, but then she hadn't always been a vamp. She'd been mortal too once, like Dillon, but that had all seemed a long time ago now — another life almost. Sometimes, on lonely nights, she longed for the days before the curse, before the need to feed, before the need to keep to the shadows lest her skin burn and her body get sick.

She pushed the memory of that existence out of her mind. *Best not to think of that life. Best to forget who you were back then. No point dwelling on the past. This is who you are now.*

Slipping her key into the lock, she turned it, letting them both into the ground-floor apartment then she reached up to flick on the light switch to illuminate the roomy hallway.

"Hey, nice place," Dillon said, blinking and rubbing his eyes as he took in his new surroundings.

"Yeah, it's not bad, I guess," she said, shrugging. "Come on through to the lounge. I'll make you a drink."

Willingly he allowed her to lead him across the small hallway into the spacious and minimally decorated monochromatic lounge. She could feel his eyes on her ass as she walked, and she purposefully added a swing to her step to give him a little extra something to look at. Not that he was going to have any problems getting hot for her, but it definitely wouldn't hurt to turn it up a little. She didn't want to take any chances, and something about this guy made her body need to know what it felt like to have him in her — on her — now.

And aside from the pure carnal desire coursing through her that told her she just had to ride this hot piece of man into the cushions on her leather sofa until they were both totally satiated, keeping him in a state of blind lust could only benefit her other reason for bringing him back here. That way he wouldn't see *it* coming.

"Sit down there," she said, gesturing to the black leather sofa lining the back wall of the large, white-painted living room. Crossing the room, she made her way over to the curved black marble bar standing in front of the serving hatch that opened out onto the kitchen area.

"Whoa, real nice place," Dillon exclaimed, sinking into the sofa, his muscular thighs straining the fabric of his denims. God, she really couldn't wait to get him out of those jeans and run her hands over *those* powerhouses.

"What do you want? I can mix you up a Bloody Mary or fix you a Scotch and soda—or I've got vodka and mixers, brandy, even absinthe if you want some." She tapped her sharp black-painted fingernails on the smooth countertop as she awaited his response.

"Uh, can I just have a beer?"

"Yeah, I can get you a beer. Wait there. It's in the fridge in the kitchen."

Turning, she walked into the little kitchen that ran off the main living area, the chrome and glass countertops gleaming as she flicked on the neon strip light. A beer. Somehow she found his choice of beverage oddly endearing, though she didn't know quite why. But she quite liked the image of him slugging from a beer bottle, cowboy hat on his head, shirtless, with just tight denims and cowboy boots on. Wow, way to go stereotype. Mentally she checked herself. *Just because he's got the cutest ever Texas accent, doesn't mean he's got corn growing out his ass.*

"Bud okay?" she called over her shoulder, rummaging through the icebox.

"Uh, yeah. Whatever you've got is fine," he yelled back.

Reentering the lounge, she passed him the beer bottle, along with the bottle opener she'd grabbed from the rack on the wall in the kitchen. He cracked open the bottle, taking a hefty slug.

"Aren't ya gonna fix yourself a drink too?" He looked up at her curiously when he'd finished drinking, his lips glistening slightly from the beer. She felt a sudden overwhelming urge to kiss that mouth hard.

"Nah, I had enough at Vain," she said, crossing her hands behind her back as she lied.

She'd actually only had two drinks the whole time she'd been at the club, but she preferred to be sharp when she needed to feed, though she could certainly do with a drink. Though she was definitely anticipating the appetizer now that she had him sitting there on her sofa. She felt like she was going to have to psych herself up in order to sink her teeth into his cute neck.

"Let me put some music on. *You* get comfortable," she said, turning away from him again and crossing over to the digital radio sitting in the pristine black shelving that lined one side of the room from ceiling to floor. As she flicked the radio on, Aerosmith filled the air with a burst of sudden noise, and she smiled to herself, unable to keep from tapping her feet. She'd always been a classic rock girl, ever since she was old enough to remember her dad blasting it out of the stereo that had been his pride and joy. She felt a sudden momentary pang in her stomach as she remembered her father's ruggedly handsome face.

Both he and her mother were long dead now, gone in the fire that had swept through the Devereaux family home. The fire that had taken her little brother Damon too, while all of them slept — oblivious. That was the night she'd been turned into a vampire.

And if she hadn't been pulled out of the burning building by Lyra, she too would have gone up in the inferno that had claimed the rest of her family's lives. Sometimes she thought that maybe it would have been better if she *had* died that night. It would certainly have been better for Dillon if she had.

"Hey, I love this kinda music too," he said, interrupting her thoughts. He grinned at her as he bobbed his head to the beat. "My dad used to play this stuff all the damn time."

"Mine too," she said, smiling back at him and wondering if she could get away with telling him to just get naked right then and there. Jesus, he was handsome. Her gaze wandered slyly to the big bulge in his jeans and she found herself licking her lips automatically.

"Course my pa's dead now. Died two years ago of a heart attack. Raised me single-handed after my momma died of cancer when I was ten."

His big brown eyes looked so genuinely sad as he looked at her that it made her momentarily forget the unspeakably filthy visions she'd been harboring. Poor guy. Her heart went out to him. She could certainly sympathize with his situation.

"I'm sorry. I know that must be tough on you. Both my parents are dead too," she said, crossing the room to sit down beside him on the sofa and placing her hand on his arm. The feel of his solid bod underneath her palm quickly made her thoughts turn X-rated again. Maybe Aerosmith hadn't been such a good idea after all? She was supposed to be getting him hard, not making him feel melancholy.

"Yeah, well, bad stuff happens, I guess," he muttered, shaking his head as he stared at the opposite wall.

"Mmmhmm, but good stuff can happen too, you know." She sidled closer to him, allowing her leg to press against his. *Who are you kidding? Good stuff? He's about to get bitten by a vampire. How is that in any way going to be classed as a good experience?* But maybe she could at least give him the fuck of his life first. She ran her hand over his muscular thigh, allowing her fingertips to briefly brush his crotch.

"Uh...uhh," he stammered, clearly getting aroused by what she was doing.

"Ssssh," she said, silencing him by pressing her finger to his lips, "just lay back and enjoy it." She pushed him firmly back against the sofa with one hand as she straddled his lap.

"Wha…? Mmmm…"

He didn't protest as her mouth met his and she felt his strong hands on her back, pulling her in as she ground herself hungrily against him. God, she was so damn hot for him. Her panties were soaked already and neither of them had even gotten out of their clothes yet.

"See? Not so bad, is it?" Smiling, she looked down into those deep brown eyes as she continued to circle her hips, gripping him with her thighs.

"God, you're a sexy woman, Lola," he groaned, plainly struggling with his arousal as his cock strained against the denim of his jeans.

Oh, he was definitely not going to be a disappointment in that department. Fuck, she wanted to feel that thing thrusting up inside her already.

"Don't fight it," she whispered, leaning in to nibble his ear. "It's better that way." Her lips moved down to his neck, alternating light kisses with little nibbles. All she had to do was puncture that tender flesh and voila, her snack for the night would be fixed. But first she was going to ride the hell out of the big, throbbing cock she could feel nudging up against her.

Mmmm, he smelled so good, his aroma all woody and masculine. She took a deep breath as she nuzzled into his neck. He worked his broad palms over her back, cupping her ass and kneading it, pulling her hips against him as their tongues entwined.

"God, you're so hot," he moaned, tipping his head back as he pulled her closer to him, the desire in his voice blatant as he thrust his hardness up against her tight, black latex-covered crotch. Her predatory eyes couldn't help but stare at the exposed flesh of his throat, but though she was damn hungry and it would be the perfect time to sink her teeth into his neck, the desire to fuck him was far stronger than her blood hunger right now.

He roamed clumsy fingers all over her corset, trying and failing to unlace the ties that held it together.

"Let me," she breathed into his ear, as deftly she worked her fingers to assist him, unlacing the garment and revealing her bare breasts to his grateful eyes, grinding her hips against his denim-clad cock.

Groaning, he picked her up, her legs locking around his waist as he stood up, the corset falling to the ground as he bore the full weight of her with his strong body. He kissed her passionately on the mouth, crushing his lips against hers, then allowing them to roam down to her neck where he nibbled lightly. She moaned, throwing back her head. His mouth on her felt so good like that, almost like he was going to suck *her* blood. *What are you thinking? You're supposed to be the vamp here, and right now you're not being a very successful one.*

"Get your pants off," he said, his voice thick with lust.

Huh, what? The commanding way he delivered the words was practically making her cream right then and there. Wasn't he supposed to be a shy guy?

He threw her against the black leather sofa, tugging down her tight black pants insistently, and she writhed urgently, squirming in an effort to peel off the constricting latex as she tried to help him maneuver them down. What the hell had happened to the nervous guy she'd met in the club? He was acting like a man possessed now.

As his head bent to her bare flesh, she couldn't help but cry out as he kissed her sex lightly, then extended his tongue to lap at her as her sharp fingernails interlocked in strands of his dark hair.

"Oh, you like me tonguing that hot pussy, don't you?" He broke off from what he was doing to look up at her with a rakish smile, as she frantically pushed his head back down again, urging him to continue to pleasure her.

"Don't stop, please," she begged, her body undulating at his expert ministrations. "Jeez," she groaned. He started to push up into her with his tongue, using his broad hands to spread her thighs to get at her easier.

"Damn, you've got me so hard for you," he said, breaking off momentarily from attending to her wetness. She pushed his head back down again, starting to buck her hips in a fast, frantic rhythm against his tongue. Surely she wasn't going to be able to hold back if he kept on doing that?

"I'm gonna come," she panted, her breath coming in jagged spurts now as she locked her legs around his neck, her entire body abuzz with sensation. He never stopped his tongue working her, sweeping down through her wet folds to tease, then swooping back up to her swollen clit to suck and lick at the little nub. All the while she cried out in ecstasy.

"That's it. Good girl. Come on my tongue," he encouraged, looking up at her from beneath his dark eyelashes as she writhed helplessly beneath him.

"Good girl." Yes, she wanted to be a good girl, his good girl. The thought made her horny as all hell.

The sight of his handsome face looking at her like that while he spread her, coupled with the thought, was enough to push her over the edge. Crying out, she came heavily, just as he had instructed, her body twisting as her long legs bucked and shook from the force of her orgasm.

"Yeah, that's so damn hot," he drawled, his accent laden with desire. "Now you gotta do something about this." He groaned, getting to his feet as he eagerly fumbled for the fly of his jeans. Unzipping, he levered out his cock and it sprang free, hard and throbbing, the head bulbous and glistening, as a bead of pre-cum oozed out temptingly.

"You going to be a good girl again and suck it for me?"

Something about the way he said those words made her want to do whatever he told her to. Though she'd just come, she felt herself twitch with anticipation, as obediently she sank to her knees, reaching her hand out to encircle the base of his thick shaft.

"Oh yeah, that's it. Hell yeah," he grunted as she extended her tongue to flick around the head of his cock, her lips encircling it. Yep, she was bona fide aroused all over again now. The salty taste of him filling her mouth was making her drip.

His fingers guided her head, forcing her to accept more of his cock into her mouth and making her gag just a little from the effort, due to the size and thickness of him. She made as if to stop for the merest of seconds but his hands prevented her, guiding her, gently.

"Keep going," he groaned, closing his eyes, the sight of him standing above her as she attended to him on her knees an unbelievably arousing one. This was something different entirely. She was normally always the one giving the commands. No guy had ever had the confidence to take charge like this with her before.

Rhythmically she began sucking his cock, stroking him simultaneously as the fat length slid deeper into her mouth, until it could go no farther. She could tell he was close to exploding. Hell, she felt close to the edge again herself, though the thought of him coming in her mouth was kinda hot. She didn't want him to blow his load until she'd experienced what it felt like to ride that cock.

"Keep doing that, you sexy bitch, and I'm gonna come in your mouth," he grunted, as if reading her mind.

Sexy bitch? Good girl? No one had ever said things like that to her before. They were usually just grateful she was fucking them. Why was this turning her on so much?

Bending forward he reached down to twist her bare nipple and she jumped at the sensation. He grinned wryly, pulling her to her feet and embracing her body with his solid frame, his arms encircling her. His cock pressing against her made her feel as though she were drugged. All she could think about was giving herself over to this man, letting him do whatever the hell he wanted to her body.

"Get on the sofa and spread your legs for me." He spoke the command huskily and she nodded, trembling from the anticipation she felt at the prospect of having him inside her and allowing him to push her back against the soft cushions.

"Good girl. Now show me what I get to fuck."

Jesus, he was so dominant. It sent waves of raw need coursing through her. She wanted him to fuck her like an animal. Spreading her thighs obediently, she allowed him to pull her pants entirely off, tossing them to the floor, so she could spread her legs wider. She heard the snap of a condom as he slid up her body and suddenly, that hard, prominent cock was pressing against her, the burning heat of it seeming to sear her tender flesh as it sought to find its way to her hot, wet entrance.

"Fuck, I need this," he groaned, pushing his swollen cock into her, and she cried out again, this time clinging to his neck as he took her. He didn't hold back, pistoning his cock, rhythmically and fast, her slick arousal lubricating his urgent thrusts, his hungry grunts intermingling with her moans. Squeezing him with her thighs, she pulled him into her, encircling his back with her legs as his lips found hers hungrily again. She was so damn horny she couldn't think straight, couldn't see straight. She was completely unprepared for this.

"Oh shit, I'm gonna come in you soon," he warned, his body tensing up as it prepared for his orgasm, his solid shoulders and back rigid with contracted muscle. Her fingers scrambled over his tight, white T-shirt, practically tearing it off his body as she struggled to ease the material over his head. She wanted to feel skin-on-skin contact, flesh pressed against flesh, and the sensation didn't disappoint, as the hard planes of his broad bare chest finally mashed against her own, softer one.

"Come in me. Come in me," she moaned in his ear, arching her back against him as he thrust repeatedly into the very core of her.

"Yeah, you want it, don't you? Fuck, I'm just gonna use that sexy body to come now," he growled, his voice husky as his cock pumped in and out of her, the friction from his crotch rubbing her clit most deliciously and causing her own desire to build again. His confidence was an incredible turn on. He was making her act in a way she never had before.

"Oh, oh, yes, I want it," she cried, her sex dripping with arousal as his cock swelled up inside her to obscene proportions. He drove his orgasm home, his thrusts becoming more urgent, she clawed at his naked back, undulating in the waves of pure pleasure his pulsating cock was delivering to her.

"You're gonna get it all now."

"Oh my God," she moaned, opening her thighs as wide as she could manage allowing this hard, hungry man to totally take over her body. *Use me. Fuck me and use me.* She wanted him to use her. The realization made her body spasm and a cry of ecstasy escaped her lips, the pleasurable sensation that hit her causing her to rake her fingernails down his back.

Afterward, she lay there, with Dillon collapsed on top of her as gradually her breathing slowed and her heart stopped pounding nineteen to the dozen. This man, this stud, had been responsible for giving her not one, but two orgasms in the space of twenty minutes. She couldn't remember the last time she'd come so quickly with a guy, let alone one as hot as this, and never twice in such a short space of time. And he was so damn dominant too.

It had taken her by surprise how aroused she'd gotten by being called those names and commanded in that way, but it had been an unbelievable turn-on. Then again, she never usually went for dominant guys, or was it just the fact that she reduced practically every guy she met into a lump of quivering jelly? Who knew? Anyway, boy, had she picked well tonight.

Was there anything wrong with this guy? She was starting to seriously doubt whether she could sink her teeth into his throat and bite—

"What are you doing?" The teeth biting into her neck were sharp, causing her to wince in pain.

"Sorry, babe," he said, panting as he looked up at her sheepishly. "I got carried away," he added in explanation, grinning as she visibly relaxed.

"Hah, for a minute there I thought you were gonna tear in to my jugular," she joked, shaking her head. *That had caught her off guard. Usually she was the one doing the biting.*

"Nah, don't worry. I ain't gonna pull any of that freaky vamp stuff on you," he said, kissing her on the nose, then on the lips.

Freaky vamp stuff? Hah. If only he knew, he'd probably hightail it out of here quicker than you could say howdy. She allowed him to remain collapsed on top of her as his body relaxed against hers, spent now, his skin slick with the exertion of sex, a fine sheen decorating his well-muscled back. Damn, he was a serious ten out of ten. There was no way she could mark that perfect flesh. *Fail, Lola. Come on. Pull yourself together. What kind of self-respecting vamp are you? Do it now. There's still time while he's not expecting it.*

"That...was the hottest fuck I ever had," he said, looking up at her from under his floppy fringe, his dark eyes looking intense and utterly irresistible.

"Wow, umm...talk about a compliment," she replied, feeling momentarily and quite uncharacteristically self-conscious. "I have to admit. Things did get kinda heated, huh?" she added, smiling back at him. *No shit, there was so much heat going on if things had gotten any hotter, the fire trucks would have to have come put out the blaze.*

"*You* have to be the hottest woman I ever met," he said, rolling off her and throwing his head back against the couch as he inhaled deeply.

She couldn't help but notice the way his strong neck was exposed in that position, how easy it would be just to sidle on in there and pounce. All she would have to do is pretend she was planting a little kiss, then whammo, she wouldn't be hungry anymore. At this rate she was in serious danger of becoming undernourished like Brandon. So why did she feel unable to move? Why was her body betraying her by refusing to act?

"Hey, you ain't so bad either, cowboy," she joked, playfully swatting him with his white T-shirt.

He wrinkled up his nose, pulling a face.

"Sorry. Didn't mean to sound like Drago. Wouldn't want you thinking I'm the kind of girl who jumps to conclusions."

"Actually though, you know you're kinda right," he said, grinning as he turned his head lazily to look at her.

"I am?"

"Yeah. My pa had a ranch back in Texas. I grew up on it, so I ain't no stranger to saddling a horse or two."

This was too fricking perfect. A genuine cowboy — and a hot one at that — had just given her the best sex and orgasm of her life. Two of them, to be exact. *Stop thinking about his charms. You have work to do, my girl. Don't forget the reason you brought him back here in the first place.*

She'd have to stall him a bit. That way she could work her way up to it. She just had to forget about those handsome, chiseled features, that charmingly adorable manner of his and those rock-solid abs, and start thinking of him as dinner. Hurriedly she got to her feet, reaching for her corset to protect her modesty again.

"Uh I'll just get you another beer," she muttered, fastening the corset around her waist again as she hastily laced it up.

"Wow, you really are too darn good to be true, ain't ya?" He grinned at her, eyeing her up and down with an appreciative glance.

Why, oh why, does he have to look so disarmingly attractive?

"Oh, this girl has a dark side. *You* just haven't had occasion to meet it yet." She winked, turning away to go to the kitchen. *And if you keep up the perfect guy act, you aren't going to anytime soon.* Why couldn't he turn out to be an arrogant asshat after he'd had his pleasure — or at least a little slow? Why did he have to be so God damn perfect?

Swinging open the fridge door, she reached for a cold bottle of beer, grabbing another for herself. Screw thinking clearly. She needed to be a little mellow if she was gonna do what she needed to do.

After returning to the lounge, she plopped down beside him on the sofa, reaching for the bottle opener that lay discarded atop the chunky black marble table in front of them.

"Here," she said, thrusting a beer under his nose. "Nice and cold, perfect for the cool down." She grinned, noting the sweat still slicking his muscular frame.

"Thanks," he said, flashing her with *that* smile as she took a swig of her beer. "Wow, do I need this," he added, taking a slug himself. "You wore me out."

"Well, I guess I owe you, though, for coming to my rescue in the club and protecting my honor," she said, pulling an expression of mock innocence.

"Oh, that? That was nothing, darlin'. The dude was an asshole."

It was the accent that did it. Normally if any other guy had called her *darlin'*, she would have barfed on the spot, but somehow, with his softly spoken Texan drawl, *he* made it sound irresistible. She knew she couldn't go through with biting him, at least not now. *Way to go, loser. That means you won't feed tonight.*

Yeah, she'd go hungry, she knew, and she'd definitely suffer for it until she found another target. But one look at that perfect face and she somehow didn't mind going a little hungry. Besides, he had already more than satisfied her in other ways. Either way, she knew she just wasn't going to be able to bring herself to do it, which all added up to one thing. She had to get him out of here. There was no way he could stay. As soon as the sun came up, she'd be vulnerable and that would be way too risky.

"Drago *is* an asshole." She grinned, nodding in agreement. "He's kind of used to getting his way and he hasn't been able to get it with me, which is why he's kinda sore about it."

"Well, I'll say one thing," he said, looking her up and down. "Dude's certainly got good taste in women. You are one fine lady." He pursed his lips and let out a low, appreciative whistle.

"I try to please," she said, feeling slightly embarrassed and really not knowing what to say. Why did she suddenly feel shy as all hell? She *never* felt shy. She was the one who was always in control. What the hell was going on tonight?

"Well, ya certainly know how to make a guy feel welcome," he continued, still smiling at her.

Stop looking at me like that with those big, brown puppy eyes. Now she was even starting to feel guilty about kicking him out. What on earth was this guy doing to her? She had to get him away from her, and fast, before she turned into a gooey marshmallow, incapable of doing anything but drooling at him and simpering like a damn fool.

"So do you live far from here?" She had to try to successfully manage to steer the subject away from her hospitality.

"I live on the other side of town—near the woods, other side of the tracks. Know Morningford Heights?"

"Morningford Heights? You must be pretty loaded then." She was a little taken aback. He seemed so down-to-earth. She really hadn't expected him to say he lived in the most exclusive area in town. And she had thought *she* was doing okay with her luxury condo. Morningford Heights was seriously swank.

"Yeah, my pa left me some money when he passed. I was planning to use it for a down payment on a house for me and my fiancée. But after we broke up, I used it to get the hell out of Dodge and move on."

"So why did you come to Burley Falls?"

"Dunno really. Just stuck a pin in a map and followed the trail. Guess you could kinda call me a bit of a nomad."

"Wow, pretty adventurous then."

"Suppose so." He shrugged with a rakish grin. "I can be a lot more adventurous, missy. You ain't seen nothing yet."

The way he was looking at her brought a flush to her cheeks almost instantly. The man was bona fide sex, one hundred ten percent, no doubt about that. Just thinking about him thrusting inside her made her want him all over again. But now she *had* to get him out of here. She couldn't risk him still being here in the morning when the sun rose. That would be far too dangerous.

She reached across the table for the silver cell phone she'd discarded there when they'd first come in. Picking it up, she pretended to be reading her messages, still keeping one eye on Dillon, as bare-chested he slugged at his beer, looking way too damn sexy. She quickly tapped at the keypad, typing in the words to Max.

Max, can you call me and pretend there's been an emergency? I need to get Dillon outta here.

Max shouldn't be too long responding. That's if he hadn't gotten lucky and found a hot guy of his own to take home. Then he would probably just turn off his phone. She'd just have to hope there hadn't been any hot gay guys at Vain tonight. Her bladder suddenly felt uncomfortably full. "I just have to go to the restroom," she said, jumping to her feet swiftly.

"Sure. I'll wait right here, sexy," he said, winking. She couldn't help but smile to herself at the cheesy line as she walked away.

When she returned, however, she was surprised to see him sitting there on her sofa, his handsome face wreathed in a scowl.

"Hey, what's the matter—" She stopped abruptly as her eyes fell to her cell phone in his hand.

"Someone tried to call you. It was a wrong number, so I didn't bother hollering for ya," he said, his tone sounding dark.

"Oh, umm…okay," she floundered, not quite understanding.

"Then when I hung up, this flashed up," he said, thrusting the cell toward her and tapping the screen to indicate what she should focus her eyes on. "I guess you forgot to press Send."

She craned her head to look at the cell phone's screen but she already knew what she would see. Internally she cringed, her cheeks burning with shame.

"Uh, it's not what you think," she stumbled, trying to cover her tracks.

"Yeah, you know what? Don't worry about it. You don't have to get your friends to haul my ass outta here. I'm a big boy. I can find the exit all by myself," he muttered, getting to his feet and reaching for his white T-shirt.

She watched helplessly as he pulled it over his head, covering up those washboard abs and well-defined pecs.

"No, wait—" she started, but he interrupted her, tossing her phone on to the table.

"Look, don't worry about it, okay? I get it. You had your fun and now you want me outta here." His jaw tightened as he turned away from her.

"It wasn't like that—" Futilely she called after his retreating back as he strode from the room. But it *was* like that, she knew. Hadn't getting him to leave been exactly what she'd intended? She heard the front door open and slam. His footsteps echoed down the pathway, getting fainter and fainter as he walked away from her. She felt a little strange. Why did she feel that odd twinge in her gut? Was it guilt? Or something else?

Well, it wasn't as if she had another choice. She *had* to get him out of here. It would have been far too dangerous to have him here in the morning, when the sun came up. He might have tried to open the blinds or something then her secret would have been exposed. She'd been photosensitive ever since Lyra had taken her mortality that night. So photosensitive, in fact, she couldn't be exposed to sunlight for more than five minutes straight before getting very sick indeed.

Even the daylight coming in from an open window could make her feel quite ill. She recalled Lyra's words to her that night, as she'd lain among the charred rubble of her former home, the smell of smoke and burning flesh filling her nostrils, as sorrow had filled her heart.

'You won't be able to feel the sun on your face ever again. The sun is your greatest enemy now. You must stay away from it at all costs. You're one of the chosen now, and you carry the blood of the ancient ones in your veins.'

She hadn't known it at the time, but she'd since found out there were different types of blood curses, depending on who you were bitten by when you got turned. Now she knew some of the other vamps in Burley weren't photosensitive—like Drago—because they hadn't been turned by a pure form, and she also knew some other bloodsuckers like Max and Brandon who were ultrasensitive to UV light, just like she was. They must have been turned by a pure blood vampire like Lyra too.

Shrugging, she sank down into the soft leather of the couch, deciding the slight melancholy she was feeling must be due to the fact she hadn't fed in days. Tipping her head back, she yawned. Boy, she was feeling decidedly sleepy. She should go to bed, but she really couldn't seem to drag herself off the sofa. Her eyelids began to feel heavy as she felt herself slowly begin to doze.

In the morning you'll feel better and tonight will all seem like a hazy memory. The last thing that flashed through her mind right before she sank into a deep sleep was the way Dillon had looked as he entered her for the first time, his muscular, athletic body rippled with tension, his expression hungry with lust as he dominated her.

Chapter Three

It was afternoon when she woke, moving her head groggily from side to side as her eyes tried to focus. Her muscles ached and her body felt stiff and sore from having spent a night on the sofa instead of in the comfort of her bed, and when she swallowed, her throat felt dry and icky. Recalling the events of the night before, she groaned aloud, closing her eyes again. It had all gone so well too, until she'd gone and put her damn foot in it — or more like put her cell phone in it. So well, in fact, she hadn't been able to follow through on what she'd originally set out to do.

Her entire body felt as if it'd been bruised all over, and she urgently needed to feed. Her stomach was strangely hollow and rumbling ominously, and her left eye had started to twitch, the way it always did when she was running on empty. Looking up at the clock on the wall, she saw it was four p.m. It had been four a.m. when Dillon had left. She usually fell asleep around six a.m., just before dawn broke, but last night she'd been exhausted, both mentally and physically.

Typically she woke up around five p.m. in the winter months. It was just easier that way, since she needed to keep to a nocturnal schedule. In the summer, she kept even later hours, sometimes not rising until eight. Now it would still be bright outside, so she wouldn't be able to go out just yet.

Tonight she'd go to Vain to find another target all over again. Maybe this time, though, she shouldn't make the mistake of picking one so cute she couldn't actually go through with biting him. Sinking back into the cushions of her sofa, she closed her eyes, thinking to herself she'd shower and get ready around six, then hit up the club at eight.

* * * *

Entering the club at eight-thirty, she looked around to scope out who had already arrived. Vain never really started to heat up until around ten p.m., but she still liked to come talk to Max and hang out, and to sip on a drink while she checked out the arriving club goers. Tonight, it looked like there were a fair amount of people here already. The club was rapidly starting to fill. Was there some kind of special event going on or something? She spied Max mopping up some sort of spillage at the bar and decided to head on over to ask.

"Heyas," he said, greeting her with a grin.

"Hey, Max." She smiled.

"How did your evening with Mr. Muscles go last night?" he said, winking.

"Superhot but I feel guilty."

"Why guilty? Did you take a little too much or something? That's unlike you. You're usually Miss Responsible."

It was true, she wasn't irresponsible, unlike Drago, who cared nothing if his victims lived or died. There had been rumors that some of the people seen leaving the club with Drago had never been seen again.

Of course that was just rumor, but she'd seen the missing person posters and some of those faces did look awfully familiar. No one could prove anything, of course, and anyway, it kind of helped when your father was one of the wealthiest guys in town like Drago's was. Money talked, and it could also stop people whispering in the right quantities.

"Nah, I couldn't go through with it. I had him leave. Well, sort of. It's a long story," she said, sighing as she remembered.

"Whaaat? You take home a hot guy like that and you don't even *try* and have sex with him? Girlfriend, I am disappointed in you," Max chided, shaking his head at her.

She smiled. "Oh, I didn't say we didn't have sex — just that I didn't bite him."

"Oh, you *dirty* girl. Okay, spill it. I want details. What were those muscles like when you got the shirt off that hot bod?" Max leaned forward, eagerly resting his chin in his hands and looking for all the world like he were a kid excited for Christmas to come.

"Just as perfect as you imagined they would be...then some," she said, grinning.

"And the...?" Max raised his eyebrows at her, waiting for her to say more.

"And the what?" She looked at him, pretending not to understand, though she knew all too well what he was hinting at.

"The pants department, of course. Did Mr. Perfect live up to expectation?" Max licked his lips.

"Oh, in every way possible," she bantered back, smiling like a cat who been given a big ole saucer of milk. "Twice in fact," she added, her smile broadening.

"*You* are one lucky lady," Max said, shaking his head. "I can't even get a decent guy to talk to me, let alone come home with me."

"Yeah, well, I don't feel so lucky right now. I haven't fed in an age," she said, leaning on the bar heavily.

"Hence why you're here tonight, I'm guessing? But you still haven't really told me, why exactly *didn't* you take a little sanguine loving from Mr. Perfect?"

"Uh, I dunno. It's really weird but I just couldn't do it," she said, frowning. She wasn't lying. She really didn't know why she hadn't been able to go through with biting Dillon.

"Oh my God, surely not? Is the infamous man-eater falling for Mr. Buff?" Max stood, looking at her, an expression of mock shock on his face.

"Oh, pfff, I could care less about him. So what? He's handsome and not bad in bed? Okay, great in bed," she conceded, grinning as Max raised his eyebrow.

"Sooo? Did you get his number? Did you give him yours? Oh my God, please say you're going to see him again. The two of you would make an absolutely *perfect* couple."

"I'm really not looking for anything like that right now." She couldn't afford to develop feelings for anyone, not with the life she led—especially not after what had happened with Rory.

"You're *never* looking for anything like that. It's not fair. You've got a conveyor belt of eager guys willing to queue up to be with you while I languish alone, yearning for Mr. Right to walk into this dive and sweep me off my feet," Max said, pretending to swoon dramatically.

She couldn't help but grin at Max's over-the-top clowning around. He never failed to make her smile.

"So what happened when he left then? You said it was a long story?"

"Oh, that." She sighed, rolling her eyes.

"Mmhmmm."

"You better fix me a drink if you want me to tell you *that*."

"Let me guess…a Bloody Mary?" He grinned.

"You know it. Oh, and make it extra bloody."

"Girlfriend needs to feed," Max said, laughing as he turned to fix her drink.

"Girlfriend needs the bathroom," she said, grinning as she added, "I'll be right back."

Returning, she saw Max had put her drink to one side of the bar, and she made an eager beeline for it.

"Lola, someone's been asking about you," Max said, interrupting her as she sipped at the thick tomato-colored liquid.

"Who?"

"Turn around and you can find out. He's seen you and he's coming on over."

Turning around as Max instructed, she caught sight of Dillon walking toward her, a sheepish-looking smile decorating his handsome face. Jesus, he looked even hotter than she remembered. *But what the hell is he doing here?*

"Uh, hi," she stammered, feeling more than a little flustered.

"Hello, Miss Sexy Pants," he said, winking as he looked down at her tight black latex pants. She wasn't wearing the exact same pair she'd had on last night. She owned at least ten pairs of them, but she hoped he didn't think she hadn't changed her clothes, all the same.

"I'm uh...really sorry about last night," she ventured, looking down at her feet. She'd never felt this awkward around a guy before.

"No, *I'm* the one who should be sorry," he said chivalrously. "I shouldn't have reacted the way I did. It was your right to want me to leave. I shouldn't have chucked a fit on ya about it."

"Hey, it's okay. I think you're forgiven. I actually had a really good evening. I umm...enjoyed your company," she said, smiling. *And your cock.* He was just too darn sweet, though. Her heart couldn't help but melt at his apology, not that she'd even been mad at him to start with.

"Oh, I had the time of my life. It ain't every day a guy meets a woman who's beautiful, smart *and* completely charming. Gonna take me a quite a while to get over that," he said, shaking his head as his eyes met hers, looking her up and down with undisguised lust. She shivered, the hairs on the back of her neck standing up. Why did she feel as if she were standing naked in front of him? There was so much chemistry between them that it should be practically illegal. Just looking at him made her think about how much she wanted him pressed up against her, hard and breathing heavy.

Flustered by the thought, she pretended to focus on Max, who was busy stacking glasses. She really didn't know what to say in response to his comment, and for some reason, her stomach was doing peculiar little flips. It must be because she hadn't fed yet.

"Awww. You're sweet to say that. Can I get you a drink?" She turned back to Dillon.

"I was gonna order a beer actually, but can I get you one?"

Ever the gent. She smiled to herself. There was something just so irresistibly attractive about that. "Got one," she said, holding up her Bloody Mary as she bent her head to sip at it again through her straw.

She noted how his eyes strayed to her cleavage and she couldn't help but mentally congratulate herself on the top she'd chosen to wear. The low cut white silk, spaghetti strap top allowed a generous amount of décolletage to be displayed and Dillon certainly seemed to be appreciating it. She'd dressed extra sexy tonight because she knew she had to pick someone up. After all, if she didn't feed tonight, she was gonna get really sick, real quick.

Dillon motioned to Max, indicating he should come over. Looking a little flustered, the dark-haired bartender approached with a smile.

"Hey, buddy, can I get a beer please?"

"Sure," Max said, shooting her a quick look and winking.

"What do you want? We have it all." Max gestured behind himself in a wide, sweeping motion. "We've got Stella, Budweiser, Cobra—"

"Just a Bud will do, my friend."

"One Budweiser coming up, sir," Max said, walking over to the little fridge where the ice-cold beer bottles were stored.

"So what are you doing back here?" She took another slurp of her Bloody Mary.

"Ah yeah." He shifted from foot to foot, looking a little embarrassed. "I guess I kinda forgot to ask for your number so that I could ask you out to dinner to apologize an' all. I was gonna swing by your house to drop you a note or something but then I remembered you two were on friendly terms, so I thought he might know how to find ya," he said, gesturing over to Max.

"Hey, like I said, it's really okay. You don't have to apologize to me."

A crestfallen expression creased Dillon's handsome features. Out of the corner of her eye, she saw Max glaring at her.

"It's okay. I know when to back off. I can take a hint. But it was sure nice to see you again, Lola. Max," Dillon added, nodding briefly at Max in polite acknowledgment, as he turned to walk away.

She felt an odd pang as she watched his flannel-shirted back walk off.

"Hey, wait," she called after him. He spun around to face her again, his brown eyes hopeful. He was just too sweet, not to mention damn attractive. There was no way she could let this guy walk out of her life, especially not when he had been so charming.

"That dinner invitation still open?" she said, looking at him with a grin.

* * * *

They spent most of the evening together, dancing and drinking, talking and laughing. Not only was the sexual tension between them sizzling, but Lola marveled that the pair of them seemed to have so much in common. In fact, she'd never met a guy before who was so damn easy to talk with.

But as she glanced around the club while lounging at the bar with Dillon and slurping on her third Bloody Mary, she began to feel the familiar waves of panic surge through her stomach. She was having the time of her life, unquestionably, but she needed to feed, and if she didn't, she would suffer, plain and simple.

How on earth can I get rid of him without offending his feelings all over again? The last thing she wanted was Dillon thinking she didn't like him, because she really did. She paused mid-sip as the realization hit her suddenly. Did she really just think that? That she actually liked him?

In more than a 'I just wanna bang your brains out' kinda way? Well, while she certainly wouldn't mind a repeat performance of last night, to her amazement she had to grudgingly admit she *was* starting to have feelings for him. No man had managed to make her feel this way, not since she and Rory had broken up. She knew she was going to have to deal with the way she felt about Dillon at some point, but right now the urge to satiate her hunger was paramount. She felt seriously weak and her stomach was growling alarmingly, the way it always did when she was near empty.

"Hey, you okay?" Dillon cut into her thoughts, his eyes full of concern.

"Yeah, I'm fine," she said, lying through her teeth and hoping she sounded convincing. She really didn't feel well at all, but how the hell could she tell him the truth?

"You know, this place? It's kinda gothy in here, sort of like a vampire's lair or something," he said, looking about him at Vain's black and purple decor.

"Hah. That's one way of putting it, I guess," she replied, smiling at his words. If he only knew half the clientele here were vamps that came to prey on unsuspecting clubbers, he'd probably hightail it out of here and never come back again.

"You're a real vamp, ain't ya?"

Startled by his words, she turned to face him. "What do you mean by that?"

"Whoa. Easy now. It was supposed to be a compliment," he said, smiling nervously and holding up his palms.

A compliment? What the hell was he talking about?

"He means you're one sexy-ass man-eater," Max said, chipping in swiftly to defuse the situation. "Sorry.

Couldn't help but overhear," Max added, shooting a warning look at her that told her to stop getting all paranoid.

Whew. She felt the relief flood her body as understanding dawned. Still, if only Dillon knew how near the mark he had really been by that off-the-cuff comment.

Her gaze drifted to the balding guy at the end of the bar who looked like he had been indulging in one too many sunbeds. He winked at her leerily as he slugged his beer, and she felt herself immediately recoil at the sleazy gesture. That guy really shouldn't be continuing to drink. He was already more than worse for wear. But he'd be the ideal target for a quick bite, and she wouldn't have to even take him home. If she could just get him to come for a little walk with her.

"Hey, you wanna dance to this? It's my favorite song." Dillon interrupted her train of thought again, grabbing her by the arm as he attempted to tug her out onto the dance floor.

"W-wait—" she tried to protest weakly, but the loud thump of the bass drowned out her objections as reluctantly, she allowed him to pull her away. She shot a last lingering look in Mr. Sleaze's direction as the crowd of heaving, sweaty bodies on the dance floor swallowed them up, obscuring him from her vision. *Great, there goes dinner.*

Dillon started to grind her, placing his arm around her lower back and circling his hips against hers, and she felt her body involuntarily responding to his touch as the beat pumped through them. She could feel herself becoming aroused. Why did he always smell so damn good? He craned his head to her ear, brushing his lips on the underside of her lobe and sending a delicious shiver down her spine.

"You're the hottest woman here," he murmured. "I want you so bad. Feel how hard you make me." He wasn't lying. The bulge in his jeans testified to his feelings. She felt his hand encircle her ass, his fingers kneading the flesh, then sliding between her legs to brush tantalizingly through the flimsy fabric of her pants. Her breath caught in her throat. He was making her feel like she was gonna lose all control of herself, smack bang in the middle of the club.

He pulled her to him with a growl, the thumping bass of the music seeming to pulsate in time with her pounding heart. His hard body embraced her, enveloping her entirely. She hooked a leg around his waist as they ground to the beat, her mouth parting to accept his tongue. She hoped no one could see just how hot she was for him. She was behaving like a lust-crazed teenager. All she could seem to think about was getting to that cock, getting him naked, feeling that hot, muscular body crush hers with its raw power again.

"I'm gonna take you outside and fuck you up against a damn tree," he growled, the rough scratch of his stubble grazing her cheek and making her breath come even faster.

Shit. He was making her body feel all kinds of crazy, but more than that, her heart was feeling stuff she hadn't felt in years — things she'd sworn she would never allow herself to feel again.

Snap out of it, Lola. You can't let him get to you like this. He'll find out the truth, and you can't ever let him. Remember what happened with Rory? She winced momentarily, remembering the pain all too well.

No, this was far too dangerous. He was getting way too close, *and* she had to feed. But somehow she still found herself tipping her face up to his again as his lips sought hers. She could feel the throbbing hardness of his cock through his denims as he ground his body against her, their tongues entwining as they kissed, and she couldn't help but yield. Her heart started to thump so hard that it felt like it might jump right out of her chest. She could hear the blood pounding in her ears. She had to stop this, had to resist. She had to tear herself away from him.

"I'm sorry. I have to go to the bathroom. I really don't feel so good," she said, breaking off the embrace abruptly and turning away, panting as she tried to collect herself. She walked quickly across the dance floor, the sea of bodies swallowing her up before he even had the chance to reply and make her change her mind.

As she made her way through the club back to the bar, she saw Mr. Sleaze still sitting there, his bald spot illuminated by the club's neon lighting. Passing him, she shot him an encouraging wink. *This should be an easy one to hook. The dude's tongue is practically hanging out of his mouth.* Out of the corner of her eye, she saw Max frowning at her.

"Where's Dillon?" He mouthed the words as she approached, but she just shrugged in response, resting her elbows on the slightly damp countertop.

"Hi, Max," she said breezily, as if nothing were up, but the look she gave him warned him to keep his mouth shut. Max seemed to comprehend because he said nothing, turning away instead and pretending to busy himself with the glassware. Sleaze shot her another glance, his eyes appraising her hungrily as he licked his greasy lips. He was making her slightly nauseous, but the feel of his blood in her stomach would have the opposite effect, she knew. Now all she had to do was wait for him to approach her. Returning his gaze, she flashed her most disarming smile at him again.

Straight away, he was up off of the barstool and sidling over to her.

"Hi," he said, extending a hand as he introduced himself. "I'm Dave. Can I get you something to drink?"

"Uh, sure, that'd be great," she replied, looking around nervously, hoping Dillon hadn't followed her off the dance floor or come looking for her. Dave clicked his fingers, as if to summon Max's attention. *God, this guy is a complete joke.* Ever the professional, Max turned around, a fixed smile on his face.

"How can I help you, sir?"

"Can I get a Scotch and soda and the lady will have a…" Dave paused, turning to her questioningly.

"Bloody Mary," she replied, nodding politely and smiling.

"Bloody Mary. Wow, do people even drink those anymore?" Dave grinned, looking from her to Max then back again, as if he'd just said the funniest thing in the world.

"Oh, Lola takes her drinks how she takes her men." Max smirked as he turned away to fix the order. She stifled a giggle watching Dave frowning as he tried to work out exactly what the comment had meant.

"Err…and how's that?"

"Oh, spicy and strong, of course," Max said smoothly, spinning round and placing a perfectly mixed Bloody Mary, complete with celery garnish, on the polished black marble countertop of the bar.

"Ah, right." Dave looked visibly relieved. "I thought you were gonna say she likes them bloody."

"Haha. Afraid I'm gonna sink my teeth into you?" She grinned, sidling up alongside him and squeezing his arm as she reached for her drink.

"Hey, I don't mind a little biting, you know," he said, a creepy smile stretching over his middle-aged features. *Ugh.* He had yellow teeth. One thing she could never overlook was bad personal hygiene. The dude was gross. His blood probably tasted disgusting. She gave a little internal shiver of disgust. She had to be honest, though. Right now it didn't matter. Her inner tank was nearly dry. It was Dave or nothing.

"Was that little shudder you imagining what I could do to that sexy, tight, little body of yours?" Dave winked at her seedily, and she tried to suppress the urge to be violently sick. She didn't want to look at Max. She knew he'd be cracking up laughing. Momentarily unable to speak, she took a sip of her drink to stall for time instead, trying to force herself to formulate a suitable reply.

"Oh, well, it might be," she purred, recovering. "But you know, I'm the kind of girl who craves a little excitement."

"Oh yeah? You're a real wild one, eh?" He raised an eyebrow.

She nodded, trying to hold back the irresistible desire to laugh at just how sleazily desperate he was.

"Mmhmm, I admit it. I like it a little spicy, just like Max said. Guess you could call me a thrill seeker," she intimated, passing her tongue over her scarlet lips. Wouldn't hurt to get him thinking about how good that tongue would feel all over him, even if she were thinking of using her mouth for purposes other than pleasuring him.

"Oh man, I like that." He moaned, his eyes practically bulging out of his head. The guy obviously couldn't believe his luck. Let's face it. The last time he'd probably scored with a chick her age, his mark had probably had a few teeth missing and a drug habit too.

And she'd be willing to bet her last dollar he'd *still* had to pay for the privilege.

"Tell you what," she whispered, leaning in closer to him, "why don't we both go and get a little fresh air. It's getting a little warm in here, don't you think?" She tilted her head, gesturing in the direction of the exit.

"Oh yeah," he said, nodding enthusiastically, his head bobbing so vigorously it reminded her of one of those nodding dogs you often saw sitting on the dashboard of hillbilly vehicles. She smiled to herself as she took him by the hand, leading him toward the back door at the rear of the dimly lit club, located past the restrooms.

The door was always left unlocked. Dana, the owner, always kept it that way just in case anyone might want to use it. The anyone in question largely translated as hungry vampires in need of somewhere to bring their prey for a quick feed. Technically the door was supposed to be a fire escape. Most of the regular clubbers never even knew it was left ajar, and those seeking a nicotine fix usually always congregated around the front of the club.

Pushing open the door, they stepped outside into the moonlit night. She pulled the door shut behind them, careful not to allow it to close completely. Outside was pretty dark, the only light coming from the neon lit sign rotating atop the club that proclaimed its name proudly in fluorescent lettering.

Dave stood there hesitating, half turning to her then away again, as if he were waiting for her to make a move. She moved closer to him, placing her hand on his chest as she smiled up at him, forcing herself to swallow down the revulsion she really felt as she met his eyes.

"Mmm, it's nice out here," she said, her voice purposefully throaty as she tried to project her best 'come ravage me now' eyes at him.

"Oh yeah," he said, looking her up and down in that sleazy way of his again. "It's real nice," he added, running his hands over the bare skin of her arms as she moved in closer. Tipping her face up to meet his, she willed herself not to cringe as his lips met hers. She forced herself to yield to his tongue, which seemed to be rotating with alarming speed, almost as if it were on the spin cycle of a washing machine.

"Mmm mmmm mmmph," she protested, breaking off the kiss. *Ewww, his breath is stale.* She feared if she didn't stop, she would gag everywhere. *Careful, Lola. It won't do to be sick on dinner. You don't want to scare him away too soon.*

"Mmmm, you like it, babe. I know you like it," he said, moving in closer to her and forcing his body up against hers. She could tell he was aroused and the thought made her feel instantly repulsed, but she didn't betray her disgust, choosing to smile mysteriously at him instead.

"Ohhh, I like it all right," she purred, running her fingers over his chest. "But I like it a little rougher too," she added, gazing right into his eyes. He looked like he was about to explode. If she wasn't careful, she'd probably give him a heart attack.

"Oh, you do, do you?" He grabbed her around the waist, pulling her closer, his fishlike mouth opening and closing as he attempted to clamp his lips on hers again. Pushing him away with all her might, she kept a smile on her face as he stumbled back against the wall, the look on his face one of definite surprise at her strength. Well, good, because the kind of rough he'd thought she meant definitely *wasn't* what she had intended.

"Not that kind of rough," she said, shaking her head but still smiling at him as he looked at her in confusion.

"You're strong —"

She silenced him abruptly, moving in close and placing a finger on his lips. Strong? Boy, he really didn't know the half of it. Since she'd been turned, she was easily able to overpower most mortal guys if ever she ran into any trouble.

"Ssssh," she hissed, planting a featherlight kiss on the side of his cheek, as her fingernails raked down his chest over the thin white cotton button-up shirt he wore.

"*This* kind of rough," she whispered, bending her head to his neck and opening her mouth to reveal perfectly white sharp incisors. Puncturing the skin, she sunk them deep into the tender flesh of his neck. The hit was instant, the pungent taste of his blood hitting the back of her throat sharply as she began to drain him, her starving stomach greedily absorbing every last life sustaining morsel.

"Mmmphh —"

He attempted to struggle as she continued to feed on his neck, not that his protestations would do him any good. He might as well give into the embrace but, either way, she didn't have to worry. Soon he'd be too weak to protest anyway. She knew she needed to take a lot tonight, much more than she usually required, and though he would eventually recover, there was no way he was going to be able to get away anytime soon.

Her mouth worked hungrily to drain him, the blood filling her body with the energy she craved as she sucked his neck, her fangs piercing his skin in just the right place in order to extract exactly what she needed.

The liquid pouring into her imbued her with the strength she'd been hungering for, restoring her and making her whole body buzz with an electric excitement as she fed on him greedily, her hands gripping the tops of his arms.

"Mmmm," he murmured weakly, attempting to turn his head as his eyelids fluttered drowsily. She had to pull back or he was going to be out for hours, but how could she stop now? She was so damn hungry. Just a little more... Surely to take just a little bit more wouldn't be so bad?

Just then, she heard a sudden bang as the fire escape door flew open violently, hitting the outside wall, startling her enough to make her break off. Drago's face grinned out menacingly from the darkness of the shadows, his arrogant features framed by his cap of blond hair.

"Having a little fun there, are we, Miss Devereaux?" Drago's grin broadened.

"Uhhh, we were just talking," she floundered, wiping her mouth in an attempt to disguise the evidence of what she had actually been doing.

"Oh really? Looked like you were doing something else with your mouth from where I was standing," he smirked. Dave made a noise, a stifled choking sound, his eyes rolling back weakly in his head as his body swayed heavily from side to side. She'd taken too much from him. He was far weaker than she'd realized. He really needed to sit down. It would be a good three or more hours at least before he would be recovered enough to stand on his own two feet.

"He's sick. Help me get him away from here and sit him down somewhere?" She looked at Drago pleadingly.

"Oh, need my help now, do you?" Drago's smirk grew even wider. God, she hated him. Why was he so damn arrogant all of the time?

"Please don't be an asshole now," she muttered, rolling her eyes. Just then Dave began to moan loudly, as if he were in pain or something. Damn it, he seriously needed to hit the deck.

"What's in it for me if I help you?"

"What do you mean, what's in it for you?" She frowned. What was he trying to insinuate?

Drago looked over her body lecherously. "Oh, I think you can guess," he said, grinning obscenely at her, his pointed incisors sharp and slightly yellow-tinged in the neon light.

She gave a little shudder. There was no way she was going to let him come within one inch of her if *that* was what he was thinking. But then, if she told him in no uncertain terms just how disgusted the thought of him touching her really made her feel, there was no way in hell he would help her. No, she would have to play this smart, act like she was flattered by his attention—like she was grateful—considering the offer even. Then, after she had gotten the help she needed from him, she'd just tell him thanks but no thanks. Even Drago wouldn't go so far as to force himself upon her, would he?

She nodded at him in what she hoped was a fairly noncommittal manner, as she continued to attempt to prop Dave up. The guy was rapidly becoming harder and harder to hold upright. She was extra-strong, but not strong enough to support a complete dead weight.

"Please help?" She looked at Drago desperately. Grinning, he moved to assist her, the smug expression on his face communicating his obvious pleasure at the fact she seemed to have no other choice but to agree with his sleazy proposal. Working together, they managed to loop Dave's arms about their shoulders, bearing his weight they as slowly guided him around the side of the club.

"Where shall we take him?" She looked at Drago nervously. She really wasn't used to her prey flaking out on her like this. Usually they were just a little woozy after and within twenty minutes or so, they were good to go again. This time, though, she'd definitely gone too far. She should never have waited so long to feed.

"We'll take him to the park, leave him under the big oak tree to pull his shit together," Drago replied, his green eyes intense in the artificial luminescence of the club's sign. Of course, she'd forgotten about the park — the perfect safe spot for Dave to get his strength back where he wouldn't be noticed by anyone. Nodding her consent, she allowed Drago to steer them away from the club, down the street that led to the spacious leafy park the local residents of the Falls liked to congregate in on sunny days.

* * * *

At the park, they settled Dave under the big oak tree, against the thick bark of the trunk, his body slumping in a half-upright position.

"Will he be okay if we leave him here?" She shot Drago a concerned look.

"Don't see why not — unless something wicked comes this way," he added, grinning at her leerily.

She shivered. The way he was looking at her felt sinister, predatory even. Trying to push the thought out of her mind and keep the conversation breezy, she forced herself to wear a bright smile. "Well, thanks so

much for helping me out. We should be getting back to the club now, I guess. I told Max I was popping outside for some fresh air and he'll be wondering where I've —
"

She gasped as suddenly Drago was on her, pushing her up against the roughness of the tree trunk and running his hands crudely over her body. He crushed his lips to hers, making her gag as he attempted to force his tongue into her mouth. Averting her head, she tried frantically to push him off her.

"Drago, get off me," she protested, beating her hands upon his chest, but it quickly became apparent she wasn't going to be able to fight him off. Drago was more than a match for her. They both had superhuman strength, but the fact that he stood over six feet tall and had at least twenty pounds on her meant he definitely had the edge. She felt his hands working at the zipper of her corset, and a frantic panic rose in her throat.

"Come on. Don't be such a prude. I know you gave it up to the cowboy. I saw the way you two were dry humping each other in the club," Drago leered.

"I said, get off me!"

"Oh, don't play coy. I bet you showed him a *real* good time." He hissed lecherously into her ear, causing her skin to crawl with displeasure.

"Get away from me, creep." Struggling to push him off her, she tried to turn her head away from his lips. There was a rustling in the bushes somewhere behind them then and panicked, she looked about, trying to discern the source of it. Was someone else here? Whoever it was couldn't discover Dave, not while she and Drago were both still here. What if he woke up and told them what had happened?

"Come on, you little tease. Give me some of what you gave up to Dillon," Drago sneered, leering at her, his breath hot on her cheek.

"Drago stop—" Her words of protest were interrupted as a fist connected with the side of Drago's face, causing him to stumble backward clumsily, his ass hitting the grass and twig-strewn floor.

"Get the hell off her, asshole," a stern male voice warned, seemingly from nowhere.

But she knew that voice. It was familiar. It was...Dillon? She wheeled around, her heart giving a strange little skip as she caught sight of his strong, muscled frame. The flannel shirt he wore only served to make him look even more handsome—handsome, but angry. His jaw tightened as he regarded Drago down on the floor, scrambling around in the dust as he frantically attempted to collect himself.

"What the fuck?" Drago scowled as he clutched at his jaw. Even in the dim light of the park, the swelling on his face was obvious. He was clearly going to be sporting an impressive bruise for the next week or so.

"Next time pick on someone your own size, creep," Dillon said, spitting on the ground to emphasize the point as he put an arm protectively around Lola's shoulders.

Drago got to his feet angrily.

"You've made a big mistake, man," he said, pointing a finger at Dillon. "You obviously don't know who my father is."

"Dillon," she insisted, pulling him back by his shirt as enraged, he started forward toward Drago. Drago began to back away as he saw Dillon lunge but stopped, feigning bravery when he realized she had managed to placate him.

"And you? You're gonna regret this too," Drago threatened, turning his venom on her.

"Get the hell out of here," Dillon snarled, lunging for him again and forcing Drago to back away, still spitting threats.

"You're both gonna pay. Mark my words," Drago muttered, as finally conceding defeat, he skulked away, his eyes still nervously on Dillon as the shadows of the night swallowed him up.

When he was gone, Dillon turned to face her, the concern plainly apparent in his brown eyes. "Are you okay?"

"Uh, yeah, I'm fine," she mumbled, feeling embarrassed and slightly confused. How had he found her here? And had he noticed Dave yet? Maybe if she could distract him, he wouldn't notice the glaringly obvious fact that there was a guy semiconscious on the ground.

"Did that asshole hurt you?" Dillon brushed the side of her cheek tenderly. "If that jerk harmed a hair on your head, I swear I'll—"

"Let's walk," she said, interrupting him swiftly as she took him by the arm, her tone falsely bright.

"Uhh, Lola..."

She stopped, steeling herself for it. Damn it, she'd thought she had almost gotten away with it.

"Yes?" She looked up at him innocently.

"I dunno if you've noticed, but there's a dude asleep up against that tree," he said, frowning slightly as he regarded Dave's slumped form.

"Oh...uh...yeah, I saw him when we came into the park, saw him in the club earlier actually. He's had a bit too much, I think," she fumbled, hoping the fact she was lying through her teeth wasn't too transparent.

"What were you doing here with that Drago asshole anyway?" Dillon turned to face her looking puzzled. Now how the hell could she answer that?

"Oh, uh, I got sick again on my way out of the restroom. I think I musta drank more than I could handle, 'cause all of a sudden I felt like I was gonna pass out. Drago offered to walk me outside for some fresh air, but then he hit on me and wouldn't take no for an answer," she said, surprised at quite how easily the lies leaped from her mouth.

"What a jerk," Dillon said, scowling and shaking his head.

"Hey, I should thank *you*, though," she said, squeezing his solid biceps as she looked up into his handsome face.

"Me?"

"Mmmhmm. You saved me from that asshole *again*. Seems it's starting to become a habit of yours." She grinned, poking him lightly in the side.

He grinned back at her.

"Hey, anytime. It's a pleasure to put that ass where he belongs...on his ass," he said, his eyes twinkling. "But what did he mean by you don't know who my father is? I mean, who *is* his father, some kind of a big deal or something?"

She rolled her eyes.

"Pretty much, yeah, actually. He's mega rich and he's also the local police commissioner so, yeah, you *could* say he's kinda of influential in Burley Falls."

"Yeah? Well, I don't give a crap who Daddy is. I ain't scared of him nor his jerk of a son. That punk better run damn fast if I see him around again," he muttered, kicking at a leaf as the two of them walked out of the park, leaving Dave still slumbering heavily up against the bark of the old, gnarled oak tree.

Lola gave a little shiver as she remembered Drago's words and the way his eyes had looked so laden with hate as he'd made his bitter threats. She hoped they were nothing but empty words, but knowing Drago's monstrous ego, she feared otherwise. He was certainly one person who would harbor a grudge. Tucking into Dillon's arm for comfort, she fell into step with him as they strolled, squeezing at the muscle of his arm affectionately.

God, he was so solid. It was such a damn turn-on. Now she'd fed, and gotten Drago off her back, her thoughts had emerged from survival mode and begun to turn to far more hedonistic pursuits.

"You know, I think you should forget all about Drago and let me take you home and reward you with a nice cold beer for your efforts instead," she said, smiling as she spoke, though her eyes communicated to him that clearly she was offering a lot more than just a chilled beverage.

He turned to her, a darkly mischievous look in his brown eyes.

"Home, eh? Who says we need to wait until we get to your place for you to reward me?"

She didn't understand what he meant for a beat, but by then he was kissing her, urgently and with force, hungrily tearing at her clothes. She remembered his words in the club and her body gave an involuntary spasm of desire. Did he really mean to take her in the open air, where anyone could potentially see them?

"Oh," she cried, as he tore at the straps of her top, pulling it down, revealing bare flesh, erect nipples. She wanted him to push her down in the dirt, mount her like she was nothing but a vessel for his hot, hard, horny body, ride her into the ground until she were entirely spent.

"God," he groaned, reaching for her breasts, bending his head to suckle them. "You're such a turn on. You drive me wild."

"Yeah? Gonna show me how wild I make you?" She flicked a mischievous glance at him, the question intended to goad.

It had the desired effect. He growled and put his hands on her shoulders, pushing her down, down onto the grass, ripping at her pants, practically shredding them from her body before she barely even had a chance to catch her breath.

"Oh," she cried, as he spread her legs wide, his eyes hungrily drinking in what lay between with naked lust as he fumbled to free his cock. It sprang free, throbbing and hard, evidence of his desire, and she took a breath, her body spasming with want for him to fill her with it.

"This good enough proof for you," he grunted, pushing into her, his hands splaying her wide lewdly, as his hips started to buck and thrust. She could feel the twig-strewn grass on her back, but she didn't care. All her body could do was respond to this man's touch, to conform to the primal call of desire that held both of them so firmly in its grip.

His cock felt so fat inside her, urging, surging, and filling her so entirely that she could think of nothing but that big, beautiful thing and how much pleasure it was giving her to have it thrust into her. He didn't stop. Like a wild animal, he fucked her — on the ground, the bare earth, just like she had willed him to, only this was better, hotter, and rawer than any fantasy.

"You like this in you, huh?" He thrust deeper into her wetness, the action having the effect of exciting her even more.

"Y-yes," she said, writhing and panting beneath him, her hair spilling from the neat high ponytail she had fashioned it into hours earlier to cascade out behind her like a dark cloud of silk.

"You want it harder?"

It wasn't really a question. From the wild look in his eyes, she knew he was going to do exactly as he pleased.

"Yes," she whispered, unbelievably aroused both by the way he was speaking and the way his cock was satiating her body's primal need to be filled.

"Say it. Tell me how much you love my hard cock inside you," he ordered her, his voice commanding and throaty with want for her.

"Please fuck me harder. I need it," she whispered into the musk of his neck, his biceps bulging with effort as he pushed deeper at her request, making her drip with arousal at the sight of them.

"Oh yeah," he groaned, thrusting deeper, forcing her thighs to widen as he plowed her, his muscular body tensing as he fucked her on the ground of the tree-lined pathway.

"Harder?" he asked, pulling out and thrusting back in again when she nodded her assent, then, "Harder," again, without waiting or needing a response this time, as her body shook and a wild moan came from her lips.

"Good girl," he groaned, holding her as the ecstasy swept through her. "Come all over my cock," he encouraged, continuing to thrust and causing her body to shake with a second spasm, extending the wave of her pleasure.

Then as the last of it racked through her pleasure-addled body, he took her, claiming her body as his own possession, her eyes rolling blissfully back in her head as she lay there spent, his cock using her soaking wetness, his hard muscular body finding its own release.

"Jesus Christ," he moaned into her ear, grunting as he came, his cock throbbing as it pumped, his body a solid wall of muscle as she held him, her fingers caressing the cord of muscle that ran down the side of his well-defined torso.

She held him till he finished, held him on top of her, feeling his heart pounding against hers, and held him after too, when he murmured kisses into her hair, the heat of his body compensating for the coolness of the evening air.

There was no doubt about it. Risky as it was, she needed this man. It was biological, pure and simple. She had no choice. For the moment, she would just have to find a way of feeding her addiction to him, while keeping her true nature a secret.

Chapter Four

The next day she awoke at five p.m., her body mildly aching from the exertions of the night before, but feeling perfectly content nevertheless. She lay on her back in the comfortable queen-size bed she slept in, staring up at the white stucco ceiling and grinning to herself as she recalled what had occurred between her and Dillon. Less than twelve hours ago, they'd tumbled through her front door hot and sweaty from their sojourn in the dirt and hungry for each other all over again.

She remembered the smooth flash of Dillon's tanned flesh and the hardness of his body urgently pressing against her own as he'd moved on top of her, this time between silken sheets, groaning his satisfaction into her ear as he'd guided himself inside her. She recalled the way she'd raked her nails down his back as he'd entered her, her legs hooking around the broadness of his back as she'd arched her own, moving against him in rapture.

She remembered too, how, in the throes of passion, he'd whispered in her ear, *'Whose are you?'*

And how, lost in her own ecstasy, she'd replied, letting him know that in that moment at least, he possessed her utterly. It was a new and strange feeling for her, this yearning to submit to someone, but the possibilities of pleasure it provided were far too tantalizing to turn away from.

Still smiling, she hummed to herself as she stood up, swinging her legs over the side of the bed and reaching for her red silk robe. Thankfully she'd managed to get Dillon to leave before sunrise without raising his suspicions, so it looked like her secret was safe for another day. He'd told her he worked for a local engineering firm over in Morningford Heights, so she'd encouraged him to leave in the early hours, on the pretense that he'd have more time to collect his work stuff and ensure he got there without being tardy.

Dillon made her feel so cared for, yet he was spontaneous as well, not dull at all. Every time she was with him, she felt a ripple of anticipation, but he also seemed to possess the peculiar ability to make her feel so completely safe somehow too. He was the perfect mixture of dominance *and* tenderness, with a hefty pinch of solid reliable masculinity, and that mixture was a heady and intoxicating brew. So intoxicating, in fact, that she was actually thinking about when she could see him again. Should she call him?

She shook her head. Lola Devereaux, Burley Fall's infamous man-eater and heartbreaker, the girl who left men discarded behind her like used tissues, was now actually worrying and obsessing about some corn-fed farm boy from the back of beyond.

But what an irresistibly sexy corn-fed farm boy. If ever there was a man who fit the phrase 'the perfect catch', it was this one. But despite his passionate words in the heat of the moment last night, she certainly hadn't caught him yet. Did she want to catch him? She checked herself. She was starting to sound like her grandmother when she'd used to get on to Lola about how to snare a guy. Frowning, she struggled to remember the conversation Dillon and she had shared the previous evening.

"You're really cool, ya know?" he'd said, as the two of them lay together, all tangled up in the black satin of her bedsheets after a third passionate bout of lovemaking.

She wrinkled her nose as she looked at him.

"You're soooo corny," she replied, teasing him gently, as lightly she nudged him in the ribs.

"Corny, eh?" He grinned, moving on top of her and covering her with the powerful, masculine lines of his body as he planted a kiss on the top of her forehead.

"You weren't saying that five minutes ago," he added, his eyes sparkling. "Oh, please give it to me harder," he said, donning a falsetto voice and screwing up his lips in a comedic pout.

"Ugh, you joker, get off me. That's because you weren't being corny then," she said glibly, poking her tongue out at him and making to push him off her. He caught her gently by the wrist, pinning it back over her head as he looked into her eyes, an earnest expression on his handsome face.

"Hey," he said, his tone suddenly serious, "I mean it, though. I love hanging with you. And it's not just the sex, though that's dynamite. It's..." He paused, his voice trailing off as a dark expression crossed his face, as if he were unsure whether or not to continue.

Not sure what to say in response and not wanting him to feel uncomfortable, she'd decided to change the subject, resorting to her old standby of cracking a joke to lighten the mood, even though a part of her — a large part — really wanted to probe him further to ask just what he'd meant.

"Oh, not just the sex, huh?" she said, digging him in the ribs again. "Saying you love my insanely bad coffee-making skills, are ya?"

Shaking his head at her, he grinned wryly as she arched under him, smiling to herself as she felt him becoming aroused again. Reaching up, she entwined her arms around his strong neck, pressing her face to his as their mouths met.

That had been the end of that conversation and the start of a decidedly nonverbal and rather more physical one. What on earth was she thinking, though? She was a *vampire*. She certainly couldn't afford to develop feelings for someone, especially not a mortal.

But he had definitely intimated that he liked her, hadn't he? And it was clearly more than a one-time encounter that the two of them had shared. Though it wasn't like he had asked her to date him, was it? *Ugh.* She was so damn confused. Life was so much simpler when you *didn't* meet a great guy, especially when you were a vampire.

Why couldn't Dillon just be like all the other guys she had met? Fine to hang out with but she had never obsessed over any of them — besides Rory, of course. *Yeah, and remember how well that turned out.* She should just forget about it. Dillon probably had. She'd wager *he* wasn't obsessing over every single word she had uttered. Anyway, if he wanted to see her again, he knew where she lived. He knew where she liked to hang out. He could come find her. She wasn't going to call him up and risk rejection.

No, she was Lola Devereaux. She didn't chase some guy, even if he did have a maddeningly attractive smile and a jawline so perfectly etched you could cut glass with it. Even if he had a way of talking absolute filth to her at just the right moment and in just the right way in order to make her cream her expensive silk panties.

Her mind made up to forget all about Dillon Chambers, she crossed the room, padding across the fluffy white carpet to the adjoining bathroom. She'd shower and get dressed, then head for Club Vain and get straight back on the horse—find some guy to take her mind off Dillon and she'd soon forget all about him and the dumb idea that she could possibly have any kind of a sustainable relationship.

Just then her eyes alighted on the piece of paper that seemed to be tucked under the small vase on her dresser. That hadn't been there yesterday. Curious, she walked over to it, carefully easing it out from under the base of the glass.

Really enjoyed myself again, beautiful. But then, anytime with you is special. Hope I can see you again? I gotta run an errand after work today outside town, but I'll be thinking of you. How about dinner Thursday night? Call or text me to confirm and I'll pick you up at seven if that's good with you. My treat, of course. D x

Why did her heart feel like it was in her mouth as she read the words? Just what kind of effect did he have on her exactly? She wasn't sure precisely but she knew her pulse rate must be through the roof right now.

He had said he wanted to see her again and that he would be thinking of her. He had actually written down his fricking feelings on a piece of paper. She pressed the paper to her lips, kissing the handwriting absentmindedly. God, what was she doing? She was behaving like he was her first crush.

She'd text him back immediately to confirm tomorrow's dinner date, of course, then she'd jump in the shower and head to the club. She just had to tell

Max her news. She couldn't keep it to herself or she'd burst with excitement.

* * * *

Arriving at Club Vain, Lola immediately sensed something was wrong. Everyone seemed to stop and stare at her as she walked in, and she could hear the whispers behind her back, though she couldn't make out what the hell they were saying. Why were they looking at her like that? What was going on?

Max shot her a look as she approached the bar.

"Not you too," she muttered, frowning at him. "What the heck is going on?"

"You haven't heard?" He raised an eyebrow at her and she shook her head. Hadn't heard what? What on earth was he talking about?

"No, what?"

"Remember the balding guy that hit on you last night? The one you took outside for some—ahem—fresh air?"

"Yeah, what about him?"

"He's dead."

"*What*?" The blood seemed to drain from her ears. But how? He was still breathing when she and Dillon had left him behind.

"They found him in the park this morning, dead from massive blood loss."

"How, Max? I didn't... You can't think... Are they saying *I* was somehow responsible?" Her voice almost a squeak, pleading, desperate.

Max's face was grave. "Lola, honey, it's not me you have to convince, though I should warn you that you might have a job assuring people of your innocence."

"Why? What are you saying?" Her eyes were wide as, panicked, they searched Max's face for answers.

"You were seen leaving the park last night," Max said, his tone matter-of-fact. "You and Dillon both. And after what Dillon did to Drago's face, people are gonna have a hard time believing he *wasn't* capable of hurting that guy."

Drago. Drago was behind this. She just knew it.

"Max, you have to listen to me," she said, leaning across the bar. "Dillon did nothing except defend me from Drago. Drago tried to hit on me and I refused to play along, so he got fresh with me, trying to force himself on me. It's damn lucky Dillon was there to rescue me or God knows what would have happened." She gave a shudder. She really didn't want to think about *that*.

Max nodded slowly.

"Max," she gasped, clutching at his forearm. "Max you have to believe me."

Max gave a heavy sigh.

"You know I do, honey, but you gotta admit the whole situation paints the pair of you to be guilty as all hell. First, there's the fact that *you* were seen leaving the club with the dude. Then Dillon whales on Drago's ass *again* then both you *and* Dillon are seen leaving the park together? People are saying Dillon killed him and you helped him cover it up."

"Why would they say that?" She didn't understand. Why would people be saying *Dillon* killed Dave if she was the one who'd been seen leaving the club with him?

"Because since everyone knows about Dillon knocking Drago on his ass in here the other day, he doesn't exactly seem like Mr. Easygoing. And people know you two have kind of a thing going on. It's not hard to put two and two together and make crazy jealous guy gets mad because his girlfriend went off with some other guy."

"I'm not Dillon's girlfriend," she blurted out, as if that made a difference to the whole awful situation. She knew what Max meant, and she knew how everyone else would think. Oh God, Drago had set them up so perfectly, and stupidly she'd just walked into it. This was what he'd meant when he'd threatened them both. In fact, she'd wager that he'd probably been planning something like this all along. Drago's ego had been rankled ever since Dillon had first put him in his place the other day, and she'd been stupid enough to hope he would let the insult to his pride slide.

"I suggest you tell Dillon to stay low profile for a while," Max warned. "At least while the police investigate the details." She nodded. She'd have to tell Dillon, and she'd have to tell him soon. He might change his mind and get home early from his errand or something and then he might come looking for her here. Why, when things were going so great with a guy she actually liked, did something have to come along and royally mess things up?

It's your own fault. You took too much blood. If you hadn't drained him, you wouldn't have needed to get the guy away from the club, and Drago wouldn't have been able to kill him. If the man was dead, then it had to be Drago who was responsible. She was certain of it. But how could she prove it? It was the year 2015. No one believed in vampires except other vampires. And *they* certainly weren't about to prosecute.

Even Drago's own father didn't know his son was a vamp. She didn't know when exactly it was that Drago had gotten turned, but she knew it had probably been around the time of the fire that had killed her family.

She remembered he'd seemed different to her after that — not just more arrogant, but something else too — and somehow she'd just known. Then the rumors had started. Coincidence? Perhaps. A lot of strange things had seemed to have happened in Burley around that time.

'You have the blood of the pure ones in you now, Lola. You will not see me again but remember my words, for my hope lies with you. The pure ones must ensure that justice triumphs. We may be immortal but we are not monsters, Lola. We must find a better way of living among the humans. You must never forget this. Never forget your conscience.'

Lola tore herself away from the memory of the words the fiery-eyed vampire had uttered to her as she had lain gasping amid the ashes of her family's ruined home. Lyra's words hadn't made too much sense to her then and even though eight long years had passed, she wasn't a whole lot closer to understanding them now. But she couldn't afford to dwell on such things at present. There was no time to lose. She had to get out of here and call Dillon. She knew she wouldn't be able to get a decent signal on her cell in Club Vain, even if she could have heard herself speak over the thumping bass.

"I have to get out of here," she mumbled to Max, turning away from the bar and making her way hurriedly through the club, the mass of bodies parting temporarily to let her through.

* * * *

The doorbell rang at exactly six-thirty p.m. and Lola flew to answer it. She already knew it would be Dillon, having spoken to him over the telephone yesterday after leaving Club Vain. She'd fretted over whether they should cancel their dinner plans, since half the town was already convinced of their guilt, but he'd insisted on keeping the date. Though he had acquiesced to bringing dinner to her instead, promising to cook her up a storm. Not that she was complaining. A man who could cook was totally irresistible. She only wished it was under better circumstances.

"Hey, beautiful," he said as she opened her front door, her gaze alighting on the open neckline of the plaid shirt he wore that exposed the smooth tan flesh of his chest. Even now, amid all her panic and stress, she still had time to appreciate how hot he was. She knew the rumors racing around Burley Falls must be stressing him out, but his appearance certainly didn't belie them. He looked smolderingly sexy tonight, even though he was dressed fairly casually.

"Hey, you," she said, smiling at him, but she knew her eyes betrayed her fears as she looked about nervously. Despite her unease, she still felt the powerful spark of attraction that crackled between the pair of them right there as he looked at her. His eyes sparkling naughtily and looking for all the world as if he were mentally undressing her. The thought made her shiver with anticipation at what he might do to her later, but then, as she remembered their current predicament, she turned her lustful daydream back to worry, looking nervously about the street to see if anyone was watching them. Sensing her anxiety, he took her by the forearm, guiding her firmly back into her apartment.

"Brought all the ingredients for tonight's cookout," he said, grinning as he held up the brown bag of groceries.

She nodded tersely, trying to smile, though she was still feeling a little tense.

"Hey, it's okay. No one saw me coming up the path," Dillon said, attempting to placate her. She shook her head, smiling. It was as though he could read her mind, sense what she worried about, like he knew exactly how to handle her. She'd never met a man who seemed to know her so well, so quickly before — not even Rory.

"Good. Sit down. I'll grab you a drink?" Bobbing her head, she gestured to the leather sofa.

Dillon grinned again, reaching into the baggie and withdrawing a bottle of wine.

"No need. Thought we could share this together? That's if you like red wine," he said, looking at her hopefully. She nodded, reaching out for the bottle and rapidly scanning the label. The corny graphic on the front of the bottle depicted a shadowy figure clad in a black cape bending his head over the silhouette of a girl as if he were about to sink his teeth into her neck.

First Bite. Sinfully good, the label read, and she tried hard to suppress a giggle, not wanting to offend his choice. It looked awfully cheesy. She hoped it didn't taste as tacky as it appeared. Then again, she probably shouldn't be so surprised. Dillon didn't strike her as a big-time wine drinker.

"Hah, don't worry about the corny ass label. The shopkeeper told me it won the silver award for best new wine this year. Plus, I thought it was pretty apt for my vampy chick," he said, grinning.

Oh boy, if only he knew...

"It's perfect," she said, smiling at him. "I'll just go grab two glasses." Back in the lounge, after she'd cracked open the bottle and poured them each a glass of the rich, red liquid, she relaxed back against the soft leather of the sofa, taking a large gulp of the wine. Surprisingly, it didn't actually taste bad at all.

"Mmm, this is quite yummy," she said, holding up her glass to the light and examining it. "So before we get into the heavy stuff, how did your errand go last night?" An odd look passed over Dillon's face, a strange expression she couldn't quite fathom.

"Oh, you know," he said, shrugging his shoulders, "work stuff, nothing you'd find exciting." Why was he acting like he had something to hide? Was she just imagining it?

"Uhh, well, try me," she said gently, attempting to coax a little more information out of him.

He took a deep breath and exhaled, the sound whistling through his teeth.

"Trust me. Some things it's definitely better you don't know," he replied, his jaw tightening as he clammed up. Now what the hell did that mean? *Some things it's better you don't know?* Was he seeing another woman? *Oh my God.* Her heart started to pound. He was married. He was fricking married. She was an idiot. No wonder he had seemed too good to be true. He *was.* The guy was a total lying, cheating asshole.

"You're married, aren't you?" She fixed him with a hard stare. Hah, let him lie his way out of *that.* Well, she'd enjoy watching him squirm. The way he'd played her, toyed with her feelings like that, led her into thinking there might be something more between them, when all along he was just after sex. Men, ugh.

"Nope. I'm not married."

"Then what?"

"I can't tell you. I want to, but I can't—at least not yet. You're just gonna have to trust me on this one."

Gonna have to trust him on this? What the hell was he talking about? She narrowed her eyes at him suspiciously. *Why is he acting so weird?*

"Dillon, look, I'm gonna ask you one more time and I expect you to be straight with me okay? Are you married?"

"Look, I told you I'm not married, okay? Maybe this is a bad time for me to be here," he said, starting forward as if to get up from his position beside her on the sofa.

Great. Way to go Lola. Kill conversation before it starts. *You had a great looking, considerate, sexy man bring you wine and offer to cook for you, and you couldn't be satisfied with that? Now you've pissed him off with your insecurity, and all he wants to do is get the hell out of here. You better think fast, my girl.*

"Dillon, wait," she said, gripping his forearm and squeezing it as he turned to look at her, his face still stony.

"I'm sorry," she said, trying to placate him, "but I don't understand why you can't tell me where you were last night." Her eyes searched his questioningly, silently willing him to fess up, but though his expression softened, his tone was still determined when he spoke.

"You're gonna just have to trust me on this," he said again, his eyes earnest as he took her by the shoulders, and though he was smiling at her, somehow his brown eyes seemed a little sad.

She nodded, letting the matter go, not wanting to push him anymore. They had enough to worry about at the moment, what with Drago and the tacky rumors spreading around Burley about Dillon's involvement in Dave's untimely demise. Uncovering the mystery of Dillon's secret would just have to wait.

"Okay, okay," she said, indicating her reluctant agreement as she gave him a thin smile. Dillon cupped her face gently.

"I promise I'm not gonna let you down," he said.

"I trust you," she murmured, returning his gaze, and even though she knew it was completely illogical, she meant it too. There was something about this man that *did* make her feel like she could depend on him, that he wouldn't let her down, even though logic told her she should still have doubts. But they had other, more important things to concern themselves with right now, like a potential murder charge.

"What about the rumors half the town is talking about, though?" She shot him an anxious glance.

"What is half the town talking about?"

"That you killed that guy because he was hitting on me, then I helped cover it up," she said, biting her lower lip.

"Why would they say that? That's ridiculous." He frowned, his thick eyebrows knitting together.

"I don't know, but they're saying it. Maybe it's because they saw me talking to him in the club," she said, shrugging. She would have to be careful what she let slip. Too much and she'd completely blow her cover. Not enough and he'd soon suspect that she was concealing something.

"You spoke to him?" Dillon looked surprised.

"Uhh, yeah at the bar. Max was there. He saw him. He came over to me actually. He was acting like a bit of a sleaze. Asked me if I'd like a drink, I said no, of course," she said, hoping desperately that it wasn't too obvious she was lying through her teeth.

"Why didn't you tell me you'd spoken to him?"

"I don't know. I guess I didn't figure it was too important. What does it matter anyhow?" She looked at him curiously. Why was he asking so many questions? Was it possible he suspected something?

"Lola, that dude is dead. The police are gonna want to speak to everyone who was seen talking to him. So if he was seen speaking with you, which is mighty likely otherwise why else would rumors be flying around, then you're gonna be a natural suspect."

"Yeah, I guess. I didn't think of it like that," she mumbled, feeling relieved he didn't seem to be acting suspicious or questioning her version of events.

"So the last time you spoke to him was when you were at the bar with Max?" He fixed her with an inquiring look.

"Uhh, yeah. Well, no, actually. I felt really sick so I went to the bathroom, then outside for some air. He must have followed me outside. It was kind of creepy."

"He followed you outside?" His tone was incredulous. "So you went to the bar before you got sick? I thought the reason you left me on the dance floor was because you were already sick?"

Dammit. Her story was falling apart. She had to think quickly.

"Uh, it was. I mean...I was," she fumbled, reaching desperately for something that sounded vaguely plausible and failing to find anything.

"Then I sure don't understand. Why did you go to the bar before you went outside for some air?"

"I'd already been to the bathroom once, after I left you on the dance floor, then when I came out, I couldn't find you so I swung by the bar to ask Max if he'd seen you," she lied smoothly.

Dillon nodded, digesting the information.

"I see. So that was when the sleazy dude hit on you?"

"Yeah, then I got sick again and had to go back to the restroom. After I came out, I hit the back door for some fresh air. That guy followed me out and started hitting on me again. He was coming on really strong, acting really drunk. I started to feel real sick, kinda like I was gonna faint. So I had to sit down, to try and keep myself from passing out. And that was when Drago came out."

"That little punk. What does he have to do with any of this? And why were you with *him* exactly?" Dillon said, scowling as the conversation turned to the subject of Drago.

"He helped me get away from the sleazy guy. He offered to walk me home to get some fresh air."

"Drago helped you?"

"Well, at first. This guy was coming on really strong, and I wasn't feeling so hot. I figured Drago may be an asshole, but at least he was a familiar asshole I could handle. I figured wrong, I guess," she said, hanging her head as she chewed her lower lip again.

Is Dillon buying any of this? She flicked him a quick glance, trying to gauge his mood, but his expression was unreadable. *It sounds plausible, doesn't it? My version of events?* And it wasn't like she could tell him what she'd really been doing outside with Dave. He'd think she was some kind of monster.

"If Drago ever so much as looks at you again—" Dillon threatened, stopping surprised as she pressed her finger to his lips.

"Don't. You can't let him get to you. I told you he was trouble and look where threatening him got us. Into a whole big pile of trouble, that's where."

"I don't care," he muttered stubbornly. "Just 'cause his daddy's Lord High and Mighty don't give him the right to put his hands all over my girl."

She blinked, slightly taken aback at the force of the outburst, as her brain tried to decipher why what he'd just said seemed so important.

"Damn, I'm sorry," he said, shaking his head as he brought his hands up to the sides of his face. "That dude just makes me so God damn pissed whenever I think of him."

"Sorry. What for?" she said, looking at him, confused. Had he meant to say it? Did he really think of her as his girl? Did she want to be? The answer was screamingly certain in her brain. She knew she didn't even need to give it a second thought. *Yes, yes, and oh my God, please, yes.* Trying to stifle the broad grin rapidly spreading over her face, she patted his arm in what she hoped was an encouraging manner.

"For being a presumptuous ass," he finished, clearly disgusted with himself. "I'm acting as bad as Drago did with that possessive crap. I know you're not my girlfriend but..." He faltered, his voice trailing off as he looked up at her, hope shining in his eyes.

"But what?" *Please say it again. Please say it again.*

"Uh well, I know it's kinda dumb of me to ask and I know you prolly got ten thousand better offers, but I'd really like you to be my girl, " he said, his cheeks flushing red as he turned his head away from her in embarrassment.

"Sorry," he added under his breath, as if he expected her to reject him.

He was a puzzle, so dominant and confident in the bedroom, so capable at protecting her, yet somehow she sensed he had a vulnerable side that needed nurturing. She couldn't prolong his agony any longer, not while inside she was silently screaming with joy at his words.

"The answer's yes, by the way," she replied, leaning forward and tugging at his shirt sleeve, unable to keep the smile from spreading over her face this time.

"You're serious?" He turned his head to look at her, his eyes genuinely incredulous as he took in her expression.

"Mmhmm. And you're wrong. I haven't got ten thousand better offers at all. My best offer recently has been Drago, and well, we all know how that turned out."

He grinned at that.

"You really want it to be just you and me?"

"Yes. Stop making it sound like I'm signing up for something bad, because I'm not. You're a great guy. Any girl would be lucky to have you," she said, laughing and squeezing his arm.

"Guess you wouldn't say that if you knew all about me," he said. "But I'll take the yes and run with it," he joked, leaning forward to scoop her up in his arms, toppling her back against the cushions of the sofa as he moved on top of her.

"Oh yeah? Man of mystery, huh?" She looked up at him and pawed the open neckline of his red and blue check shirt. He looked so handsome like that. She just wanted to tear the damn shirt off him. Was she crazy? What girl in her right mind would turn him down? She was sure most of the female population over the age of eighteen in Burley Falls would literally queue up for a piece of his fine ass.

"If only you knew," he muttered, swooping down to nuzzle at her neck, which had the effect of making her shiver in pleasure as his lips and the rough scratch of his stubble brushed against her own smoother skin.

"Oh, I'm sure it can't be all that bad," she said, half moaning, half speaking the words as he continued to give her neck attention, and her mind began to turn from the conversation they were having to the delicious tingle that was starting to spread from between her legs.

He grunted in response, his cock thickening as he responded to her body, his hands palming her flesh, eagerly searching over the silk blouse she wore, then unbuttoning it hastily until it fell open, displaying the raspberry silk bra she'd put on in anticipation of his visit.

His response was immediate, his hands on the silken cups, fingering and flicking her nipples, which stood out through the flimsy material, testifying to her arousal.

"Excited, huh?" He looked at her for an answer as he encircled her nipple, twisting.

Squirming at his touch—which made her feel aroused despite the uncomfortable sensation it provided—she found she didn't know how to respond. A flare of embarrassment was rising up in her at her own obvious eagerness to be dominated by him, and she couldn't seem to form logical thoughts, let alone a comprehensible sentence. She chose to merely nod dumbly instead, casting her eyes to the ground. *What is going on? Why is he making me feel so nervous?* She was Lola Devereaux, yet in this moment, she felt quite unable to look this man in the eye.

"Good girl. Now get on your knees. Unbutton my fly and take my cock out. I want you to suck it real good for me." His tone was tender, yet utterly in control. All the reserve he had displayed earlier gone now as lust took over, and the primal way he took charge of her felt like the most natural thing in the world.

Nodding her assent, she unzipped him, levering his thick, veiny cock out of his pants and obediently bending her head to it.

"Ahh," he sighed, looking down at the sight of her on her knees, as her lips closed around him. He moved his hands to her shoulders, the touch of him gently commanding as her head began to move back and forth, pleasuring him.

"Good girl. Suck it real nice. That's it. You like sucking my cock, don't you?"

"Yes," she moaned on to his length, her pussy dripping with arousal. What was she doing? Her head was spinning. She felt so out of control, like she wasn't in command of her own body. Did she like feeling that way? Was that why she felt so damn turned on?

The ache between her legs was so unbearable that she found her fingers slip between them to stroke lightly over the silk of her panties. He shook his head.

"Uh-uh. No pleasure until I say so. Understand?"

She nodded.

"Good girl. Now stand up and bend over the sofa." He helped her to her feet as she carried out his desire, hesitantly bending over as he had asked. She felt a little silly, but her body was on autopilot now, driven toward one goal, to feel the hard thrust of him inside her once again, so she did as he commanded her unquestioningly.

He pushed up the short skirt she wore, exposing her panties and the curve of her derriere. She was soaking wet with arousal. She knew he must be able to tell just how turned on she was, and the anticipation of how he might take advantage of that made her thrill with desire.

"Oh, very nice," he whispered, bending over her as his thick digits brushed wet silk, "but I think someone needs to be taught a lesson about waiting for orders."

Not understanding what he meant, she wondered momentarily what he was doing, as his hands left her body temporarily. She heard the creak of his belt as he eased it from his jeans, then the kiss of leather as he took her wrists behind her back and bound them quickly, before she had the chance to protest. Would she protest? Or did she want to be bound, restrained, unable to defend herself, barely able to move?

The way her body responded to the new sensation of having her wrists secured told her everything she needed to know.

"That's better," he said, tugging on the leather and forcing her to arch her back. He pushed the silk of her panties roughly aside, entering her wetness and making her gasp out loud.

"Oh, oh," she cried, her head twisting one way then the other at the delicious torment. She needed more, wanted him to put more fingers inside, wanted him to put them all inside.

"You want to be fucked by me, huh? By my fat cock?"

"Yes," she cried, practically screaming the word. She could take no more of the sensations flooding her overstimulated body. If he didn't take her right this moment, she feared she'd go mad with lust.

"Beg then," he urged, the word simple but potent.

"Fuck me, please."

"So who's in control here?"

"Y-you are," she said hesitantly, unsure where exactly this was going but wanting to know all the same.

"And who tells you when you can get pleasure?"

"You. You do?"

"That's right. So in the future, no touching until I say so. Understand?"

She thought about it for one single second before nodding her agreement.

"Ye-yes."

"Good girl. *Now* you can have your pleasure," he said, pulling her panties back wider and pushing his full length deep into her as he yanked on the leather that bound her.

It was too much. The tug of leather reinforced his dominance over her, and coupled with the anticipation she had been feeling, sent her body over the edge as she came heavily over his cock.

As she cried out in ecstasy, he drove his cock in deeper, his body replying to hers in silent rhythm as he rode her hard and wild, any way he wanted until the hardness of him erupted in a feral groan and his frantic thrusts ceased.

"You're mine now," he whispered in her ear as they recovered, his body covering hers, his hand still holding the makeshift leash that held her wrists bound, and the words silently thrilled her.

His, she was *his*. She belonged to him. Somehow — and she didn't know how — he filled up the empty void inside her and made her feel whole again. As she lay there, breathing hard, she thought how somehow when they fucked it always felt deeper. She wasn't corny enough to call it making love exactly, but it was as if — when their bodies joined together — their wild spirits communicated the deepest yearnings of their souls.

He was her answer, and she was his. And though she had no idea how practically they would ever be together, this much she knew now, at least.

Chapter Five

The next day Lola woke early to a loud knocking on the door, the sound hammering and insistent. She quickly flicked a glance at the clock on the bedside table. Five-thirty p.m., it would just be growing dark outside. She lay there for a moment, hoping whoever it was would figure that no one was at home and go away, but the incessant banging continued. Begrudgingly, she rubbed at her eyes, blearily attempting to clear the sleep from them, as she tried to arouse herself from what had been a rather pleasant slumber.

"Coming," she yelled out, hurriedly pulling on a white turtleneck sweater, the material's tight fit emphasizing and complimenting the curves of her figure. Hastily she reached for the black skinny jeans draped over the back of the oak chair that stood at the end of the bed.

The chair had been Grandma Devereaux's. It had belonged to Grandma's mother before her and was something of a family antique. Lola wasn't sure how old it was exactly, but the aged patina on the grain told her it had been around a good number of years. She'd inherited it when Grandma's house was finally cleared out last year after standing empty for the five years since her death. Most of the rest of Grandma's furniture was in storage, and she didn't really have anywhere to put it since the ornate oaks and rich mahoganies that Grandma and Grandpa Devereaux had favored didn't exactly fit in with her monochromatic theme, but she'd not been able to bring herself to part with the chair.

She finished pulling her jeans on, quickly smoothing down her bed-rumpled hair as she made her way to answer the door.

"Miss Devereaux?" The officer's face was inquiring as he looked up at her. He was youngish, though he had to be at least five years older than her. She reckoned him to be about thirty. His light brown curly hair framed a pleasant, honest appearing face. Some might even call it a handsome one, though he couldn't hold a candle to Dillon. There she went comparing everyone to Dillon again. Jesus, she was obsessed. She nodded at the officer in response. This had to be about the murder surely?

"You probably already know what this is in conjunction with, Miss Devereaux," the officer said, as if reading her thoughts. She noticed he hadn't come alone. To his left stood a twenty-something, sensible-faced redheaded woman, dressed in the same standard-issue force uniform as he was. The woman gave her a sympathetic, if no-nonsense, smile, and Lola smiled politely back at her in return. Well, at least they both looked fairly friendly. She turned her attention back to the male officer, who stood there, politely waiting for her to respond to his question.

"Uhh…yeah… Yeah, I do have an idea. Would you both like to come inside?" She gestured behind her, into the hallway, but the officer shook his head firmly.

"No, miss. I'm…I'm sorry," he stammered, as she raised an eyebrow at him. "I'm sorry, miss, but I've instructions to take you down to the station for questioning."

They were hauling her ass down to the station? Wow, Drago must have really persuaded his father to do a number on Lola. Then again, a guy had wound up dead and she supposed somebody had to account for it. The police were only doing their job after all. It wasn't their fault they were trying to apply human laws to vamps who operated somewhat above the law—or was that under it?

Whatever… It didn't really matter. The important thing was to cooperate with them—whatever they wanted—so that their suspicions weren't raised. That included going with them voluntarily and telling them what they wanted to know—or at least, what they needed to know. Nodding her head, she looked at the pair of them, smiling resignedly as she shrugged her shoulders.

"Sure, no problem. I'll help any way I can. Lead the way," she said, as the redheaded woman took her by the arm and guided her firmly to the police car parked outside her apartment.

* * * *

They let her out four hours later, after repeatedly asking her for an account of the night Dillon had rescued her from Drago. She'd told them nearly everything that had happened—how she'd spoken with Dave in the club, how Drago had offered to walk her home, then hit on her, refusing to take no for an answer. She'd told them too, how Dillon had come to her rescue and how the two of them had walked home to her apartment afterward.

Of course she'd had to leave out the part about how she'd hit on Dave first, figuring him to be a likely food source, as well as the part about Drago being a vamp, because — face it — if she *had* told them, they would probably have looked at her like she was crazy.

Most people didn't believe vampires really existed, at least not until it was too late. Had Dave believed in vampires? Probably not or he might not have wound up dead. Somehow she couldn't shake the feeling that she was at least partially responsible for his death.

No sense feeling guilty after the fact now, Lola. Face it. You're a monster. Might as well embrace who you are.

But she knew she could never fully embrace that part of the curse, the terrible hunger that if left unchecked could drive her to endanger others in a way that scared her. Dave may have been a sleaze, but he definitely didn't deserve to die for it, especially not by Drago's hand. That was the frustrating thing, not being able to tell the police that Drago was responsible.

Oh, she didn't have any proof, but she had more than a hunch who was really behind all this. And, as usual, Drago would walk away from it all scot free, with not as much as a smear on his reputation. The cops would search for a suspect, and eventually, unable to find anything concrete and desperately needing to tie up loose ends, they would lay the blame on a likely sucker, most probably a felon with a prior rap sheet.

Well, that was too bad, but even worse would be if somehow she and Dillon got caught up in it all. There was no way she was going to allow Drago to try to frame them both. Pacing the final few blocks home, she felt confident that Dillon and she would both soon be discounted as having anything to do with the murder. Though the questioning earlier had been extensive, the two officers had been friendly and the interview seemed to go well. And neither of them had acted like they'd disbelieved her version of events.

After slipping her key into the lock of her front door, she stepped inside, clicking the door shut behind her. A nice hot shower was what she needed, followed by a large glass of wine.

She'd not showered since yesterday evening and her dark hair was tangled and unkempt. She'd freshen up and see if she could get in touch with Dillon again after. As soon as she'd been released, she'd called his cell but he wasn't picking up. Figuring he must still be busy at work — probably fixing a customer's car — she'd left a message instead. Why hadn't he responded to her yet? Was he regretting asking her to get serious the previous evening?

Stop obsessing. You're behaving like a schoolgirl over this guy. She remembered his sexy growl as he tugged on the leather of the belt that had bound her wrists and gave a little shiver as she crossed the hallway to pad slowly up the stairs to the bathroom, where the hot steam of the shower awaited her.

Just as she'd peeled her clothes off, discarding them on the bed ready for her shower, the cell phone she'd left on top of her dresser rang out sharply. Groaning, she reluctantly crossed the room to answer it. Who was it now? This had better be important?

"Hello?"

"Lola?"

Max's voice? "Max?"

"Yep, it's me. You okay?"

"I'm fine. Why wouldn't I be?" She was losing patience now. All she wanted to do was jump under the shower's hot stream of water and forget about everything.

"It's Dillon. Something bad has happened…" Max's voice sounded grave and she suddenly felt a sinking feeling in the pit of her stomach. What did he mean something bad? Dillon couldn't be hurt?

"Max, is Dillon okay? Is he sick?" Her voice was urgent as she spoke, the fine hairs standing up on the back of her neck.

"He's not hurt, and he's not sick." She heard herself audibly exhale at the words.

"Then what?"

"He's been arrested on suspicion of murder."

"*What?*"

"Drago took great pleasure in telling me. Apparently some guy told the cops Dillon attacked him two nights ago. I don't know the details. Drago was gloating too much to tell me properly but I suggest you come down to the club. Maybe you can speak to Drago and find out more."

"How come Drago told you? Is he the only one who knows anything about this?"

"Duh. His daddy is Commissioner. Of course he knows. But I wouldn't say he's the only one, at least not now. Rumors are flying around the place like wildfire."

"Okay, I'll be right there. I just need to go shower and freshen up," she said grimly as she hung up.

* * * *

Arriving at the club, she gave a cursory nod to Tony, the broad-shouldered bouncer who worked the door. He smiled back at her politely but his expression didn't seem to be his usual friendly one. There was something else in his eyes tonight. What was it exactly? Why was he looking at her that way? Had he heard the rumors too? She didn't know, but she couldn't hang around to find out. She had far bigger problems to deal with. Pushing open the glass-fronted door of Club Vain, she strode through the plush purple carpet of the reception area on stiletto heels, making her way over to the black-painted double doors that led into the club beyond.

As she entered, she rapidly became aware of the eyes that seemed to follow her as she picked her way through the crowd, the sly glances shot her way by the regulars at Club Vain. Max hadn't exaggerated. It obviously wasn't just Tony on the door who'd heard the rumors.

Well, let them look. She wasn't going to let them see how scared she really was. She'd dressed with extra care tonight, knowing full well that as news of Dillon's arrest spread, she would likely be the center of attention by association. The scarlet silk dress flattered her every curve and sheathed her body snugly, the material draping expertly to enhance her assets to the maximum. Pair that with the black patent spike heels that had cost almost as much as the annual gasoline bill for her car and she knew she was dressed to kill. Hopefully not literally, though she would have to do all she could to hold herself back once she saw Drago.

That little punk, as Dillon had called him, had caused some serious trouble — trouble that Dillon might not be able to get out of. Why was it exactly that as soon as she found a decent guy who she actually could consider dating, Drago and his ego had to go and spoil everything?

She spied Max at his familiar position behind the bar and made a beeline for him, maneuvering her way through the crush with expert ease.

"Hey, Max," she said somewhat mutedly as she propped herself up at the bar.

He raised his head, giving her a thin smile. "Hey, sweetie, you okay?"

She sighed. "I guess. I tried to call Dillon after you called me, just in case, but he didn't pick up his phone. Then I called the station but they wouldn't let me speak to him and they wouldn't tell me anything. They wouldn't even officially confirm they had him in custody since I'm not his next of kin."

Max gave her a sympathetic glance as he patted her forearm. "How about I make you a drink. Extra strong Bloody Mary?"

She shook her head. The thought of anything remotely resembling blood was suddenly making her feel a little queasy. After all, it had been her own damn thirst for the stuff that had wound up getting Dillon in trouble. If she hadn't needed to feed, she wouldn't have needed Drago to help her walk Dave for air. Then Dillon would never have wound up in jail.

"Nah. Just a vodka — on the rocks, no mixer. Actually, make it a double. I'm gonna need some Dutch courage if I'm gonna talk to Drago."

"Yeah, he seemed pretty pleased with himself when he stopped by for a drink with his obnoxious friends earlier," Max said, shaking his head. Drago's friends were pretty notorious, almost as snotty nosed and spoiled as he was. The crowd he ran around in was almost exclusively vamps, and every one of them had parents who dripped money.

"Where is he now?" She looked around the club, scanning the crowd as she tried to pick out Drago's bright blond head.

Max shrugged as he turned to fix her vodka.

"Dunno. He's about, though. He asked after you. Said he'd be expecting you." She rolled her eyes, great. Drago obviously fully expected her to beg him for crumbs of information. Well, she wasn't going to give him the satisfaction. If he wouldn't do the decent thing and tell her what he knew, she'd just have to find some other way.

"Ta-da. One double vodka on the rocks," Max said, handing her the ice-cold tumbler.

"Thanks," she said, knocking back the liquid, the ice chinking against the rim of the glass. She swallowed the contents, the neat alcohol burning slightly on its way down into her stomach, but it did what she'd hoped, taking the edge off her frazzled nerves nicely and providing her with a pleasantly numb sensation. One more and she'd be ready to face Drago. She turned back to Max.

"Pour me another?"

"Careful, Lola. You don't want to get wasted," he warned.

"Eh, I can handle it. Trust me. I'm gonna need to be a little gone to talk to Sir Spoiled Brat, otherwise I might not be able to hold back. I just can't believe he would go this far," she said, taking another glance around the club and chewing absentmindedly on her lower lip. Her eyes fell on a crowd gathering around one of the tables in the corner of the room. Squinting she walked forward, peering through the bodies bumping and grinding on the dance floor to try to discern what all the fuss seemed to be about.

There was Luke, Drago's friend, and there was Sam. *Ugh, he is as snotty-nosed as Drago.* And there was Drago's sister, Marie, the tall, thin, blonde girl dressed head-to-toe in black designer garb. Just then, the hubbub around the table parted temporarily and Lola saw Drago himself, seated on one of the club's chunky red leather chairs and holding court as people thronged about him.

He's probably regaling them with tales of Dillon's guilt and loving being the only one to have insider information on the hottest topic to hit Burley Falls.

"Here," she heard Max say as he thrust the newly made drink at her.

Accepting it gratefully, she took a large swig before handing it back to him and turning to make her way toward where Drago's crowd gathered.

"Good luck," Max called after her, as she made her way through the heaving club, the intrigued eyes of the club goers following her as she moved. Arriving at Drago's table, she stood there for a moment, feeling confused as the throng of people clamored for his attention. Should she wait for the crowd to part before she approached him or should she just jump right in there and force her way through? The Dutch courage she'd imbibed prompted her to take the second course of action, and with a firm set of her jaw, she began to ferret her way through the crowd that gathered around Drago, muttering the odd excuse me, as she pushed her way forcibly to where the king awaited his court.

As Drago caught sight of her, a smile of pure satisfaction spread over his spoiled features.

"Why look who it is. It's little Miss Devereaux herself," he drawled, arching an eyebrow as he cradled a tumbler of what looked like whiskey in his hand.

Resisting the impulse to lunge for his throat and begin throttling, Lola bit her tongue, forcing herself to take a deep breath before she spoke. What was she planning to say to him? She hadn't really thought about it but she better think fast. Drago was waiting for her response, and she could feel the eyes of his entourage keenly watching their exchange. Fortunately for her, Drago was the first one to break the awkward silence.

"Come to ask me what I know about Dillon?"

"No. Well…maybe. I mean, I already know he's been taken in for questioning. What more is there to know?" She hoped she'd come across fairly nonchalantly and not betrayed the desperate uneasiness and panic she was feeling inside. It wouldn't do to let Drago know just how anxious she really felt. That would only serve to feed his power trip.

"Oh, I think you'll find there's quite a bit more," Drago said, rubbing his chin smugly as he smirked at her from his position ensconced in the leather armchair.

"Like?" Lola tried not to let her irritation show but she was close to slapping him. Dillon was in a jail cell because of him. It was all she could do to restrain herself. No wonder Dillon had socked him one. If it wouldn't make a bad situation worse, she swore she'd do the same thing herself and not regret it for an instant.

"Well, like the fact some random guy told the police Dillon tried to attack him. Showed them his neck wound and identified him in a lineup. Apparently it was completely unprovoked. The dude said Dillon was like an *animal*." Drago grinned with satisfaction, his pale blue eyes boring in to Lola's face as he watched her reaction to the news.

"What?" She couldn't believe what she was hearing. Dillon, guilty of assaulting someone unprovoked? He couldn't be guilty. Dillon wouldn't just hit someone out of the blue like that. There must be some mistake.

"Oh yes," Drago continued, his lips curling over sharp teeth in a pleased expression as he leaned forward. "Your little boyfriend is going to have to answer a lot of very difficult questions. And if he can't give the right answers, then he's going to be going away for a very long time indeed." Drago sat back, satisfied he had made his point, as she stood there in front of him feeling dumbstruck, not knowing quite how to respond.

"It's you who's done all this, isn't it? You're bitter and sore because you couldn't stand up to Dillon and because I rejected you, so you made up lies and used your fathers influence to get him arrested," she said, spitting the words out angrily as she pointed a finger at him.

"Careful," Drago warned her, "you're making a spectacle of yourself. But maybe that's because you feel a little guilty yourself about Dillon's arrest?"

"Why the hell would I feel guilty about Dillon getting arrested when everyone knows it's *you* who was really responsible?" She fixed him with an accusatory stare.

She knew the crowd of hangers-on huddled around Drago and her were watching and listening to the two of them trade barbs, and she knew too that even more rumors would be flying around Burley Falls after tonight. *Well, let them talk. Perhaps a little speculation over Drago's apparent innocence will help Dillon's cause.* Drago brought the glass he was holding up to his thin lips, draining the last of the contents elegantly, the amber liquid disappearing down the back of his throat as he smiled in satisfaction.

"Because everyone knows it was you who enticed the dead dude outside. I for one saw you. You can't deny it. As for your boyfriend? Well, he has a temper on him, that one, doesn't he? Guess Mr. Perfect got jealous." Drago grinned, his expression menacing in the dark shadows of the club. Casually he held out the empty tumbler he was holding in his right hand, gesturing for a member of his entourage to take it.

Frustrated, she stifled the urge to scream, clenching her fists as she spun on her heel. She couldn't stand to hear Drago gloat a second longer. Turning her back on him, she plunged back into the mass of bodies populating the dance floor.

"Lola Devereaux?"

The voice that came from somewhere behind her was softly insistent, and she felt the arm gently tugging at her elbow. Spinning around, she turned to face the owner of the voice. A dark-haired, fairly unassuming-looking man who appeared to be in his late thirties stood looking back at her. She didn't recognize him. She'd never seen him in the club before, and she would remember if she had too, for despite his rather nondescript appearance, she had an excellent memory for faces.

"Yes?" Raising her eyebrow she looked at the stranger suspiciously, waiting for him to explain himself. Who was he? And how did he know her name?

"I have some information that might be of interest."

"What kind of information?"

"Information regarding the death of Dave Eversham."

The dead guy. Instantly her guard went up. This better not be one of Drago's twisted attempts to rile her.

"What about him?" She narrowed her eyes at the man, staring at him intensely as she tried to figure him out. Visibly he recoiled, and she smiled to herself. She knew she could be pretty intimidating when she chose to.

"Well?"

Furtively he looked around, as if he were making sure that no one was listening to their conversation. Taking her by the arm, he gestured over toward the booths lining the walls of the club.

"I think we should sit down somewhere a little more private?" He looked at her pleadingly.

She considered the question a moment, still suspicious, before nodding her assent.

He turned, threading his way through the club and Lola followed his white T-shirt-clad back, her interest piqued. What information was he talking about? What could he know that she didn't already, if anything?

"You're probably wondering what this is all about and who I am," he said, giving her a slightly nervous smile as they both sat down opposite each other in one of the booth's lining Vain's purple walls. She noted he had pleasant eyes and an honest-looking face, though she knew better than to judge a book by its cover. Still, she sensed she could trust him.

"I'm a bit curious. I must admit," she said, nodding and returning his smile with a brief, small one of her own.

"I'm Jim Cavanagh, reporter for the *Burley Chronicle*. I have some information—" He stopped suddenly as she held up a hand, making as if to get up from the chair.

"No, sorry. I'm not going to answer any questions. You'll have to get your story another way Mr....Callahan, was it?"

"It's Cavanagh, but please, listen a minute. It's not you I want to question."

Frowning, she looked at him, not understanding. "Then who?"

"Actually I don't want to question anyone. As I said, I have some information — sensitive information I think could be of interest to you."

"So what is this *information*?" Perhaps she was giving him a hard time, but he wasn't exactly telling her everything. Why all the cloak and dagger stuff?

He leaned forward, beckoning her to come closer. "This morning I was approached by a witness who saw a man in Burley Park with Dave Eversham shortly before he died. A blond man...someone who very definitely wasn't Mr. Chambers."

So, it *had* been Drago. Her suspicions were correct. And there was a witness? One thing was for sure. Whoever it was, was in danger. There was no way Drago was going to allow anything or anyone to incriminate him.

"Mr. Cavanagh, I'm sure you're already aware this information is highly sensitive. Your witness...is he or she aware of this fact?"

Jim nodded, his head bobbing enthusiastically, a furtive look in his eyes as he scanned the club to ensure no one had noticed them. She really didn't blame him. Drago had spies everywhere.

"The witness is a he. And, yes, he's aware, but rest assured, the only person who knows what he saw is me. And the only person I've told about this is you, since you and Mr. Chambers are the only people I can trust."

"How do you know you can trust me? Or Dillon, for that matter?"

He smiled. "Well, since you and Mr. Chambers are in the frame as prime suspects, I think the pair of you are probably the only two people in the whole of Burley

Falls that I can know for sure aren't covering up for Drago Graythorne."

Nodding thoughtfully, she stared across the table at Jim, her eyes not focusing on anything in particular as her brain scrambled to make sense of things.

"Is your witness prepared to give a statement to the police about what he saw?" It was unlikely, though. After all, who in their right mind would dare to defy the juggernaut that was the Graythorne family?

Jim pulled a face. "As I'm sure you can appreciate, this is very sensitive. But if the source's anonymity could be assured, then perhaps…yes."

"But it would still be this one man's testimony against Drago's." She lowered her voice to a hushed whisper before continuing, "It *was* Drago your witness saw, wasn't it?"

"It was." The whisper that escaped Jim's lips was almost imperceptible but the resigned head nod he gave told her everything she needed to know.

"The court would never hear of it," she said, shaking her head. "It would never fly, and this witness — whoever he is? He'd have to leave Burley Falls forever. Hardly worth it, especially when I don't see how it would help Dillon any. I'd tell your witness to just forget about what he saw, if I were you." She shrugged resignedly as she stood up.

"Wait," he protested, clutching at her arm.

Confused, she looked down at him, her brow furrowing.

"There's more."

She sat back down in the chair again, rolling her eyes slightly. *This better be good.* "There is?"

"Yes. There's photographic evidence. The witness took several pictures with his mobile phone. Now, they aren't the best quality, but even so, it's pretty clear who the attacker is and who he's with."

She sat bolt upright in her chair at that. *Did he just say photographic evidence?* But that changed everything. Surely even Drago couldn't argue against solid proof like that?

"Do…do you have the pictures?" She held her breath. She hardly dared hope. Jim nodded, his mousy brown mop of curls bobbing up and down as he gave her a small, thin smile.

"I do. I have them safely stored in an encrypted file on the computer at my office. And I think if we can persuade our witness to approach the police, we might just be in with a chance of clearing your boyfriend's name."

"What's in it for you?" Her eyes narrowed at him. Cynical as it might sound, in her experience, *no one* did anything purely out of the goodness of their hearts.

Jim shifted slightly in his seat, visibly uncomfortable, his eyes avoiding her gaze as he stared at the tabletop.

"Well, if we *do* manage to break this case, it *would* make a good story for the *Chronicle*," he said, still averting her gaze. Ah, of course, a journalist. She should have known his priority would be getting a good story. Well, she wouldn't complain about that. If the evidence he possessed helped clear Dillon's name, she'd gladly write the damn story for him.

"Sure," she said brightly, laying her hand on his shoulder.

Visibly he relaxed at the tone of her voice.

"If you can help get Dillon and me out of this mess, I think you deserve a scoop." She grinned. She still felt like she couldn't quite take it all in. Her brain was reeling from Jim's revelations. She'd known Drago had to be responsible, but the fact that someone else had witnessed him with Dave *and* had the photographic evidence to prove it was mind-blowing. Surely this had to prove Dillon's innocence?

"Hah, thanks," Jim said, returning her smile, though she noted he was still looking around furtively to see who might be observing them. Drago's reputation obviously preceded him. She didn't blame Jim for his caution. After all, he had stumbled across some dangerous information — the kind of information certain people would kill to get their hands on and destroy. And Drago had killed at least once, of that she was more than certain, and she'd hazard a guess that he wouldn't hesitate to kill again.

"I'd like to see the pictures. Is it possible?"

"Yeah, of course, we should set up at time to meet," Jim said, nodding.

"Can I see them tonight?"

Time was of the essence and she wanted to ensure this guy was the real deal. There was no use barking up the wrong tree. The witness could have been confused. He could have been drunk. He could have wrongly identified Drago. She needed to see those pictures.

Jim paused, considering her request.

"Okay," he said, "I'll drive you in my car. But we have to make sure no one sees us leave together. Meet me in the car park by the green Vauxhall Astra in fifteen minutes? My car's the one two rows from the back." He looked at her to assess her reaction as she nodded her acquiescence.

"Sure. Ten minutes and I'll follow you outta here," she assured him.

* * * *

Thirty minutes later, Lola was ensconced in the offices of the *Burley Chronicle*, peering at the grainy images on Jim's computer screen. The building was deserted since all the staff had long gone home, and she and Jim had taken extra care to ensure no one had seen the two of them leave together, but even so, she couldn't help feel a vague sense of unease. If Drago or any of his goons found out what Jim had discovered, both their lives, as well as the witness', would be in danger, and Dillon could kiss goodbye to his freedom. They had to make certain they played this right.

Lola leaned forward as Jim clicked through the sequence of images on the computer screen. In the first few, she could only make out two shadowy shapes, one lying slumped against the old oak tree in the park where the confrontation between Dillon and Drago had occurred, and the other, a thin figure, clad in dark clothes, standing with his back to the camera, the only identifying feature being the thatch of bright blond hair that topped his head.

As Jim clicked on, the angle changed slightly, as if the person taking the pictures had changed position. Now it was possible to see the blond figure's face in side profile, a profile that looked all too familiar. There was no mistaking the owner of that aquiline nose and haughty bone structure for anyone else but Drago. The snaps continued, the photographer angling the camera and zooming in closer as Drago began to bend down to the figure on the floor menacingly.

The slumbering figure slouched against the tree seemed unaware of his horrific future fate, even as the pictures showed Drago bending his head to the man's neck. Lola had seen enough. Turning her head away from the images, she took a deep breath. She wasn't squeamish but there'd been something about the look in Drago's eyes that was deeply unsettling.

"Are you all right?" Jim's voice pierced her thoughts.

"Yeah, yeah," she said, steeling herself. "I'll be okay. It's just a bit disturbing. That's all." But why was the sight of another vamp about to sink his teeth into an innocent man's neck so disturbing? Hadn't that been exactly what she herself had done to the very same man just a couple of hours earlier that night? Didn't that make her a hypocrite of the highest order?

That's different. You didn't intend to kill him. But she'd known there was a risk. There was always a risk. And that hadn't stopped her, had it? It was all her fault—Dave's death, Dillon's arrest, everything. She should never have allowed herself to become involved with Dillon. She should have learned her lesson after what she had done to Rory.

"Lola?"

"Uh, sorry, I was just thinking. Surely this clears Dillon now? Especially because the pictures are time-stamped?"

"That's the idea. But we still have to convince the witness to testify. And you know how hard that's going to be," Jim said, smiling tentatively at her.

Lola nodded. Hard was a definite understatement. Try impossible. If there was anyone in this town, vampire or otherwise, who was prepared to go up against Drago and his powerful father, then she had yet to meet them. Taking a deep breath, she shot another look at the screen. An image of Drago, eyes rolling back in his head, a dark line of blood trickling from his thin lips, assaulted her senses. She closed her eyes, mentally willing the image away.

"Have you kept a copy of these anywhere else?" She looked at Jim quizzically. They had to make sure the evidence was safe. It was Dillon's only chance. Even though the file was encrypted, she still didn't feel completely reassured. If Drago somehow got wind there was pictorial evidence of his guilt, he would definitely send his goons to break into the newspaper's offices.

Jim paused, considering something. Reaching into his pocket, he pulled out a small black rectangular object, holding it out for her inspection. Confused, she crinkled up her nose. What was it?

"Have 'em stored on here," Jim said, tapping the object with his index finger.

"What's that?"

"USB flash drive. You just plug it into any computer's USB port, then you can upload and access the files. Here. Take it. I'll make another copy for me," he said, placing the object into her palm. Feeling slightly bewildered, she accepted it, closing her fingers around the small, square object.

"But why don't *you* just keep it safe?"

"Because if anyone finds out what I know, they'll come after me. And you can be sure they'll try to destroy the evidence. So it's important you keep a copy too."

She nodded, a shiver running down her spine as an unwelcome thought flashed through her head. Knowing Drago, it wouldn't be just the evidence he would want to destroy. Pushing the thought away, she forced herself to focus on the present. No use thinking of what might happen. They had to concentrate on clearing Dillon's name.

"The witness? Do you know his identity?" She narrowed her eyes as she looked at Jim.

He nodded, slightly hesitantly.

"Yes...but—"

"Don't you think I should know that too, just in case the worst happens?"

"Uh, well, he asked me to keep his identity secret until we could be very sure we could build a water-tight case against Drago. And I have to respect his wishes. He's been very brave in coming forward."

She sighed, nodding reluctantly. Great, so if Drago did come after them, then she wouldn't be able to name the one and only person who could possibly help clear Dillon's name. Well then, they'd just have to work fast to ensure that they could get the witness to testify.

"So we need a solicitor, I take it?" She looked at Jim questioningly.

Jim nodded. "We do. And I happen to know a rather good prosecuting attorney. I'll call her first thing tomorrow and see if I can get a morning appointment to speak with her. You can come with me if you can make it?"

Panic gripped her in the pit of her stomach, its icy fingers coiling around her intestines as fear coursed through her. How could she? She couldn't last five minutes in sunlight without burning and blistering up, never mind sit for God knows how long in an attorney's office in the middle of the day, not to mention the drive all the way there. But what could she say without arousing suspicion? *Think, Lola. Think.*

"Uh, actually I can't," she said, trying to inject what she hoped sounded like a disappointed note into her voice. "I've got a really important prior engagement with one of my big clients," she added, hoping Jim wouldn't require her to expound on what exactly it was that she did.

"Oh, okay. What is it that you do exactly?"

Hunt and stalk innocent humans and suck their blood? Then leave them in a weakened state at the mercy of other vamps with more sinister intentions? Somehow she didn't think that answer would go down too well.

"Interior design. I work freelance. Just getting started really but it's beginning to pick up." Amazing how easily lies flew off the tongue when necessary. She felt a little guilty lying to Jim when he was obviously placing his trust in her but it wasn't exactly like she had another choice, was it? Anyway, it was only a white lie. After all, interior design would be what she *would* want to do if she wasn't an accursed vamp. She'd always had a flair for design but it was pretty darn hard to decorate people's homes when you couldn't even open your own curtains for fear of burning unless you'd covered yourself from head to toe in thick black fabric first.

"Oh, awesome, do you have a website?" Dammit. Why did journalists have to be so nosey?

"Uh, like I said, it's just getting started really," she said, floundering. "I'm hoping to get one built soon, though," she added, smiling politely.

"Sure. I know a great web designer if you'd like me to put you in touch. I know she'd give you a discount. She's a personal friend," Jim said, smiling back at her. Okay, this was getting way too intense. She needed to steer the focus away from her career — or the lack of it — and back to getting Dillon out of jail.

"Tell you what," Jim continued. "If you're going to be busy all day, we can go see my lawyer friend at her home in the evening. I'd rather you were with me, since you were the one with Dillon that night. Lydia doesn't usually take out of hours appointments, but she'll see us as a favor to me."

"Another personal friend?" She raised an eyebrow at him. How many personal female friends did this unassuming-looking man have? Jim laughed broadly, the smile reaching his brown eyes this time, as his face creased with amusement.

"Hah. Not what you think, Lola. Much as I'd love to play the great Casanova, Lydia and I are and have always been strictly platonic. But as a journalist, I've done her a few favors in the past, so I figure she owes me one."

She grinned. "Okay. Well, tomorrow evening would be much better. What time were you thinking?"

"I'll call you to let you know, but should be around eight p.m. She doesn't live too far from here. I'll come pick you up of course."

Eight p.m. Phew, the sun would definitely have gone down by then.

"Sure, no problem," she said, replying smoothly, breathing an internal sigh of relief.

"Okay, well, we'd better get out of here now," Jim said, getting to his feet and reaching forward to flick the monitor off.

"I'll drive you to your place," he added, and she bobbed her head gratefully, following his lead and standing up. Tonight had certainly been eventful, but for the first time since Dave had been found dead, she felt hope in her heart instead of the dreaded sinking feeling she'd been carrying around with her.

Chapter Six

Sitting in Lydia Balmain's front room with Jim beside her, the two of them perched on the edge of a maroon-colored sofa, Lola smiled politely as Jim made introductions.

"Lydia, this is Lola Devereaux," Jim said, turning to Lola then back to the cool blonde sitting elegantly ensconced in the armchair opposite, observing Lola with a detached, professional-looking smile.

"Hi, Lydia," Lola ventured, feeling a little shy. She was never normally flustered in social situations but the woman's professional manner made her feel like she was awaiting her fate in a head teacher's office. She needn't have worried, though, for Lydia smiled warmly, her genuine expression illuminating her features and crinkling up the corners of her sea-green eyes.

"Nice to meet you, Lola. Any friend of Jim's is welcome here. So what can I do for you exactly? Jim tells me you're looking for some legal advice on the Eversham case?"

"Uh, yeah. My uh, friend Dillon...he's been arrested on suspicion of murder. The police won't tell me the exact details, but I think they're trying to put the blame on him for the death of Dave. I mean...Mr. Eversham," she said, correcting herself. It definitely wouldn't do to appear disrespectful about a dead man in front of the lawyer she was seeking assistance from.

"Please do go on, Lola." Lydia frowned, her brow furrowing.

"Well, I know that Dillon couldn't have had anything to do with it. The last time either of us saw Mr. Eversham was the night he died, and we left him in the park and very much alive when we went back to my apartment. Dillon was with me the whole night, until he had to leave for work in the morning." A vivid memory of Dillon on top of her as the two of them writhed in her bed came to mind then and she hoped the woman couldn't tell from the guilty look on her face what she was thinking about.

Lydia nodded thoughtfully, scratching the side of her face with a perfectly manicured beige fingertip. Everything about the lawyer looked expensive and classy, from her flawless complexion to the subtle caramel highlights in her glossy blonde bob. Sitting there in her tailored, light gray flannel skirt suit, she appeared the epitome of the successful law professional.

"So Dillon was definitely with you the whole night? He didn't leave your apartment at all?" Lydia looked at her questioningly.

Lola shook her head vehemently. "No, I told you he went home with me and stayed with me until the morning, when he left for work. But that's not all. There's photographic proof too..." She looked at Jim, unsure of whether she should continue. He nodded encouragingly at her.

"You can trust Lydia. She's a good friend. Anything you tell her will remain utterly confidential," Jim said, giving her a reassuring smile.

Lydia nodded her agreement.

"Of course. But I must say I'm rather interested when you say you have photographic evidence. I take it you mean of Dillon and yourself? I'm afraid it will still be incredibly hard to prove he wasn't at the scene of the crime, unless of course you have another witness apart from yourself who can corroborate his alibi."

Lola shook her head in protest. "No, not of Dillon and me. Evidence of someone else with Mr. Eversham. The real killer. With him at the time he was killed — committing the actual crime." Lydia's elegantly arched eyebrows shot up in her head as she leaned forward.

"You mean to tell me you have photographic evidence of a murder?"

Lola nodded, her gaze meeting Lydia's earnest sea-green one.

"That's exactly it."

"But how?" Lydia frowned, looking confused. Lola glanced at Jim, willing him to continue. After all, he was the one who knew more about the source of the information than she did.

"After the *Chronicle* reported the murder, a witness approached me with the info. He'd been walking by the park late when he saw a man lying on the ground and another man he recognized standing near him. He wasn't sure what he was witnessing, so decided to snap it," Jim said, answering Lydia's question smoothly.

"What I don't quite understand is, why didn't your witness call the police if he thought he saw something suspicious?" The lawyer narrowed her eyes, giving Jim a thoughtful look. They really were quite stunning eyes, Lola thought, feline shaped, the aqua color enhanced by striking gold flecks decorating the iris.

"Because of who the suspect is. And he wasn't sure if he *was* witnessing something suspicious. He thought it might be some kind of game or weird initiation ritual. Then after he read about the vic's murder in the *Chronicle*, he knew he had to tell someone."

Lydia stretched, tilting her head to one side, and exposing the slim flesh of her delicate neck. Lola felt a shiver run down her spine as she noted the flush of the hemoglobin beneath the woman's pale, translucent skin. *Stop that. Now is definitely not the time to be thinking of satiating your appetite for blood. Remember what got you into this mess in the first place.*

"What do you mean by weird ritual? What was he doing exactly?" Lydia finished stretching, straightening up.

"The attacker was seen bending down to the vic and biting him on the neck. The witness saw blood spurt out from the man's neck and in the pics we have, you can see him with the man's blood running out of his mouth," Jim answered, relaying the information matter-of-factly. Lola watched Lydia's response as she took in Jim's words. The woman looked a little shocked but retained her air of professional composure.

"You mean, he bit him and drank his blood like he was a vampire?"

Jim nodded.

"Just like that."

"And the official cause of death is?"

"Heavy blood loss, caused by a fatal wound to the neck—a wound that punctured his jugular."

This time Lydia couldn't quite manage to hide her surprise. She started to say something then stopped, her mouth hanging open as if she couldn't quite believe what Jim had said. The woman looked at Lola then back to Jim, as if searching for answers to help her make some sense of what she'd just been told.

"Do...do you have the pictures with you?" Lydia finally found her voice again, though she seemed extremely flustered as she spoke. The account had obviously disturbed her. Most sane, normal people would be disturbed. *Not you, though. You don't deserve to feel. You're a vampire, a monster.*

Jim nodded his head, reaching into his pocket to retrieve an identical USB stick to the one he had presented to Lola the previous day.

"We do. I have them here on this. Is there anywhere we might...?" Jim's voice trailed off as he looked around Lydia's spacious living room for evidence of a computer.

The lawyer smiled. "I don't keep a computer in here, probably because I'm surrounded by them all day long, but I have one in the study. Or I could fetch my laptop, if you like?"

"Study sounds great," Jim said as Lydia rose to her feet, indicating they should both follow.

If Lydia was surprised before she'd seen the pictures, then after she saw them, she was gobsmacked. The lawyer's eyes bulged with disbelief as Jim clicked through the shots while they stood around the stylish white iMac perched atop the polished oak desk in the center of Lydia's study.

"As you can see by the time stamps, this puts the guy in the picture very firmly with the victim at the time he would have been killed," Jim said. Lola couldn't hold back any longer. They needed to get what they had come here for, assurance that if they could persuade the witness to testify, they would have a solid case. It was

Dillon's only chance to clear his name. She felt a pang of sorrow as she imagined his handsome face locked behind the bars of some dingy prison cell.

"Well, that's definitely not Dillon in the pictures, but I know exactly who it is," Lola said, tapping the gruesome image on the screen with one sharp, blood-red fingernail.

"And who *is* it exactly?" The lawyer looked at her questioningly.

"Drago Graythorne. You might have heard of his father." Lola uttered the words casually, but the sharp intake of breath that escaped Lydia's perfectly glossed lips assured her there was no need for dramatic effect. The lawyer obviously knew all about the Graythorne family and the power and influence they wielded in the Burley Falls community.

"So you see, it's crucial we find out if this evidence is enough to convict. Because if it isn't, the consequences could be dire for everyone involved," Jim said, his face grim.

"And that's where you come in," Lola cut in, looking at Lydia hopefully, her pulse in her throat with anticipation at what the lawyer might say.

The woman nodded slowly, blinking slightly as she collected herself. "If you have a solid witness who doesn't have any prior serious convictions and is prepared to make his identity known, then, yes, you potentially could have enough to build a case," Lydia replied, looking from Jim to Lola.

At the sound of the words, Lola felt waves of relief coursing through her body. Thank God for that. Now all they had to do was tell the witness what Lydia had told them, get him to testify, and Dillon could walk out of jail a free man.

"I should warn you both here, though," Lydia continued, "a solid case doesn't always mean a conviction. I've had cases before which on paper were a shoo-in, but as we all know, the law doesn't always work that way."

Lola knew what the woman's words meant. Judge Graythorne had a long reach and a huge influence on justice in Burley Falls. This wasn't going to be a walk in the park.

"But the witness refuses to testify unless we can be assured of a conviction," Lola said, a sinking feeling beginning to take the place of the relief.

"Then you have to work on strengthening your case to make it as watertight and irrefutable as you can, and get the very best lawyer you can afford," Lydia replied.

"Would *you* consider representing us?"

Lydia's brow furrowed as she considered the proposition. "I... Well, I don't think I'd really be suitable," Lydia floundered, looking to Jim for help.

Jim merely shrugged, grinning. "Don't look to me for assistance," Jim said, shaking his head. "I think you'd be perfect. You're the best lawyer in Burley Falls, hands down. Hell, make that in the whole damn state." Lydia stood there looking helpless for a moment or two as though she were trying to find the words to gracefully extricate herself from what was being asked of her. Now was the time to apply a little gentle arm twisting.

"I'll pay well," Lola said, shooting a pleading look at Lydia. "Please, my parents... When they died, they left me some money...quite a large sum of money — more than enough to pay for Dillon's legal fees." Even though doing so would probably bankrupt her.

Lydia shook her head. "It's not that, Lola. It's just that I really don't know whether I'm prepared to take on a case involving someone as high profile as

Commissioner Graythorne's son. I've worked damn hard to get where I am today. This could jeopardize everything for me."

"But imagine what it could do for your career if you win, Lyds," Jim chipped in. "It would be a landmark case," he added with a flourish, as if he were challenging Lydia to accept.

The lawyer paused, obviously considering the tempting carrot that was dangling in front of her, then to Lola's dismay shook her head again, the beveled curves of her neat blonde bob swinging. Lola felt her gut twist. She *had* to say something to convince Lydia. They needed someone like her on their side. Not only was she an excellent lawyer, but if Lydia was hesitant to take on the case, despite the fact that she was a good friend of Jim's, then there was a high chance no other lawyer would dare even touch it. "I know how highly Jim regards you, and we really need a lawyer we can trust or Dillon hasn't got a chance. Please, Lydia?"

Mentally she willed her to say yes. There was a long pause as Lydia stood there, not saying anything, just looking from Lola to Jim then back again, the silence seeming almost unendurable. Lola could hardly bear to hear the words that would surely come next from Lydia's mouth and half wanted to block her ears to prevent having to hear them.

Lydia gave a long sigh, the breath exhaling from her elegant, willowy frame.

"All right then. I'll represent you, but on one condition." Did she just say she would represent Dillon?

"Anything, anything you want. I'll do anything," she replied, the words tumbling out in an excited rush.

"Well, you might want to hear me out first. The condition is if you can get your witness to take the stand without anonymity, I'll represent Dillon in court," Lydia said, her tone firm as she delivered the ultimatum.

"And if we can't?" She could hardly bear to contemplate the prospect. Lydia looked straight at her, her aqua eyes intense as they met hers.

"Then I'm afraid I just can't afford to jeopardize my position," Lydia replied, her cool gaze direct.

* * * *

After Jim had driven her home from Lydia's house, Lola was standing outside the front door of her apartment, key in hand, when her cell phone rang. She fumbled in the pocket of her slim-fit skinny jeans for the razor-thin handset, her fingers deftly gliding over the phone's smooth surface as she frantically struggled to answer the call.

"Lola?" Emotion coursed through her body at the sound of Dillon's voice.

"How did you—"

"They allowed me a phone call, and I wanted to call you, sweetheart. You mustn't believe what you're hearing. It's not what you think. I never wanted to hurt him."

Never wanted to hurt who? Who was he talking about? She fumbled in her pocket for the key to her front door, finding it and sliding it into the lock.

"I'm just glad you're safe. I'm behind you one hundred percent. I know you had nothing to do with Dave's death. I was with you the whole night. Remember?" She blushed at the memory of his strong arms embracing her as the two of them thrashed about on the dirt pathway.

"Who?" He sounded confused, not remembering.

"Dave? The dead guy who was with us in the park with Drago?" Turning the key, she opened the door, stepping through into her apartment and shutting it behind her.

"Oh, yeah, but I was talking about the other guy." Dillon coughed, the sound a harsh rasp. His tone sounded tired. They had better be treating him well. The other guy? What the hell was he talking about? Lola's brain scrambled to make sense of what he was saying. Just then it clicked as she recalled the information Max had told her, the realization coursing through her.

"So it *is* true?" She sank down on the high-backed black French Rococo–style chair that sat in the hallway, holding her breath, hardly daring to wait for his response.

"No, well, yeah, kinda. But it's not what you think, I promise you. Look, I'll explain everything to you…if I ever manage to get out of here." He sounded down, almost as if he were giving up hope. *No, you have to fight. You have to be strong.*

"I've got you a lawyer," she said, trying to make the words sound hopeful. They had the intended effect.

"Really?" His tone sounded brighter. She couldn't let him know that Lydia's offer had been conditional.

"Yes, really. A good lawyer too. Jim's a journalist, and he says she never lost a single one of her cases since she started her independent practice."

"Wait. Who's Jim?" He sounded confused and a little apprehensive, and she couldn't help but smile at his possessiveness of her. He was obviously wary at the mention of some strange guy's name, and she wasn't going to be so mean as to leave him hanging.

"Jim's a reporter. He approached me at Vain with some information about your case. Info that could really help you."

"What information?"

"I can't really say over the phone, so you gotta trust me on this one. But it's going to prove you're innocent." No point in telling him the specifics just yet. After all they had to get the witness to testify first. A tiny twinge of guilt coursed through her as she considered that perhaps she was raising Dillon's hopes only for them to be dashed further down the line, but he had sounded so down in the dumps that she had had to do something to cheer him up.

"Really?" He coughed again, the sound rattling down the line, even though she could tell he was trying to stifle it.

"Hey, you okay?" She was concerned now. He sounded really sick.

"Yeah, it's nothin'."

"Doesn't sound like nothing. Maybe you should ask to see a doctor?"

"Nah, I'll be fine."

"You can't just leave these things. It could turn into something much more serious." God, now she sounded like someone's parent. She was never usually the mother hen type, but now she couldn't help feeling concerned. In a way it was understandable. She had finally found a great guy. She didn't want anything else to happen that was bad. *But what could really be worse than being accused of first-degree murder?*

"I'll be fine. I just have this medical condition, and I need my meds, but I ran out. I was gonna pick up more supplies back at the house when I got arrested."

"Condition? What kind of condition?" Now she was really getting worried. He had to have his medication or he'd get sick.

"Uh, I've had it for a long time. It's a rare blood disorder, not usually serious as long as I stay on the meds."

"Then you have to get your meds. I'll collect them for you and bring them into the station. The cops will have to understand."

"I dunno…"

"Hey, I'll get them to you. I promise. What's your address?"

"Wha…wait, but you don't have a key," He sounded surprised and she smiled to herself again. Bless him, he was so innocent he didn't realize she had faced more than one locked front door in her past.

"Don't worry about that. I know how to pick a lock. Misspent youth," she said breezily, hoping he wouldn't question her further.

"Uh…wha…what?"

"Just tell me your address and where the meds are and I'll bring them to you," she replied, speaking gently but firmly into the small black handset.

"Can't wait to see you. I been thinking about you practically all the time in here. Thinking about all the stuff I'm gonna do to that sexy body of yours."

She thrilled at the words, an almost instantaneous reaction of excitement flaring within her as anticipation tingled between her legs. She couldn't wait to feel his arms around her again, the rough chaff of his stubble against her cheek, his hands wandering, sliding.

"Yeah? Well, then you're just have to make good on that promise when they let you out of there," she said, hoping to give him something to look forward to. God, she hoped they did let him out of there soon. Something in her yearned to be at his command again, move beneath his touch, submit to him.

"Oh, I sure will, beautiful. You better be ready for me. You been a good girl for me?"

"Of course."

"My good girl, ain't ya?"

"I am," she whispered down the handset, beginning to feel extremely aroused. She had to get off the line or she was gonna end up getting off just talking to him, and she needed to get those meds.

"Take your panties off." The words cut through her ears.

"Wha… What?"

"Come on. I know you're aching for it. Don't those pretty little fingers just want to slide into that wet pussy I know you got for me?"

"I—" She went to protest, then stopped, uselessly. "Yes," she admitted, her voice a whisper.

"So take the panties off and spread those long legs. Tell me how wet you are."

Cradling the handset with her neck, her hands flew to the zipper of her skinny jeans. Shimmying out of them as she arched her back on the chair, she stepped out of one leg then the other, kicking them to one side. Her hand moved over the cream satin Victoria's Secret panties she wore beneath, her body responding to her touch as she slid them down, kicking those away too. "They're off." She waited with bated breath for his next instruction.

"And?"

"And I'm soaking," she whispered.

"How much do you wish I was there right now, attending to that hot little pussy of yours with my mouth?"

"Oh God, so much," she groaned, her hand automatically flying between her legs to satiate the pulsing hunger that leaped through her at his words.

"What did I tell you about waiting for pleasure?"

"Wha...? How did you," she stammered. How did he know her so well? It was like he was actually in her mind.

"'Cause I know you, bad girl."

She could hear him smile as he said the words. "I'm a good girl, not a bad one. *Your* good girl."

"Mmhmm, then you're going to wait until you can touch yourself, aren't you?"

"Please," she begged, writhing on the chair.

"Wetter?"

"Yes."

"Who makes you wet? Whose big cock belongs in that hot little spot you got between those thighs?"

"Yours. Oh God, let me," she moaned.

"You may...if you say, 'Thank you for letting me finger my hot little pussy, Sir.'"

"Th...thank you for letting me touch my hot little pussy...Sir." She couldn't believe she was calling him Sir. Actually she couldn't believe she was doing any of this, but her body was on fire right now and all she could think about was how she felt compelled to do exactly as he said. Somehow he could get away with using language like that. He just sounded raw ass sexy, but she fervently hoped she didn't sound like a cheesy participant in a bad BDSM flick.

"Now you can. Stroke your clit first then slide a finger in slowly. Just one finger, mind—into that silky wetness."

"Oh, oh," she moaned, doing as he commanded, her body practically jumping at the sensation as her finger made contact with her clit.

"God, I wish I were there with you." His voice was right in her ear, hot and sexy. She could imagine his musky smell, the masculine odor of him.

"What would you do to me?"

"Everything. Now put another finger in."

"Yes, oh God, yes, I want more."

"You just want to sit on my hard cock, don't ya?"

"Yes, please, yes," she moaned, practically drooling at the thought of that beautiful, veiny shaft.

"Put another finger in?"

"Yes," she said, doing as he bid, the sensation of slowly becoming expanded turning her on even more. It was as though it were his fingers sliding inside her, prepping her before he entered her with his cock.

"How much do you need to come?"

"Oh God, so much," she groaned, "please."

"Now another."

"Four?"

"Four. God, I can only imagine how you must fucking look right now."

She could hear the blatant arousal in his voice. Sliding another finger in, she parted her thighs wide and closed her eyes, imagining he were watching her display herself for him.

"Let me, please. Let me now," she begged him.

"Now I want you to stop."

"What?" Did he just tell her to stop?

"You heard me. I want you to stop. Slide your fingers slowly out of that hot little hole of yours and stand up. Go put on a short skirt. Don't wear any panties. Then go get those meds and come to see me."

"But why?" Her brain was whirring. How could he make her stop now, when she was so close to pleasure?

"Because you need to learn that I control your pleasure. And you like it that way, don't you?" His throat rasped slightly as he spoke and he spluttered, but he still sounded sexy as ever.

"Yes...Sir," she whispered, so incredibly aroused by what he was proposing, even though she was raw-ass horny, aching to come.

"My good girl. Now this is what I need you to do for me."

* * * *

Ten minutes later, she was behind the wheel of her small silver Audi, steering her way through the streets of Burley Falls, over to the other side of town where Dillon lived. The form-fitting cream miniskirt she sported rode up slightly as her foot pressed on the clutch, exposing acres of smooth, creamy thigh. She was still horny as all hell and breathing hard, her body craving the release that had been denied her, but she knew she needed to try to focus on the task at hand.

She hadn't had much occasion to visit the Morningford Heights neighborhood often, but she knew the street she was headed to. It was, no question, one of the most sought after addresses in the area. How the hell did a humble engineer manage to live there? Now, though, was hardly the time to ponder such things. Dillon was sick and she had to get him his meds before he got even sicker. Then maybe, just maybe, he'd give her trembling and aching body the permission it needed to seek release.

Her mind turned to the instructions he'd given her on the phone. They had sounded a little bizarre.

'There's a big industrial-looking metal unit with a lock on it in the kitchen. The key to it is in the top drawer of the computer desk in the lounge. Use it to open the unit. Inside you'll find my meds. It's real cold in there, so don't burn your

fingers. Inside you'll find bottles. Take one out and bring it to the station as quick as possible after. Tell them I get real sick if I can't take my meds.'

She hoped she'd be able to get them to him without too much protest. Though his sexy voice in her ear had made her putty in his hands, she knew from the raspy way he'd sounded on the other end of the phone that he was sick. Why hadn't he told her about his illness before?

Just then a black Mercedes pulled abruptly out in front of her, causing her to slam on the brakes then the Audi came screeching to a swift halt.

"Jesus," she exclaimed out loud as the maneuver forced her back against the headrest. She sat there, breathing heavily, the adrenaline pulsing through her. Unbelievably the driver of the Merc didn't seem to care that he'd almost caused her to fly through her own windshield. The vehicle squealed as its wheels spun, the black car turning around ninety degrees as he – or she – roared off down the road.

"Of all the…"

She shook her head angrily. Whoever it was, they hadn't even stopped to see whether or not she had been injured. Wait. She recognized that Mercedes from somewhere. Didn't one of Drago's clowns drive a car like that? It would be just typical of Drago to cut her up and then take off. Obviously it wasn't enough for him to get her boyfriend fingered for a crime he didn't commit. Well, if he thought he was going to get away, literally with murder, he could damn well think again.

Revving the engine, she started up the Audi again determinedly, her jaw set in defiance as she drove. Damn Drago and his arrogant, spoiled brat ways.

Fifteen minutes later she was pulling up outside the address Dillon had given her. Morningford was well lit and even better signposted. It was pretty obvious the residents that lived here cared about their community. She looked up at the swish condominium where she was parked. The place reeked of money. There was no way an engineer's wages would pay for all of this. Dillon was certainly not telling her everything, of that she was certain. So what *was* the secret he was hiding?

Five minutes and one expert tussle with a lock later, she was sliding effortlessly through the front door and into the shadows of Dillon's darkened hallway. Looking around, she spied what looked suspiciously like a dimmer switch on the wall to her left and hitting it, found her suspicions had been correct as light flooded the spacious entrance way. Eyeing a half-open doorway up ahead, she picked her way through the apartment's plush white carpet, and pushed the door open further, stepping through into what she assumed must be Dillon's lounge area.

She saw the masculine-looking oak computer desk in the corner. She couldn't help but smile. It reminded her of Dillon somehow, so solid and comforting with its chunky square-cut legs and tough patina.

Pulling open the top drawer of the desk, she hastily rummaged through pens, papers and other assorted stationary, looking for the key. A glint of silver metal winked at her as she rifled through a sheaf of haphazardly stacked papers. *Aha, there you are, my friend.* Dillon obviously wasn't a neat freak. Well, she could forgive that. The man *was* pretty darn near perfect. Plucking the little key out of the drawer, she tucked it neatly down her sweater between her breasts. Now, all she had to do was find the meds and hightail it out of here.

Exiting the lounge, she scanned her surroundings for a door that looked as though it might possibly lead to the kitchen area. Trying her luck on the one to her immediate left, she flung it open and flicked on the light switch, realizing too late she'd walked into what appeared to be a spacious downstairs bathroom instead. She turned around and decided to try the one on her right, pushing it open then hitting the dimmer on the wall as her high-heeled boots made contact with what sounded like polished wood.

Pleased to discover she'd got it right this time, she scanned the sleek-looking chrome- and glass-covered kitchen, looking for the industrial, silver-colored unit Dillon had described to her over the telephone.

She spied a large rectangular cupboard resembling the kind that might house an old boiler, and clicked her way across the wooden floor until she was standing in front of it. Reaching out to grasp the handle of it, she recoiled immediately, retracting her hand, shocked by how cold the surface felt. Dillon had warned her the unit would be pretty chilly but she had to admit she hadn't quite been expecting *that*. It was as if the thing were made entirely of ice.

There seemed to be a little keyhole, and removing the key from where she'd tucked it, she slid it into the lock, turning it slowly until the lock clicked, then wrenching open the handle. The wave of coldness hit her, filling her lungs and making her gasp for breath. It was colder than any freezer she'd ever been in in her entire life.

Reeling a little, she tried to focus, looking over the contents. There were three shelves, the top one empty, while the second was filled with odd plastic pouches that seemed to contain some sort of frozen, dark liquid. She saw the bottom shelf was lined with the kind of brown glass bottles pharmacists dispense. Dillon must have meant for her to bring him one of these.

Reaching down, she braced herself as her fingers closed around one of the bottles. The cold was almost unbearable, forcing her to abandon her plan to retrieve the container abruptly and causing her to massage her sore, stinging fingers as she pondered how to get around this little technical hitch. She spied a tea towel hanging neatly from a chrome peg. Aha, that would do it.

She grabbed the towel, wrapped it swiftly around her hand then reached down again to deftly pluck one of the bottles.

'There's a cool bag in the cupboard drawer next to the unit. Use it to bring the meds to me.' Shivering, she pushed the unit door shut then opened the cupboard drawer to pick up a silver cool bag. She shook it open then deposited the bottle carefully at the bottom of it. Mission number one had been accomplished. She'd retrieved the meds. Now all she had to do was make sure she got them to Dillon on time.

* * * *

Arriving at the police station, Lola gave a friendly nod to Joe, the redheaded station clerk manning the reception. She'd known him ever since the two of them had been in diapers. They'd even been in the first grade class together at Burley Prep, the local community school.

"Hey, Joe," she said, tossing a friendly smile as she headed up to the desk where he sat.

"Hey, Lola, how you doing? Looking good…" Joe's voice tailed off as his gaze flicked appreciatively over the cream miniskirt and low-cut red scoop-neck top combo she was sporting.

She smiled to herself. Joe had always had kind of a thing for her, ever since freshman year when the two of them had attended the end of semester school dance together, after he had awkwardly asked her to be his date. She'd said yes and they'd had a blast, but the very next semester hunky Henry Wilkes, a quarterback on the school football team, had asked her to go steady, and any hopes Joe had been harboring were crushed.

Not that she was too upset about that, she had to admit. She liked Joe, just not in that way. But his obvious feelings for her sure as hell might come in handy tonight. Beaming back at him broadly, she fixed him with an intense violet gaze, allowing the dark sweep of her long eyelashes to flutter ever so slightly. She noted the flush that came to his cheeks. He was going to be a pushover.

"So what can I do for you tonight, Miss Lola?" Joe looked at her quizzically as she stood before him.

"Uh, well, you're holding Dillon Chambers here, right?"

Joe nodded slowly.

"Okay. Well, I spoke to Dillon on the telephone earlier and he asked me to fetch him his meds." She held up the silver cool bag to illustrate her point.

Joe chewed his lower lip, looking unsure.

"Sooo... I know it's not strictly procedure but if I could get these to him? He'll get awful sick if he doesn't take them tonight." She shot Joe a pleading look, her full lips pouting slightly as silently she willed him to say yes.

Joe didn't respond, tilting his head to one side, as if he were considering her request, while his eyes continued to appraise her.

"Please, Joe. You and I go way back and you've never let me down. " She looked at Joe beseechingly, her lower lip wobbling, as if she were on the verge of tears. That swung it. An expression of concern creased Joe's honest features as he stood up then made his way around to the side of the desk she was standing at, bobbing his carrot-colored head.

"Sure, Lola. I understand. You can go in and give them to him. He's in the holding cells. I can buzz you through."

She rewarded him with a full-on ten-megawatt beam of a smile as gratitude coursed through her.

"Awww, really? You're such a sweetie. Haven't changed a bit since high school." Leaning in to pat his arm, she planted a swift kiss on Joe's cheek, causing his already red cheeks to blush an even deeper shade of scarlet.

* * * *

Dillon lifted his head as Joe ushered Lola into the small holding cell, closing the barred door behind her and locking it.

"Buzz through when you want me to come let you out," Joe said through the bars, as she nodded her assent gratefully at him.

"Sure. Thanks a million."

The clerk bobbed his head again, turning to walk away swiftly down the corridor, keys jangling as they swung from the belt attached to his waist. She focused her attention back on Dillon.

"Hey, how are you?" She sat down on the edge of the hard, uncomfortable bunk he was perched on as she appraised him. Her body thrilled to see him again, but wait. Something was wrong. He didn't seem like his usual healthy, strapping self. This Dillon was pale and wan. He *looked* sickly.

"Eh, I'm okay. Feeling a little off color, but it's nothing to worry about. You look sexy as hell," he said, eyeing the miniskirt she wore. He coughed involuntarily, the sound a harsh, awful rasp. She placed a concerned hand on his arm.

"You sure you're okay? Sounds like a pretty nasty cough you've got there." She looked at him, her eyes raking his face for an answer.

He shrugged, managing a thin smile. "It's nothing. I just get this way when I don't take my meds. I've always been this way, ever since I was diagnosed."

"Speaking of which…" She held up the cool bag she'd brought from Dillon's apartment, shaking it. The look of relief on his face was obvious.

"Smart girl. I know it must have been some sterling effort to get into my apartment and all." His big brown puppy dog eyes shined with gratitude as he looked at her, and she felt her stomach do a funny sort of flip.

"Well, you can pay me back by taking me out to dinner when you get your ass outta here," she bantered, smiling at him, though inside she didn't feel quite as confident as the words she spoke so flippantly. *That's if we can convince our mystery witness to testify against Drago.*

Dillon grinned.

"Of course, it would be a pleasure. But I got some other promises to keep first, remember?" he said, shooting a glance at her cleavage.

She blushed at the thought, knowing exactly what he meant, what those hungry glances he kept giving her signified. She felt as though he already had her on her knees at his total and utter command. Already between her legs she could feel a pulse of desire rise.

"Pffff. Hush you and take your meds." She tossed the cool bag at him and he caught it, peering inside at the contents.

"I just brought you the one like you asked. That okay?" She looked at him as he scrambled through the bag.

"Yeah it's fine, babe. They don't keep if ya store 'em out of the cold too long anyhow."

"Can't you ask one of the officers to keep them in the station refrigerator until you need them?"

A guarded look clouded his handsome features and he shook his head slowly.

"Not cold enough. Not even close. You felt the temp in that unit for yourself, didn't you?"

"I sure did. It was…beyond freezing." She shook her head, giving a little shiver as she remembered how cold the icy unit had been when she had touched it.

"Well, that's the temp they need to be kept at, or they're darn good as useless." Dillon shrugged as he uncapped the dark glass bottle, bringing it to his lips and taking a healthy slug of the contents.

"So what's in them exactly? I mean…what kind of meds are they?" She looked at him curiously. Dillon shrugged again, but she noticed the tiniest of micro expressions as that handsome, chiseled jaw clenched — or was she merely imagining it? He tossed the empty bottle on the bunk, sighing heavily with relief.

"Oh, you know…just meds. Darned if I know. But, jeez, they must work 'cause I feel better already. Thanks, sweetheart." Reaching for her, he caught her by the arm as he bent forward to kiss her, and she found herself leaning closer in order to reciprocate, as their lips locked for what seemed like the first time in an age. She gave an involuntary moan as she felt his broad hands roaming over her back, pulling her closer to him.

How come even locked up in a jail cell this man had the ability to make her feel so safe, so protected, so damn horny?

"Damn it, I've needed you," he moaned, sighing as he caressed her back, his strong arms crushing her to him.

"I'm here now," she whispered, her heart singing at his words, the sensation between her legs expanding to a pulsating throb.

"I didn't know when I would see you again, *if* I would ever even see you again. I thought you might figure I was too much trouble—"

He broke off as she silenced him with a finger.

"Hey. You're not too much trouble. And Jim and I are going to get you out of here. We've got an excellent lawyer on our side now," she said, standing on tiptoe to plant a kiss on his lips. She crossed her fingers, wincing a little, as silently she prayed the words she spoke were true. Lydia's offer had very definitely been conditional, if they couldn't get the witness to testify without anonymity, they were clearly going to have to get another lawyer. But what kind of lawyer would take a case as high profile as this one? Only someone with a death wish and somehow she didn't think too many people around here fit that bill.

"Yeah, you said on the phone."

"Mmhmm, *and* we've got a witness." The words tumbled out too late before she could restrain herself. Mentally she kicked herself. *Way to go, Lola. Now how are you going to explain things when they fall apart?*

"Really?" Dillon's eyes lit up with hope. How could she bear to disillusion him?

"Really. So you'll be out in no time, I promise. And we can get back to happy, together. If that's what you want of course." She arched an eyebrow at him quizzically.

Yeah, that's what he wants, to be with a monster like you. Do you really think he'd want to be with you if he knew what you really are?

"Duh. I can't wait till I can hold you in my arms again properly, not in some rat-infested jail cell."

"Ewww, there's rats in here?"

"There are."

"That's totally disgusting. You should complain to one of the officers."

"Somehow I don't think they'd listen too much. I think the whole point is it's not supposed to be a walk in the park."

"Still, rats are completely gross. Somebody should definitely report that. And if you won't, *I* will."

Dillon grinned, holding his palms up in a gesture of surrender. "All right, all right. I give in already, missy. I'll do it."

"Good. Well, those meds must have done the trick. You look perkier already." It was true. His complexion was more alive, and the sparkle that usually inhabited his brown eyes had returned.

"Yeah, it tends to be pretty fast acting." He shrugged his broad shoulders and moved his hand down her back to circle her ass. The pulse between her legs expanded, and she struggled to keep focused. All her body was silently willing his fingers to slip under the hem of her skirt, to stroke the smooth, bare flesh that lay beneath.

"Uh, yeah, I'd say so. Sooo…tomorrow I'm meeting with Jim and we're gonna go talk to our witness."

"Yeah? Look, I really do appreciate you going to all this trouble for me. I don't wanna be the pain in the butt boyfriend in jail." A troubled expression crossed his face.

Even though him admitting he was her boyfriend thrilled her, she was concerned he was upset. "Hey," she said, squeezing the strong muscles of his well-shaped forearm through his flannel shirtsleeve.

"You're not my pain in the butt boyfriend, okay? You're my hot and sexy boyfriend who just so happens to have found himself in a fix, thanks to some jerk called Drago. But your amazingly gorgeous girlfriend is going to see to it that he won't get the better of us." She gave him what she hoped was a reassuring smile and was rewarded with a flash of his white teeth as he grinned at her, shaking his head in amusement.

"You're quite a woman. You know that?" His fingers slipped down, edging closer to the hem of her skirt. Her heart started to pound in anticipation as her body squirmed, desperate for his touch, inching his fingers closer, but still unbearably out of reach of where she needed them to be.

The look on his face was hungry as he regarded her, his eyes drinking her in as he pulled her on top of him, tumbling back on the low, shabby bunk that lined the small wall of the grimy cell.

"Gonna show me just how much of a woman I am then, stud?"

Laughing at her corniness, he reached up to her, pulling her body close to his as he slid his tongue between her lips, his fingertips trailing along her inner thighs.

"Oh," she moaned, her back arching as she attempted to thrust onto his hand, his touch still maddeningly out of reach.

"God, you could drive a man crazy," he groaned, lacing her fingers in his hair as he thrust his hips upward, pressing his hardness against her bare flesh.

This witness better talk soon or *she* was going to be the one going crazy. It was going to be agony to be away from this guy. She took a deep sniff of his neck as she nuzzled into him, straddling his lap and grinding like she was in heat. She felt thick fingers slide into her wetness and moaned into his mouth as he kissed her, her body spasming around his touch. The spicy, raw scent of him was in her nostrils. Even locked up in a jail cell, the odor of him was irresistible. She needed him to let her come so much.

"Good girl. No panties."

"I did as you asked me...*Sir*." She spoke the last word tongue in cheek but she wanted him to dominate her anyway.

"So I see. Undo my fly." The commanding tone was back in his voice, the words huskily delivered as he looked at her spread-eagled over him, her breasts practically falling out of the scarlet scoop neck she wore.

She didn't need asking twice. She flew to deftly pick at the buttons, freeing his thick length from its denim cage, and she gasped as he thrust up against her, hard and groaning and tantalizingly inches short of entering her.

"Stop teasing please," she begged. "Haven't I waited long enough?"

He grinned, regarding her, reaching up to cup her breast and ease it out of the cream brassiere it nestled in, closing his fingers around a nipple.

"Maybe." He reached down the side of the bunk. She could hear the clink of metal.

"What's that?"

He pulled out the handcuffs, the grin on his face widening.

"Oh, these things? I think they use 'em to restrain naughty boys and girls."

"How the hell did you get hold of those?"

"Dunno. Found 'em under that bunk. Security in here ain't exactly top notch, it seems." He thrust his cock up against her, causing her to temporarily forget everything but the desire to have him inside her, hungry and thrusting again.

"What are you planning to do with them?" The question came out as a desperate squeak.

He sat up, his hands encircling her hips as he hoisted her around his waist and got to his feet in one decisive movement.

"What are you doing?" She tried to protest, but he hushed her with his mouth, carrying her across the floor of the cell until they reached the bars looking out into the brightly lit corridor. It was there he set her down, her skirt around her waist, her breasts spilling out, her lips swollen from his kisses.

"Turn around," he instructed.

"What? But we can't. Someone might come."

"Turn around," he insisted, and despite her protests, she found herself doing as he'd ordered.

"But someone might see us."

"Joe's the only one in the whole damn jailhouse. And I saw the way he was looking at you. If he saw you like that, he'd probably thank me for it."

She felt the cool kiss of the steel handcuffs as he took one of her wrists and fastened it to the cell bars, then placed the other in the manacle to join it. Her cheeks were burning. How could he say those things?

"You wouldn't let him see me like this?"

He paused, considering a moment. "Maybe. If I was in a generous mood. No touching, though. No one puts his hands on my woman or he has me to answer to."

"But…but—" She went to protest again, but the feel of his hard cock thrusting as his body pressed her up against the bars silenced her. He reached his rough hands around to twist her nipples and she cried out.

"Kinda turns me on, the thought of guys getting all hot over you—never being able to have you, seeing your mine, knowing I'm the lucky guy that gets to take you like this, spread your legs and fuck you like the sexy bitch you are," he growled into her ear, making her body quake and her legs tremble with excitement at the erotic possibilities he was filling her mind with.

"Take me," she breathed, her hands clasping the cell bars, her breasts mashed up against the metal with every new thrust his searching cock made into her.

"Jesus, you're so fucking wet," he groaned, his thrusts becoming more and more frantic, sliding his hands between her legs to pull and pinch her clit as she couldn't help but cry out loud, in that moment not caring who might hear her.

"Oh God, I'm coming," she cried as he fucked her roughly, stroking fast over her slippery little nub and causing her body to tip into convulsions of pure bliss. She thought she heard a noise at the end of the passage, and for one split second, panic coursed through her, but the riskiness of the situation merely heightened the thrill spiraling through her fired-up body, and she moaned with abandon.

"Not yet," he said, pulling out and biting her ear, leaving her standing there, back arched, her ass high, her pussy aching for him to fill where he had been only moments before.

"Please," she cried, her body twisting slightly, wrists straining against their prison, her need for him so great. The few seconds he made her wait seemed like forever before he finally gave her what she wanted. He plunged back into her with a heavy growl, his mouth on her neck, biting as he grunted, "Now," and his own release hit as she felt the hot spurt of his cum.

Panting, she tried to right herself after but she found her legs failed her. He caught her, helping her to stand as she tried to catch her breath, her heart still pounding. Never had she experienced anything like that and she'd had some pretty wild times. This guy had total control of her body and if he kept this up, he was gonna rapidly gain control of her mind and soul to boot.

"Well, uh...that was pleasantly unexpected." He grinned.

"You're unbelievable. I thought you were supposed to be sick," she said, just staring at him.

"Eh, takes a lot to knock me off my feet. Mind you, you managed that when you walked into my life."

"Oh God," she groaned, "you cheeseball."

"Careful," he warned, "I might leave you like that. I have the key, remember?" He dangled the silver key in front of her nose with a smirk.

"Yeah, but then who'd be there to save your sexy ass...hmmm?"

His face darkened.

"Wish to hell I didn't have to put you through this. Makes me feel kinda pathetic."

Pathetic? Hardly. This man is alpha all the way.

"Trust me. The last word anyone would ever use to describe *you* would be pathetic," she said, shaking her head again as he made to release her.

"Oh yeah, is that 'cause I'm all man?"

"Now if we're talking about the word corny, that's a whole different— Stop it. I'm ticklish!" She squirmed as he tickled her sides.

Laughing at her helplessness, he raised a dark eyebrow. "Ticklish, huh?"

"Mhhhmmm."

"Well, *maybe* I'll stop if you give me something in exchange." Trying to keep an expression of mock seriousness on his face, he looked in to her eyes, his own dancing mischievously.

"Hrrmm, what might that be exactly?" Of course she knew exactly what he wanted, but she still enjoyed teasing him all the same. After all, what girl in her right mind wouldn't want a handsome cowboy begging her to kiss him?

"I think you know what," he growled, his voice throaty as he bent to cup her face. Looking up into his strong, handsome features, she felt her stomach flutter. God, she could lose herself in those dark eyes. She wanted this man so much. Reaching up to stroke his cheek, she parted her lips, half closing her eyes.

"Oh, I might have some idea, Mr. Chambers," she said, purring the words as he craned his head down to nibble at her neck, her lips gently brushing his earlobe as he lifted his head back up to her kiss her passionately.

Chapter Seven

The next day she woke early, ready for her meeting with Jim and the mystery witness. She felt primed with hope, and a renewed determination to get Dillon out of the hell that Drago had put him in coursed through her, firing her up. Drago had really gone too far this time. His family might be practically almighty in Burley Falls, but even he couldn't get away with murder.

She dressed quickly, pulling on a pair of black tailored cigarette pants and a scarlet roll-neck sweater, and sweeping her long, dark hair up and off her face in her trademark high ponytail as she stood at her dresser. After reaching out for the tube of scarlet lipstick that had become something of her signature color, she applied the cosmetic deftly, pausing briefly to check her appearance in the mirror.

The face that stared back at her was undeniably striking. With her porcelain pale skin, the dramatic hairstyle she sported showcased her elegant bone structure, and the slash of scarlet at her mouth screamed femme fatale. She was a man-eater all right and the only guy who could tame her was locked up in a jail cell. She blushed at the memory of the night before. Dillon had been wild and hungry and she was more addicted to him than ever. She still couldn't quite believe the grip he had on her, the way he could make her forget herself and give herself over to total pleasure.

Glancing at the little LED clock perched on her bedside table, she saw she had to leave, and fast, or she'd be late to meet Jim. She'd promised she would be at his apartment by five-thirty p.m. and the clock's neon face informed her it was already five. Swiping her car keys from the dresser top, she hastily headed for the front door, pausing to retrieve her phone before she exited, slamming the door firmly behind her.

Arriving at Jim's, she locked the door to her car with a beep, clicking her stiletto heels up the path to his front door where she pressed the buzzer firmly. She waited a minute or so, then pressed it again, holding it down more firmly just in case it hadn't been loud enough the first time. Still no answer.

Damn it, he must still be showering up or something. Well, she couldn't just stand around on his doorstep like this. Digging her cell phone out of her pants pocket, she began to dial Jim's cell phone number. The handset rang and rang but still Jim wasn't picking up. Eventually it clicked through to voice mail and feeling mildly frustrated, she hung up. Perhaps he hadn't turned his phone on yet. Maybe it had run out of battery and he'd been charging it overnight?

A sudden brainwave struck her as she remembered Jim writing down his house phone number in the office of the *Burley Chronicle*, just in case she needed to reach him there. After reaching into her other pants pocket, she removed her sleek black leather wallet then opened it and rummaged through it to the section where she had stuffed Jim's card. She pulled it out and her eyes quickly scanned the reporter's messy scrawl. She punched in the digits on her cell.

The phone rang and rang, unanswered. Okay, now this *was* getting a little odd. Where the hell was he? He better not have forgotten all about their meeting and stayed late at work like he had said he usually did. What if he'd left his mobile phone behind that day? Perhaps she should call his office, just to make sure?

Feeling irked, she keyed in the number for Jim's desk phone then placed the handset at her ear once more, waiting to see if there would be any response. Five rings she counted and nothing. Six, seven, and she was just about to hang up when she heard a voice on the other end.

"*Burley Chronicle*, can I help you?" The voice sounded older, a lot older than Jim's.

"Uh, yes," she floundered, feeling caught out and not quite knowing what to say. There was silence on the other end of the line, as whoever it was patiently waited for her to explain.

"I just wondered if Jim Cavanagh was still at the office?" Holding her breath, she crossed her fingers, hoping the voice would say yes and the mystery would be solved.

"Cavanagh?" The voice sounded slightly incredulous.

"Ye…yes," she stammered, suddenly feeling unsure, she certainly didn't want to land Jim in any trouble.

"I'm his boss. He's not been in at all today. Didn't ring in sick, either. You know anything about that?"

"No, no, I'm just a friend of Jim's. He's not picking up his cell so I thought I'd try and catch him at work is all," she said, hoping she didn't sound like she was lying her ass off.

"No, he's not here. Odd he's not picking up his cell, Cavanagh normally always picks up, unless he's asleep or drunk."

"Uh, well, umm, sorry to bother you, and thanks for the information," she said hastily, wanting to get off the line.

"No problem. When you find him, tell him he better have a good excuse when I get a hold of him."

After she'd hung up, she mused over what Jim's boss had told her. The fact that Jim hadn't come into work that day, wasn't picking up his phone *and* was seemingly nowhere to be found was more than just a bit odd, especially considering they had arranged to meet at five-thirty and it was now almost a half an hour later. What if something had happened to him? Something bad? Perhaps he'd fallen over and hit his head. Perhaps he'd been lying unconscious since this morning? Perhaps he wasn't breathing even?

Well, there was only one way to find out, wasn't there? With a quick glance to check that the street was clear, she pulled her wallet out of her pants pocket again, opening it and removing the small silver lock pick she always carried with her.

Slipping it into the keyhole of Jim's front door, she began to work the lock with practiced ease. A minute later, she heard the familiar click as the lock gave way, a smile of smug satisfaction creeping over her face as she pushed open the door. She was really getting too damn good at this. Jim definitely needed to step up his security. With a lock as easy as *that* to pick, anyone determined enough to break in could easily get inside.

She shut the door softly behind her and stood there, listening quietly for a moment. The house was silent. There really didn't seem to be anyone in. As she walked through the open door to her left into what appeared to be Jim's lounge, her eyes flicked from left to right, assessing the situation. The small, cozy-looking room was eclectically decorated with its tattered print wallpaper and mismatching velvety drapes, but it looked comfortable and homely, and somehow it seemed to fit with Jim's laid back, friendly personality.

There was still no sign of Jim, but *hang on a minute*, what was that? Lola's gaze zoned in on the battered brown leather satchel sitting atop the polished oak coffee table standing in front of the sofa. Jim's satchel? She recalled how he'd told her he took it everywhere with him. Apparently he never left the house without it.

"Everything I need is in this bag," he'd announced, proudly patting the tattered leather as if it were a favorite pet.

"Well, it certainly looks like it's seen some action," she'd replied, smiling at his obvious fondness for the worn-in old leather satchel.

"Oh yeah, we've been through a lot together. This little beauty contains my essential journo's kit. She's always by my side. I never leave her at home," he'd said.

I never leave her at home. But that appeared to be exactly what Jim had done. So what did that mean? Lola's mind rifled through the possibilities as she tried to make sense of the situation. Jim could have been caught short for something, maybe some milk or some other groceries, and had to step out of the door for five minutes? But then surely he'd be back by now, unless something had happened to him when he was out. Something bad, maybe?

Another thought loomed large, and she shivered, not wanting to dwell on it but unable to escape contemplating the idea all the same. What if the something bad that had happened to him had happened before he'd even left the house? What if someone had broken into Jim's house and attacked him, or what if he'd innocuously opened the door to his attacker, thinking it was her arriving early?

What if Jim was lying here now, unconscious, or perhaps even worse? She should check the other rooms. Standing around here was only wasting precious time. Striding out of the room, she turned to her right, pushing open the shabbily painted wooden door as she entered Jim's kitchen. The room was empty, the only noise punctuating the silence the gentle, constant hum of the tall refrigerator standing in the corner.

Just then, a flashing light caught her eye. Jim's Blackberry winked back at her. The little black cell sat forlornly atop the Formica of the kitchen counter. So he *hadn't* taken his mobile with him. That would explain why he wasn't picking up his phone, at least. This was definitely not looking good. Shaking her head, she walked over to the phone then picked it up to deftly thumb through the messages. Nothing untoward here, at least not as far as she could see.

A message from Jim's mother, saying she was looking forward to his Thanksgiving visit the next month, a message from one of his work colleagues asking him if he had finished the piece on the local community allotment project and would he send it through, a message sent from Lola's own phone yesterday evening confirming she would be at Jim's house at five-thirty p.m.

Wait, what was this?

Cavanagh. We'll be round tomorrow to collect that evidence. Don't even think about trying anything. D.

D? Drago? Was the message to do with the witness that had contacted Jim? If it was, then Jim could be in serious trouble. She had to find out. There was no time to waste. Who knew the lengths Drago would go to in order to cover up his guilt? After all, he'd already proved he was more than capable of cold-blooded murder.

Jim would never have been involved in all this if he hadn't been trying to help her and Dillon out. And Dillon wouldn't have been locked up on suspicion of first-degree murder if it hadn't been for him trying to protect her from Drago. *Why do I have to destroy everyone I come into contact with?* First Rory, then Dillon and now Jim. Was everyone she ever knew destined to be cursed?

She recalled her ex-fiancé's face, the expression of revulsion he'd worn when she'd finally plucked up the courage to confess what she really was. Earlier that week he'd arrested a girl called Blue outside Club Vain for sinking her teeth into a man's neck and drinking his blood. But when Blue had found out exactly whose fiancé Rory was, the girl had told him that if he was gonna haul her ass in for blood play, he should start making arrests at home first.

Guess it didn't always pay to be a somewhat infamous man-eater in Burley Falls. You kinda made enemies that way.

Rory had known there was blood drinking going on in Burley Falls. You couldn't be a long-time resident and fail to notice, but he certainly hadn't known the full story. But when he'd come to ask her the truth of the accusation, she'd decided to take the opportunity to fess up. Stupidly, she'd hoped he wouldn't reject her when he found out the accusation was true.

"What are you saying, exactly?" Rory looked at her skeptically. Standing there, by her bedroom window, her silhouette highlighted by the silvery moonlight, she lifted her head to look at him as he sat there on the end of her queen-size bed. She winced as he regarded her. He'd never looked at her like that before, with such suspicion in his eyes.

"I'm a vampire, like Blue."

"You're one of those weirdos who drink blood? You have to be kidding me."

"No, and I wish to God I was joking. But when I was seventeen years old, a house fire killed my entire family." She took a deep breath, steeling herself as she remembered that awful night – the noise, the heat, the choking, stifling, terrible smell of smoke, of burning flesh.

"I thought your family died in a car crash." Rory shook his head, his russet curls bobbing in the semidarkness, as his handsome face creased into a confused scowl.

"I told you that because I wasn't ready to tell you the real truth. I was the only one who was awake. I must have been woken up by all the smoke and I crawled to the bedroom window to try to escape. I managed to use my tennis racket to shatter the glass but I was semiconscious on the floor of my bedroom when she appeared in front of me – a woman, a vampire." Lyra. She shuddered as she recalled Lyra's pale beauty, the cool smoothness of her flesh as the vampire bent forward to cup her cheek.

"Are you freakin' for real?" Rory's face was incredulous as he looked at her.

"Yes. She turned me that night, and she saved my life." But condemned me to another kind of death. The death of my humanity.

"Why didn't she save your family then?" Rory's face was instantly suspicious.

"By the time she'd arrived, it was already too late for them. They were dead from smoke inhalation." She remembered the charred bodies that had been pulled from the wreckage of her *family home — her mother, her father, her kid brother Damon. Tears threatened to spill from her eyes at the painful memories and she felt a lump forming in her larynx.*

"Is this some kind of sick joke?" He looked at her, his eyes disbelieving.

"No. You remember how I never go in sunlight, right? You remember how I told you I had that skin condition that makes me blister up real bad?"

"So?"

"So the reason I can't go in sunlight isn't because of a skin condition. It's because I'm a vampire."

Rory still looked skeptical.

"Okay, you remember how I'd have to disappear sometimes?" she said patiently.

"So?"

"So I was going to feed. To drink blood. What that girl told you about me was true."

She saw the realization dawn in his eyes as they assessed the truth of what she had been telling him. Moving across the room to where he sat, she placed her hand tentatively on his well-muscled forearm.

"I'm sorry I kept it from you," she said, searching the gray-green depths of his eyes hopefully, for some sign of emotion.

She hadn't had to wait for long.

"Get off me, you freak," he spat, grabbing her by the wrist and shoving her arm violently away from his. Recoiling, she stared at him in disbelief. Was the man who only an hour earlier had held her in his arms and whispered sweet nothings to her now so cruelly rejecting her? He'd told her he wanted to marry her, make her his wife, love her until they were both gray and old and for all the years beyond, so how could he be acting this way now?

"Please, listen to me. This doesn't have to change anything. This doesn't have to affect us, not if we don't want it to..." She gulped, noticing his expression. The disgust on his chiseled features was evident.

"Are you crazy? You think we can be together now, after what you've told me? You think I'm going to marry a monster?" He looked at her as if she was out of her mind — this man she had known and loved, held in her arms, this man who had held her in return.

Wincing at his words, her mind had struggled to recollect itself, the verbal blow making her mentally reel and rendering her seemingly incapable of sentient speech.

"Rory, please," she begged, moving forward to reach for him, but he shoved her away again, more violently this time, causing her to stumble backward and clutch at her dresser in order to stay upright. He was acting as if she meant nothing to him, worse than that even…as if he hated her.

"Just keep away from me," he warned, standing up from the bed.

Her whole body was trembling, her legs feeling as though they might buckle from under her, the wooden dresser the only thing holding her upright.

Gathering his discarded clothes, he dressed quickly as she watched, holding her breath, too scared to say anything, too frightened to even allow the tears pricking at her eyelids to fall. She stood there clutching the dresser as he turned to look at her one last time. A full five minutes after her front door had slammed shut, she remained there, long after she'd heard the heavy tread of his footsteps crunching down the gravel pathway outside.

Her ears still rang with the last words he'd uttered as he'd addressed her for the final time before striding from the room.

"You're disgusting. Stay the hell away from me. You hear me? I never want to see you again."

Well, he'd certainly gotten his wish, because that had been the very last time.

Apparently he'd moved out of town to Snowy Brook, where Max's cousin lived. According to Max, Rory had gotten married, gained his detective badge and was now the proud father to twin girls. Lola wondered briefly what his wife was like—what she looked like, how she dressed, if she was a stay-at-home mom or not.

Not that it mattered. Whoever he had married was a normal woman, not a cursed, wretched creature like her—a normal flesh and blood woman who could feel the warmth of the sun and didn't happen to ruin the lives of everyone she came into contact with.

Ugh. She had to pull herself together. If Jim *was* in trouble because of her, then standing around here moping over the past wasn't exactly going to help get him out of trouble. *Focus, Lola. Think.* What would be the best thing to do? Drago and his goons had obviously not gotten what they wanted out of Jim. Otherwise he'd still be here, wouldn't he? So what was it they did want? The mobile phone evidence?

Hurriedly she walked back into the lounge to the tattered leather satchel still sitting on the sofa. Opening it, she hastily scrambled through the contents, closing upon a slim, plastic USB stick similar to the one Jim had brandished at her in his office. So they hadn't taken the evidence? But wasn't that what they had come here for in the first place?

A sudden chill shot through her then as the realization dawned. They hadn't taken the evidence because that wasn't their main concern. The footage was damning enough, but on its own and without a witness, it was proof of nothing. Photos could be doctored. More damaging was the fact that there was someone out there—a witness—who could testify that Drago was responsible for the murder.

Only Jim knew who that person was. *That* was why they had taken Jim. They wanted him to lead them to the one piece of evidence that could potentially destroy Drago, a live witness. And whoever that witness was, he was now in serious danger, that was for sure. She knew she had to find out the identity of Jim's secret witness, but how? *Think, Lola. Think. Where would a journalist store his secrets?*

Pulling Jim's laptop out of the battered satchel, she plopped down on to the sagging cushions of the tatty-looking sofa and flipped open the lid, hitting the Power button so the machine whirred into life.

Quickly she clicked through to the documents folder, her eyes scanning for something that might look likely to yield some sort of clue, as she muttered the names of the folders. *Articles, research, pictures, contacts, fiction* — that one must contain the novel that Jim had told her he was working on. But where would he be likely to store the information about the witness? Just then, her eye caught the name of a folder labeled *Interviews.* Interviews? Maybe there was something in there?

Clicking through, she scanned the names of the files. *Hang on a minute.* One of them — a video file — was grayed out. That was weird. The name of it was Mr. X. Peering closer at the screen, she saw a small padlock icon by the side of the file. An encrypted file? This *had* to contain something important, but how on earth to get into it?

Double clicking on the file, she was confronted with a box prompting her to enter a password in order to gain access to the document. The password could be anything. There was no way she was going to be able to second-guess it, though she sure as hell knew someone who just might be able to help her get into the file. Whipping out her razor-thin cell, she hit speed dial, tapping her fingers nervously upon the laptop's keypad as she waited for Max to pick up.

The handsome bartender was much more than just a pretty face and an acerbic wit. She remembered how he'd told her he'd majored in computer science at college and how he still liked to hack into systems he wasn't supposed to for fun every now and then. Well, maybe he could put those skills to good use, because now she needed to get into that file. If she didn't find out the identity of the witness, both Jim and whoever it was could be in mortal danger — not to mention the consequences for Dillon. She shuddered, not wanting to think about *that* awful prospect.

"Lola." Relief coursed through her at the sound of Max's familiar voice.

"Max, I need your help on something. It's urgent."

"Is everything all right?"

"No, actually. They've taken Jim. He's in danger and someone else could be in danger too."

"Wait. Who's Jim?"

"Jim's this guy from the *Chronicle* who found some evidence that totally incriminates Drago. Drago found out about it and now Jim's gone. And there's more. There's a witness, and if I can't find out who it is. He could be in danger too. I need you to break into this file on Jim's laptop for me," she said, the words falling out of her mouth in a rush.

"Uh, sure, but where are you? I'm home at the moment. You need me to come and meet you?"

"Please."

"Okay, what's the address?"

Twenty minutes later they were both sitting on Jim's sofa, the laptop on the small wooden coffee table in front of them as Max peered at the screen.

"Here. See? This is the file?" She indicated at the screen with her pinky finger, shooting Max a hopeful glance. "You think you can get in to it?"

Max shrugged.

"Dunno, but I'll give it a shot. Looks pretty standard to me. Shouldn't be a problem."

"Okay. Well, I'm just gonna go use the restroom. Be back in five, okay?"

"Sure, I'll work on this. Depending on how tough Jim's password is, this could take anything from five minutes to five hours," Max replied, bending his head to the laptop once more as his fingers tapped hurriedly at the keyboard.

Five hours? She hoped it didn't take that long. She wasn't sure if they even had five hours left to rescue Jim. Shaking her head, she got up from the sofa and walked toward the bathroom, the sound of Max's fingers tap tapping away in her ears.

She was bending her head to the faucet to splash water on her face when she heard Max's voice again, calling out to her.

"Lola, I think you better come and see this." Quickly shutting off the faucet, she hurried back into the lounge.

"What is it?"

Max gave her an uneasy grin as he gestured to the laptop's screen. "Password was easy to crack. Your guy wasn't very inventive—used his first initial combined with his surname and the four digits of his birth year."

"*What?* How did you know when Jim was born?"

"Oh, wasn't hard to find out. Dude had all sorts of info stored on this little baby." Max patted the laptop affectionately.

"Wow, you're good," she said, blinking in admiration as she stared at him. She knew Max was good with computers but she honestly hadn't expected him to be quite *that* good with them.

"Hah, not what you would expect from me, eh?"

"No, it was just so fast. That's all."

"Yeah, I guess if I hadn't gotten turned into a vamp, then I'd probably be working for a company like

Microsoft or Apple right now," Max said, shrugging, a resigned expression crossing his face.

"Yeah, that's gotta suck." She shot him a sympathetic look. Of course, Max had gotten turned right after college, after he'd gone home with the wrong guy – the wrong guy who'd just happened to be a vamp. Now the only job he could handle without getting blistered up was late-night bartending at Vain.

"Hey, we got bigger problems to worry about than my non-career as a technology whiz. You need to sit down and take a look at this," Max said, indicating to the screen again as he pulled up the laptop's video player. Jim's face popped up as the recording began, and slightly puzzled, she sat down as Max had instructed, her eyes glued to the screen.

Jim began to speak, his brown eyes earnest as he looked into the camera's lens.

"If you're watching this file, that's not a good sign and probably means something's happened to me," Jim said, his face grave. "But since you *are* watching it, it's my duty to tell the truth about Dave Eversham's death. There's someone who saw someone with Mr. Eversham on the night of the murder, at the time he was killed." Jim paused, onscreen, to take a gulp from the glass of water positioned on the desk in front of him. Her breath caught in her throat. This was it. They were about to find out the name of the witness now, surely?

"That witness is me," Jim finished, his gaze direct as he looked out through the camera's lens, his pupils seeming to bore into her own as he delivered the bombshell. What was he *saying*? He couldn't be serious? *Jim* was the witness? He had taken the pictures? But why hadn't he told her?

"On the night Dave Eversham was murdered, the man I saw with him in Burley Park was Drago Graythorne," Jim continued.

She shot a quick glance at Max, whose expression told her everything she needed to know. Jim was a dead man. There was certainly no way Drago was going to let the one and only witness to his guilt live.

Her eyes flicked back to the screen as Jim coughed, clearing his throat.

"It's probably too late now to help me, but if you're watching this, you need to get this video to Mr. Bob Lanton, editor of the *Burley Chronicle*, as soon as you can. Note down this email address and password. There are pictures stored securely that can prove the truth of what I am saying. You need to get those to him too." Jim paused to pick up a small, white piece of paper from the tabletop he sat in front of, clearly displaying it to the camera's lens. She squinted at the screen, trying to read Jim's messily scrawled handwriting.

mrx@hotmail.com
Password: evershamfiles

"But be careful," Jim warned. "The information contained in this video and stored in the email is highly dangerous. Some people will kill to get their hands on it," he finished, as the video faded to black. She turned to look at Max, whose face was as grave as Jim's had been.

"Jeez, Lola, if all that's true, your friend's landed himself in one whole heap of trouble," Max said, shaking his head. She chewed her lip nervously, mulling the possibilities over in her mind. Jim had instructed whoever found the video to get it to his editor as soon as possible. But if his editor decided not to publish the story — which was highly likely considering the serious nature of the accusations — then she would have wasted time for nothing and Dillon would still be behind bars — time that she could have spent finding where Drago had taken Jim. That was if there was any Jim left to find.

A shiver ran down her spine as she couldn't help but picture the worst. *Don't think like that, Lola. You can't think like that. It's all your fault Jim's in this mess. Now you have to get him out of it.* And get him to court so he can testify. She had to rescue him both for his own sake and for Dillon's sake. No, there was no way in hell she could turn that evidence in just yet.

"Any ideas where Drago might have taken him? You know him slightly better than I do," she said, looking at Max. Max had been Drago's former classmate in high school, after all.

Max screwed up his face, considering the question.

"Honestly, I don't know. But you could try the Hollow. Rumor has it that's where Drago takes some of his victims — the ones that don't come back."

The Hollow was an abandoned summer house located in a grove out by Winterford Lake and was so dilapidated that there was now moss growing on the moss sprouting through the cracks in the walls. She had to admit it was a pretty picturesque spot, what with the lush scenery and the lake view nearby, but the place had always creeped her out somewhat. Still, there was no time for cowardice now. A man's life was at stake.

"The Hollow it is then."

"Want me to come with you?" Max shot her a questioning look.

She smiled. Max was a loyal friend *and* a vamp too. He was definitely less likely to run in to danger than

Jim would be. Even so, vamps still had their weaknesses. And no one knew those weaknesses or how to exploit them better than Drago. No, vamp or no vamp, she couldn't afford to put anybody else in danger.

"Thanks, but I think it's better if I go alone," she said, hoping whatever she did find at the Hollow, it wouldn't be a fresh corpse.

Chapter Eight

Forty-five minutes later Lola pulled up outside the cabin, the smooth, still waters of Lake Winterford stretching out in one large, amorphous expanse to her right. After killing the engine on the silver Audi, she jumped out of the little vehicle, slamming the car door shut behind her then locking it with a beep.

The place looked deserted, and glancing nervously around over her shoulder, she hurriedly made her way to the cabin's front entrance, overgrown with the tumbleweeds and moss that grew so profusely down by the lakeside's moist, dank environment.

Pushing open the dilapidated door, she started as a cluster of spiders scuttled abruptly out from under the crook they'd temporarily made home.

Calm down, Lola. You're going to have to face more than a bunch of bugs by the time this whole ordeal is through.

Steeling her breathing, she made her way through the cabin's long, dingy hallway. The only light helping to partly illuminate her way was the moon's low, silvery beam.

There was no way she was going to be able to see a damn thing if she went any farther in this near darkness. Scrambling in her pockets, she whipped out her cell phone, flicking through till she found what she was looking for. She pressed a button and light flooded the room as the beam made the impromptu flashlight.

Thank God for technology. Now if it were only as easy to find out where Drago had taken Jim.

"Stop right where you are." The voice froze her dead in her tracks. Drago. A shiver ran down her spine as her eyes flicked wildly around, attempting to discern exactly where the source of the voice was coming from.

"Drop to your knees," he commanded, and trembling slightly, she did as he obeyed, her knees hitting the dank wooden floor of the cabin. There was no use trying to run, Drago knew this place like the back of his hand and he'd be on her in a second. She had to play this smart, try and outwit him, wait for her opportunity to escape.

She heard footsteps coming nearer, from behind her somewhere, Drago must have been in the recreation room, but where was Jim? Her pulse was in her throat, but she forced herself to calm down. She could feel Drago's presence right behind her.

"Well, look who it is," he drawled, his nasal tones snaking their way into her ears and wrapping their slimy tentacles around her senses, making her shudder in revulsion. He caressed a tendril of her hair, twisting it around his thin, bony fingers until the entire section was wound tightly.

"Little Miss Lola, here all on her own. Where's your Texas cowboy to save you now?" Drago's voice was a dry hiss, but she knew from the way he was speaking he was wearing a grin the size of Orange County. Drago liked nothing better than to be in control, and that was certainly where he was right now — in control, with her at his absolute mercy.

"I just don't know what you want," she squeaked. He still gripped her hair firmly.

"I just don't know what you want," he mocked, his voice a grotesque parody of her own as he yanked her head back so that she was looking straight into the cold, unforgiving blue of his eyes.

"Please, why are you doing this?"

"Oh, I think you know exactly why I'm doing this." He lowered his face until his nose was almost touching her own.

"I think you and your hick boyfriend have caused me quite enough trouble, don't you?"

"We haven't done anything to you, Drago."

"You've both done plenty, not to mention your journalist friend as well," he said, the spittle hitting her cheek as he spat the words. *Oh God, please let Jim be okay.*

Drago must have noticed her panic at the mention of Jim's name because he grinned sadistically, obviously pleased at her discomfort.

"Oh, is Ms. Devereaux all worried about her little journo? Don't fret, my pretty, you two will be reunited real soon," he sneered, his thin lips revealing the luminosity of his sharp incisors.

"What have you done with him?"

"*Moi*? Nothing…yet." He grinned, finally releasing his grip on her hair and pushing her forward with a hard shove.

Gasping, she managed to put her palms out, preventing herself from falling flat on her face at the last moment, but the blow still winded her, and she lay there panting on the floor, her cheek pressed against the cold hardness of the cabin's wooden floorboards.

In a flash he was on her, his breath in her ear, as he crouched over her menacingly.

"I thought we'd have a little fun together before the grand reunion, find out just what it is that Mr. Texas finds so appealing," he said, tracing his fingers down the side of her face, making her skin crawl.

"Drago, please don't do this." She yelped as he grabbed another fistful of her hair, yanking her head back again. Once more she was forced to look into those eyes, their chilling coldness making her shudder as he regarded her, an amused expression on his face.

"I don't think you're really in a position to plead for clemency, do you?" he murmured, caressing her cheek, the false tenderness of the gesture causing her to cringe with fear as he pawed her.

"Get the hell off her, scumbag, or you'll live to regret it you son of a bitch."

The words pierced the passageway, low and firm, causing her heart to soar with joy. Dillon? But how?

Confused, Drago released his grip on her, causing the side of her face to hit the floor again as she tried to twist round to see where Dillon was. There he stood, illuminated in the cabin's doorway, moonlight filtering through the top of his dark, curly hair, hands thrust deep into the pockets of his dark leather jacket. Her stomach did a funny little flip at the sight of him.

"What the fuck are you doing here, asshole? I thought the cops were dealing with your sorry ass," Drago muttered, clearly sick Dillon had somehow managed to come to her aid again.

"I bet you did, especially since you framed me, douchebag," Dillon said, stepping through the doorway. His brown eyes were full of concern as he stooped down to where she lay on the floor.

"You better not have hurt her," he said, shooting a warning look at Drago. She tried to stifle a giggle as she noted Drago's eyes, fixed warily on Dillon, as if to make sure the taller man wasn't about to make a sudden lunge for him.

"You okay, sweetheart?" Tenderly Dillon stroked her head, his soothing touch a welcome relief from Drago's manhandling.

"Yeah, I'll live," she said, scrambling to sit up.

"Here." He got to his feet again, proffering his hand to her as he stood up. Gratefully she took it. How was it he always managed to show up in the nick of time to save her ass? She didn't know but she was sure as hell relieved he did.

"Wait, where's Drago?" she blurted out, suddenly remembering the blonde vamp. Her eyes peered through the semidarkness of the hallway, trying to discern where he'd disappeared to.

"Damned if I know or give a damn about that piece of trash," he muttered, a scowl clouding his handsome features.

"No, you don't understand. *He's got Jim.*"

"What do you mean he's got Jim? The newspaper guy?" Dillon's brow furrowed.

She nodded. "I was supposed to meet Jim this evening but when I went to his house, he wasn't there. He left his bag and laptop behind, so I got suspicious. I came here looking for him —"

She stopped abruptly, eyeing him warily as the thought flashed through her mind. *How had he known?*

"What is it?"

"How did you know I'd be here?" She scanned his face warily.

"Max mentioned you might be here. He didn't say anything about Jim, though, mind you when *I* spoke to him he was knee-deep mixing cocktails," he said, grinning wryly.

"Yeah, he probably wasn't too sure what you knew or what was safe to tell you. We can't let Drago get away, we have to find him or Jim has no chance."

"I didn't see him leave, did you?" He screwed up his face.

"I'm pretty sure he didn't get past us, so that means he can't be in any of the rooms down there," she said, indicating down the slim passageway. He picked up her discarded cell, the beam still bright as he paced to the other end of the corridor, where the door to the rec room stood half-ajar.

"Nope, not in here either. But I found this." He held up a pendant, a small silver dagger suspended on a black leather thong.

She recognized the item immediately. Drago was never seen without it around his scrawny neck.

"Well, that's Drago's pendant. He musta lost it when we were tussling. But we need Drago."

"Okay, look, don't worry. We'll find him if he's not taken off already. You wait outside, I'll look upstairs. Maybe he's hiding out up there?"

She allowed him to lead her out to her Audi, and she beeped open the door then slid inside to the relative comfort of the cream leather seating lining the small vehicle. He reached in to plant a kiss on her nose.

"I won't be long," he murmured, his proximity making her shiver with sensation despite her heightened state of fear. Somehow she always felt better when he was beside her.

"Thank you for doing this," she said, smiling gratefully at him as he shut the car door behind her. She watched his broad back as he walked back into the rundown little cabin.

"Be careful," she added under her breath, her heart in her mouth as she fervently prayed he would be all right. She was confident Dillon could handle himself. In fact, she was more than certain that in a fair fight he was a match for most men. *In a fair fight.* The problem was Drago didn't like to fight fair. She shivered. She had to stop this. She was letting her imagination run away with her. Drago had likely long gone anyway. The only thing she could do now was wait.

Settling back against the comfortable seating, she closed her eyes and tried to breathe. Maybe she should get five minutes sleep to calm her frazzled nerves.

The all too familiar voice was insidious in her ears as she leaned back, causing her to bolt forward again with a start.

"I wouldn't get *too* comfortable there if I were you." *Drago. How the hell did he get into the Audi?* He must have snuck out of the front door and picked the lock of the vehicle while she and Dillon had been talking. She gasped for air when she felt Drago's icy fingers creep along her throat and tighten, and she felt his stale breath upon her cheek as he leaned forward to menace her.

"Start the car, Lola. There's a good girl."

"No." The fingers squeezed tighter, forcing her to cough and splutter.

"Do as I say or you'll regret it." He hissed, applying more pressure as, terrified, she struggled to unclasp his fingers from her neck.

"Okay, okay," she said, choking the words out, frantically struggling for air. He relaxed his grip and she fell forward on to the engine's dash as she was freed.

"Better not try anything funny. There's no big strong cowboy here to save you now. Turn the key and start her up. There's a good little girl," he said, patting her on the head patronizingly. Breathing hard, she struggled to collect herself as the engine spluttered into life. She had to time this right. Move too early and Drago would be on her in an instant, too late and they'd be too far away for Dillon to come to her aid.

"I won't try anything. I promise," she lied, crossing her fingers in the darkness and hoping against hope that what she was planning would work out. She sure as hell hoped Dillon had good hearing.

"Well, drive then. What are you waiting for?" Drago said again, shoving her forward roughly as her shaking hands reached for the clutch. The car's engine began to roar as she reversed the vehicle, turning the wheel slowly, expertly, to make it look as if she were trying to drive away from the cabin.

Trembling, she counted to herself under her breath, flicking a nervous glance at the darkened cabin as she continued to reverse the vehicle. *Five, four, three, two, wait, wait, now, go, go, go.*

She turned the steering wheel violently and the Audi roared forward, forcing the car's chassis to swing out one hundred eighty degrees as she steered it toward the cabin. Eyeing the overgrown stucco, she guessed she would have around five seconds to open the door and jump clear before impact. Could she make it? Well, she had to try. It wasn't like she had any other choice. She'd just have to hope Dillon wasn't standing right behind the wall of the cabin when the Audi crashed through it.

"Stop right now," Drago screeched behind her, his bony fingers scrabbling at her back as determinedly she drove the Audi forward. *Now.* She reached for the door then pressed down on the handle. Internally bracing herself, she sprang clear of the vehicle in a duck and roll motion, her hands protectively covering her head.

There was a terrible screech and the sound of crunching metal as the Audi collided with the wall of the cabin, then the sound of a tidal wave of bricks falling as the damaged wall collapsed. She listened for sounds of life from the vehicle but she could hear nothing.

Gingerly, she lifted her head to peek at the scene. The back end of the Audi was crumpled up like a sheet of paper, half hanging out of the cabin's by-now-destroyed front wall. A normal person would likely have been killed by the impact, but Drago would most likely just be seriously concussed. Chances were good he would survive it. He *was* immortal after all.

Concussion or not, she wasn't going to risk letting him get away this time. Lifting her head she called out the only name she knew she could rely on to come to her aid.

No reply. Where the hell was he?

"Dillon," she called again, her voice cracking with the effort. He must be upstairs right at the back of the cabin. Great. Just what she needed. Forcing herself to her feet, she staggered as she attempted to stand up, dusting off the brick dust and mud that clung to her pants as she tried to find her balance.

"Dillon," she yelled out again.

"I told you, Lola," the voice whispered, "there's no cowboy to save you this time." She felt something heavy hit her in the small of her back, sucking the air out of her lungs and forcing her to topple forward face-first into the gravel pathway.

Damn it. Drago had obviously jumped free from the car shortly after she had. Now he was going to be even more pissed. *Think, Lola, think.* She *had* to stall him. What was Drago's weak spot?

The answer was as obvious as a slap in the face. His ego, of course.

"Okay, okay, you win. I give in. Please just don't hurt me. I'll do anything you want, I'm sorry," she begged him.

His snigger told her he wasn't buying it. She knew she was going to have to try a little harder than that.

"Look, if you let me, I'll prove to you just how sorry I am," she wheedled, twisting her upper body round to face him, all too aware of how her curves were spilling out of the form-fitting scoop neck black top she wore. He may hate her right now but she knew even Drago wasn't totally immune to her charms.

His eyes proved her assumption correct, as they raked over the mud-spattered, creamy flesh left exposed by her décolleté, and though internally she cringed. She knew she had to try to work this if she were going to have any chance of eventual escape from him.

"Pathetic." He spat the words elegantly from his thin lips, his nose crinkling up in distaste. "Miss High and Mighty Lola Devereaux reduced to scrabbling around on her knees in the dirt, begging me for her forgiveness. If you really think your tawdry charms are going to save your sorry ass, sweetheart, you can think again. You've pissed me off, and that's a very stupid thing to do to a Graythorne." Lifting his hand, he made as if to strike her, and she recoiled with a yelp, her hands cradling her head protectively again.

Laughing, he paused in midair, allowing his hand to drop slowly, until his fingers traced a lazy path along her cheekbone.

"Although if you're a very good girl, they might make me go a *little* gentler on you," he drawled, his meaning crystal clear, as valiantly she tried to stifle the urge to vomit.

"I understand." She nodded, meekly bobbing her head. She had to try to trick him into thinking she had really surrendered.

"So if you're serious, start by showing me just how talented that mouth of yours is." He grinned, fumbling for his fly. He gripped the back of her head, forcing her closer to his crotch, as frantically her eyes and ears searched the darkness for a sign of Dillon, but there was no sign of him. She had to act now and act alone.

Sinking her teeth into Drago's wrist, she allowed herself the briefest smile of satisfaction as he howled in pain, recoiling from her momentarily to grab at his wounded arm. She didn't squander the opportunity, shoving him backward in the chest as he grabbed at her hair in retaliation, the gravel clinging to their clothes and scratching at their skin as they frantically scrabbled in the dirt.

She knew there was only so long she could fend him off before he got the better of her. Summoning all her strength, she employed her best assets, forcing him into a powerful thigh lock, which had the desired effect of temporarily neutralizing him.

"Dillon—" She lifted her head to yell out again, looking at the upstairs window of the cabin in desperation. "Dillon," she screamed.

Then she saw him, a dark shape in the open window of the cabin, a story above, hands in pockets as he perched on the ledge. The two of them locked eyes momentarily in the darkness and a strange charge seemed to ripple through the night. Then gracefully as a cat, he dropped down on to the pathway beside them.

In a flash of black leather, he was on Drago with a roar, pounding him and dragging him off her by the scruff of the neck, as the blond vamp uselessly thrashed about, unable to provide an adequate challenge to Dillon's superior strength. She watched, still trying to catch her breath, as Dillon pinned him in a headlock, then looked at her, his chiseled jaw set firmly in anger.

"What shall we do with him now?" His deep brown eyes had the faintest trace of amusement in them but his expression was stern.

God he was gorgeous. *My hero.*

"Lola," Dillon said again, urging her gently.

She forced herself to consider the question at hand. What *were* they supposed to do with him? "Tie him up and leave him somewhere deserted. Don't let him go until he tells us where Jim is." Yes, that would spook Drago—the knowledge he wouldn't be able to feed on any more victims. His bloodlust was so all consuming, she'd wager he'd be singing like a canary within the hour.

"You sure I shouldn't just beat the hell out of his sorry ass?" Dillon looked at her, the anger flaring in his eyes. She knew he was mad as all hell that Drago had tried to hurt her again.

"Mmmph," Drago mumbled in protest from under Dillon's biceps, attempting to squirm free from the viselike grip he was being held in. She smiled as she stared Drago straight in the eyes, the terrified expression on his face giving her a peculiar satisfaction. She didn't usually enjoy inflicting pain on anyone, but when it came to Drago, she might have to make a special exception.

"Nah, I think my idea will be a much more apt punishment. Tie him up and take him down to the basement, leave him there until he decides to tell us where Jim is. That's unless…" She paused, standing up and walking toward Drago slowly. She bent down again to cup his face and lifted his arrogant chin till he was looking at her defiantly. She peered into the icy blue coldness of his eyes.

"Unless you want to save yourself the trouble and tell us where Jim is now?" She raised an eyebrow at Drago.

He sneered, staring back at her defiantly. "You think you and your little hick can threaten me? Do your worst. My father will have the cops on both your asses before you even have time to say yee-haw," Drago scoffed, spitting on the ground. He'd obviously decided to be difficult, even though the bravado of his words was betrayed somewhat by the quiver in his bottom lip.

"Hey, watch who you're calling a hick," Dillon warned, squeezing tighter as Drago's hands desperately clutched at Dillon's sleeve, trying to pull him off. Sighing, she rolled her eyes.

"Okay, the basement it is then. We'll come back to check on him later, see if he's changed his mind. *If* we can't find Jim, of course. Otherwise we'll just leave his spoiled ass to rot."

* * * *

Twenty minutes later, after Drago had been safely deposited in the depths of the cabin's mold-infested basement and they had made their way back up the dingy steps to the cabin's entrance, she turned to Dillon.

She had been too busy fending off Drago to pay the matter much thought beforehand, but now her brain started to wonder just how he'd managed to get out of the jail cell she had left him in when she had last set eyes on his face.

"How did you get out? I mean, I'm glad you did, but how?" She shot him a confused look. He grinned at the question, his eyes crinkling up at the corners attractively. She felt a flash of lust as her eyes took in the plains of his handsome face. Why even in the most unlikely of moments, did he always have the ability to make her body anticipate sex?

"They had to release me on bail, but I've been charged and I gotta go back for the hearing on the twenty-ninth. I rang ya, but the call went straight to voice mail so I decided to hit up Vain to see if you were there. That's when Max said you were going to check out the cabin, so I thought I'd swing by." He shrugged his broad shoulders as if it were no big deal. The simple gesture made her want to hug the life out of him.

"Well, you came at just the right moment," she said, grinning back at him. It was true, she genuinely didn't think she'd ever been so glad to see anyone in her life.

"Yeah, looks like I was right on time to get that dumbass handled, eh? I can't believe he tried to hurt you again. Man, that just makes me mad as all hell," he said, shaking his head.

"Hey, don't beat yourself up over it. *You* were behind bars because of that asshole and anyway, you were here when it mattered to save my ass from that jerk," she said, moving forward in the semidarkness to place her hand on his forearm.

"I guess," he said, shrugging, "but you shouldn't have tried to come here alone. I know you were doing this for me but ya don't have to fight my battles for me. Makes me feel bad, like I can't protect you."

Could there be a guy alive who is sweeter and more considerate? "Hey," she insisted, sidling closer and pressing herself against him, "I know I don't *have* to fight your battles for you, but I wanted to help you, silly. Anyway, I had to find Jim's ass, which we still have to do. God knows what Drago's done with him." She looked up at him and he nodded.

"Of course. But first..." He paused, turning to face her, moving to cup her face tenderly as he looked down into her eyes. The electric touch of his hands caused her to shiver, and the way he was looking at her made her heart beat fast, real fast. She was crazy with lust for him but she had to admit she was feeling a lot more than just lust right now. Here she was, the great Lola Devereaux, famed femme fatale and local man-eating legend, fallen hook, line and sinker. And what was more? She didn't regret it, not one little bit.

"First what?" she whispered back, feeling as though she were drunk as he held her tightly in his arms. He didn't reply, choosing instead to answer by bending his head and pressing his mouth against hers, as with urgency she willingly responded, yielding to his touch and kissing him back with a ferocity *she* didn't even know she possessed. The two of them stood there, enmeshed, half embraced by the shadows, the heat between them causing her skin to tingle with anticipation, her pulse yammering away frantically in her chest.

Eventually he broke off the kiss, pulling back to look at her, his hands still holding her gently, as his eyes moved over the planes of her face.

"Lola," he said, shaking his head.

"What is it?" She hardly dared breathe, what was the matter with him, he was acting so strangely? Was he about to break up with her?

"There's something you should know...about me..." He stopped, faltering slightly as she searched his eyes.

"What is it?" Part of her didn't want to know, at least not if it was going to be bad news, but the other part of her wouldn't rest until she knew exactly what was on his mind. He sighed, still moving his hand gently over the contours of her face as he stood there, his eyes locked on hers. Her heart was beating so strongly that she was sure he could hear it loud and clear.

"I love you," he said simply, pressing his mouth to hers again, this time with more urgency then surged his tongue between her lips.

What? He had said he loved her. He had said those three words, those three actual words? Had he meant to say them? Her mind was racing but she couldn't seem to focus as he roamed his hands over her body, a body rapidly losing all of its self-control at the touch of his gentle but total masculinity. Never had she felt so completely out of control before, and what was more was she loved it. She felt safe and wildly unpredictable all at the same time, and the feeling was completely addictive.

He slipped his strong hands under the thin material of her shirt, making contact with the smooth, naked flesh of her back and making her shiver, the touch of his skin burning her with a curious fire as she yielded to him.

"Inside me," she moaned, feeling his hardness as he responded to her invitation, pressing against her with urgency. Roughly, he pushed up her shirt, urging her to tug it off over her head as he nibbled at her throat.

An explosion of desire welled up within her. The smell of his raw masculinity mixed with the worn-in leather of his jacket was driving her wild. Coupled with the slight menace of the cabin's darkened environment, it felt like they were the only two people in existence at that moment, the only two hearts that beat in the entire world.

He planted soft kisses along her collarbone, each one delighting her with a delicious pulse. He reached up to her bra, unclipping it skillfully and reaching forward to slide the straps off her slim shoulders, allowing the garment to fall to the floor and exposing the flesh of her full breasts.

He pulled back a second as he dropped to drink in her newly bared flesh greedily, the unguarded look of lust in his eyes plain to observe as he pulled her to him again with a groan. The cool leather of his jacket brushed against her aroused nipples, causing her to moan out in pleasure as hungrily he tongued her mouth.

"God, why do I need you all the time?" he said, bending his head to attend to her stiff nipple, his mouth enveloping and sucking on it, causing her to elicit another wild groan of lust that he quickly silenced with a kiss. She reached down to the waistband of his jeans, fumbling her fingers with urgency to unbutton his fly. She *needed* him inside her. If she didn't have him right then and there, she felt she would go crazy.

She snaked her hand into his boxers then caressed his hardness. He responded with an animal groan, crushing his lips to hers and arching his back to thrust into her hand as she used her fingers to expertly tease him.

Panting, she joined her mouth to his, still seeking his heat as she felt his hands move over the fly of her jeans, unzipping them and tugging them down. She flew to assist him, pulling off first one leg, then the other, and wobbling slightly in her haste as she yanked at the denim.

She stood before him, the only thing concealing her from nakedness was the creamy silk of the high-leg,

French-cut panties, the first thing she'd pulled on when she'd dressed so hastily.

Audibly he inhaled, the sound cutting through the silence of the night, the admiration in his eyes shining in the darkness as he drank in the sight of her.

"Man, you're so beautiful. What the hell did a guy like me do to deserve a goddess like you?" He let out a long, slow whistle, shaking his head.

His words sent a thrill down her spine, and suddenly she found herself feeling a whole new sensation. She'd always known she was attractive to men but in this moment, she felt proud to be who she was — Lola Devereaux, the whole person. Even though she knew there was so much he didn't know about her still, she felt as though somehow he knew. Somehow he saw right into her.

"I think rescuing me three times is deserving enough," she replied, brushing her lips over his as he automatically encircled her waist, seeking her mouth with more urgency now. He brushed the small of her back and she shivered at the touch of him, pressing her bare flesh against the smooth leather of his jacket as he urged down the waistband of her undergarments. She was so aroused, but what was happening between them felt different from the other times they'd been together, was tenderer somehow, though his dominance was there like an electric undercurrent promising delicious things. He was the master of her body. She knew that now and she was glad for it.

He pulled the flimsy silk down to expose the bareness of her, and she stepped out of the scanty undergarments deftly, kicking them away in one swift motion until finally she stood naked before him. She could feel the bulge of his cock as he ground it against her, feel the beating of his heart as it pulsed against her own, and she reveled in the salty taste of him as their tongues mingling made her yearn for every damn inch of him pushing with urgency into her until he could push no deeper.

"My God," he murmured, his breath hot on her neck as he used his thick fingers to probe the soft flesh between her legs. She threw back her head, allowing him to tease her expertly. Her thighs trembled as they parted at his touch. Her nipples were stiff and sticking out with desire, and her whole body was aching for him to take her, to push her down on the floor with rough urgency. She'd never felt submissive with any guy before—usually she was the one firmly in control—but with Dillon it was as if another part of her took over.

Almost as if he were reading her mind, his palms were on her shoulders, forcing her to sink to her knees onto the floor. Hurriedly, he tore off his leather jacket, bending down to place it behind her before removing the plain white T-shirt he sported underneath in one easy motion.

Now it was her turn to gasp as she saw the full perfection of his body revealed in the moonlight. She saw his well-muscled torso ripple and his strong, well-defined arms glistened in the silvery moonlight as he reached forward to press her against him, finding the heat that rose between her legs with his hands.

She was dripping wet and trembling with desire. This man's raw masculinity set her senses alive with wanton arousal, and the desire he elicited from her made her want to abandon every care she had until her body was entwined with his. Cradling her, he eased her onto her back, bending his head to kiss the corners of her mouth, and as she looked up into his eyes, she was struck by the expression in them.

For the gaze that stared back at her were not just that of a man who desired her body, but of a man that also sought the very core of her being. She knew that look. Rory had once looked at her that way, a long time ago. That was the look of a man in love.

Parting her thighs, she moaned as he eased himself between them, her hands skimming his taut flesh as his cock entered her. Pulling back slightly he kept his gaze locked on hers as slowly he began to move inside her.

"I love you," he said again, caressing her sides, her breasts, her thighs, causing delicious ripples of desire everywhere they touched.

"I…" She floundered, wanting to reply, yet somehow she felt desperately unable to speak the words. He smiled, placing his finger over her mouth as he shook his head.

"You don't have to say it," he said as he bent to kiss her, thrusting his hardness into the very core of her, filling her with a delicious sensation of being infused with every fiber of his essence.

"You're mine," he said, as he began to thrust into her with more urgency, causing her to moan out loud in ecstasy as he took her, right there on the floor, in the silence of the night, the cool breeze of the lakeside air wrapping around their naked flesh as the two of them writhed together, slaking their lust for each other on the floor of the little tumbledown cabin.

Chapter Nine

Two hours later they were winding their way through the streets of Morningford Heights, freshly showered and replenished after dropping by Dillon's condo. Lola snuggled into the sleeve of Dillon's leather jacket comfortingly as he steered his green coupe through the darkened streets. When he'd taken her on the floor of the cabin, held her in his arms and told her he loved her, it had felt as if something primal had awakened in her—a need to surrender to him totally, mind, body and soul, an urge she'd never experienced nor wanted to before. It had felt so good that she longed to feel it again, to probe the sensation and what it might mean.

"Where should we start looking for Jim?" She shot him a worried look. She really didn't have a clue where the hell Drago might have taken him. The two of them had searched all around the lakeside cabin's grounds with no luck and she was fresh out of ideas.

She could see his jaw tighten in the semidarkness of the vehicle.

"I suggest we start at Vain. Try to talk to some of Drago's little cronies, put the pressure on them a bit, see if they squeal."

"Put the pressure on them how?" She raised an eyebrow. Did he even know who he was dealing with? None of Drago's friends had any reason to tell them anything, and nearly all of them came from the same kind of wealthy families Drago himself had sprung from. Rich, privileged and insulated from the consequences of whatever they did. No they wouldn't talk.

"Oh, you'd be surprised how some people can start talking when you give them a little motivation." He leaned forward, picking up the small silver dagger now hanging from her neck – Drago's pendant.

She hoped for both their sakes he was right. Leaning back against the coupe's rather comfortable headrest, she allowed him to steer them to the little club where all this madness had started. Perhaps Dillon was right and the answer could be found within the club's four walls after all.

Entering, she noticed the place didn't appear to be as full as it usually was at this time on a Friday night. Above them, directly ahead in the glass-fronted DJ booth, a guy was halfheartedly spinning vinyl as people danced listlessly to the generic beat, but the mood in the club felt different somehow, though she couldn't figure out why.

Looking around, she scanned the crowd for the familiar faces of the regulars. Some of them were still here. There was Theresa, her opportunist eyes flicking around for suitable victims, and Brandon, standing at the corner in the shadows, the same permanently hungry expression carved into his pale features. But there was no denying it appeared that most of the usual

Friday night crowd had chosen to stay away. Chosen to...or were they too scared to show?

Rumors quickly spread in Burley, she knew, and the run of recent events had probably scared off both vamps and non-vamps alike—the former out of fear the finger of suspicion would fall on them, and the latter scared they too might wind up like Dave Eversham.

"Seen any of Drago's buddies yet?" Dillon turned to her and she shook her head.

"Nope, not a soul. It's weird. The club's half-empty. It's never been like this on a Friday night before."

He frowned, his hand massaging his chin.

"Let's head for the bar then, see what Max knows."

Max looked up as they approached, shooting a relieved glance in her direction.

"Thank God you're both safe," he exclaimed, relief palpable in his voice as she plopped down on a barstool in front of the counter.

"Hah, just, thanks to this one," she quipped back, squeezing Dillon's biceps and flicking him a grateful glance. It was true, though. If he hadn't come to her aid, who knew what could have happened to her? It didn't bear thinking about. Drago's fury knew no mercy, and let's face it, she'd certainly not endeared herself to him.

"Well, it's good to see you both," Max said, "and it's not as if we couldn't do with the extra customers," he added, gesturing at the half-empty club. "Recent events haven't exactly been good for business." He rolled his eyes.

"Yeah, I guess the rumor mill's gone into overdrive," she replied.

"Like you wouldn't believe," the bartender nodded.

"Thing is, dude, we really need to speak to Drago's crowd," Dillon said, chipping in.

"Yeah, so if you've seen anyone around who might be able to help?" She tilted her head at Max.

The bartender scowled and shook his head. "Nope. Haven't seen any of them. Oh, wait, apart from Marie."

"Ugh, Marie?"

Max nodded. "Mhhmm, the dragon queen herself," he said, pulling a sour face.

She couldn't blame him. Marie was almost as unpalatable as Drago was. Drago's sister wasn't a vampire but she *was* a superbitch.

"She's over there actually." Max indicated at the corner of the club, where the thin, tall, blonde girl stood watching the assembled crowd, sipping occasionally from a Margarita glass. Marie certainly bore more than a passing resemblance to Drago's haughty good looks.

Lola nodded resignedly, shrugging her shoulders as she tugged at Dillon's sleeve.

"Come on then. Let's see what the ice queen has to say," she muttered, turning away from the bar and heading toward the blonde, pulling Dillon behind her.

Marie raised an eyebrow as they headed up to her. Lola smiled nervously, wary of the reaction she was going to get.

"Hey, Marie. Uh, how's it going? This is Dillon. You might have heard of him?" Might have? She'd wager her best pair of five-hundred-dollar boots that Marie had heard *all* about him.

Marie nodded sniffily. "I already know who *he* is. And I bet I know why you're here too."

"Uh…" Lola floundered, searching for something, anything, to say. Feeling a bit helpless, she caught Dillon's eye, but he merely shrugged, looking equally lost for words.

"Well, clearly neither of you can seem to find your tongue right now so I suppose I'm going to have to speak for the pair of you," Marie said, rolling her eyes dramatically as if she were a headmistress reprimanding two naughty schoolchildren.

What am I supposed to say to that? She bit her lower lip, waiting for Marie to continue.

"I suppose it's about my brother, isn't it?"

"Drago?" The name came out almost like a squeak. It took a lot to spook Lola Devereaux but Marie's frosty manner was seriously intimidating.

"Exactly. You want to know where he is, I suppose?"

"Uh, not exactly." What on earth should she say? After all, she couldn't exactly tell the girl she had her brother tied up in a basement, could she? Or could she? The realization hit her like a wave as she recalled Dillon's comment in the coupe. *Of course,* by capturing Drago they had the perfect bargaining power to make Marie Graythorne tell them everything they might need to know.

"I think we better all go sit down somewhere," she said, fixing Marie with a smile, as she gestured toward one of the private booths that lined the walls of the club.

* * * *

They emerged from the club a lot wiser than when they'd gone in. Marie's obvious displeasure at being forced to reveal her brother's favorite hiding place had certainly been amusing.

"You'll be sorry for this. You should know that," Marie had threatened as they'd risen to leave, confident they had the information they needed. "I'm a Graythorne, and you'll be extremely sorry for messing with my family."

The blonde's threats didn't worry her much. Somehow she doubted anything Marie could do would be worse than the mess they were currently knee-deep in. Anyway, Jim was the key to all this. If they could get him to the witness stand to safely testify, then they could clear Dillon's name.

There would be time enough to fret about the wrath of the Graythorne family later. They had the pressing matter of a murder charge to worry about for now. After all, if they couldn't get Jim on the stand, then they didn't stand a chance of proving Dillon's innocence. And the consequences of that didn't bear thinking about.

"Hey." Dillon nudged her as the two of them walked arm in arm to his coupe. "What's the matter, thinker?"

"Oh, I'm just a little tense is all. I'll feel better once we check out the school and find Jim," she said, flashing him a thin smile.

She fingered the little silver dagger pendant hanging from her neck. Drago was always wearing it and it had certainly proved useful. As soon as Marie had seen it, her already bloodless face had paled even more.

It hadn't taken long after that to elicit the information they'd required about Drago's favorite hiding place — Waterfall High. Of course, his old high school. According to Max, even back in school Drago, had been just as spoiled and egocentric as he was now.

"Hey, we'll find Jim. Don't worry," Dillon said, placing a hand on her arm, as he unlocked the doors of the coupe with a beep.

He didn't have to add what she knew he was thinking. *Let's just hope we find him in one piece.*

* * * *

Arriving at Waterfall High, the two of them exited Dillon's coupe, leaving it parked outside the abandoned school. She slid her arm through his as they both walked up to the imposing iron gate that had been shut for almost a decade now, ever since the school had closed its doors for good.

The building loomed eerily at them in the darkness, the tall pines poking their lofty heads over the iron railings, highlighting the fact that tonight they were very, very alone. She just hoped Jim was inside somewhere, alive. Pulling the leather bomber jacket Dillon had loaned her to keep warm tighter around her shoulders, she shivered at the coldness of the night, keeping in step with Dillon's brisk strides.

As they approached the gate, they both stopped while Dillon bent forward to slide his hand through the rusted iron, drawing the bolt back with a creak and pushing on the aged gate. Slowly it creaked open and the two of them slipped through, Dillon pausing to close the gate again behind them. Though what good *that* would do to keep out Drago's henchmen if they were determined to follow, she didn't know. They'd just have to hope Marie was too worried about what might happen to her brother to tell Drago's crew where the two of them were headed.

"Where should we start?" She turned to Dillon. The place was massive—six stories high, not including the grounds running all around the school.

"On the ground floor. If we can't find him there, we'll check the basement before working our way up," he said, his expression focused as he eyed the school up ahead. She couldn't help but admire his handsome profile silhouetted by the moonlight. A wave of tenderness came over her and she leaned in to plant a soft kiss on his cheek.

"Come on. Let's go find him," she said, squeezing his biceps gently. She'd never felt this way about any guy before, not even Rory. They had to find Jim. There was no way she was going to lose Dillon now.

But you'll lose him anyway when he finds out what you really are, won't you? He'll leave, just like Rory did. He won't want to be with a monster.

What was she thinking? There was no way this could last? The best she could hope for was to get Dillon off the hook but after that, sooner or later, she was going to have to tell him what she was. Then just like Rory, he'd turn on her and walk out of her life forever. Somehow she couldn't bear to think about that.

Forcing the thought out of her mind, she clutched at Dillon's arm as the two of them walked up the shadowed pathway to the school's main entrance. The glass-fronted double doors were firmly shut but she had her trusty lockpick. Patting her pants pocket, she felt a momentary panic. Her pocket felt empty. Where the hell was it?

"What's the matter, babe?" Dillon looked at her quizzically.

"My lockpick. It's not in my pocket where I usually keep it. It must have fallen out when I was trying to fend Drago off." She noted how Dillon's lip curled slightly at the mention of his name.

"What gives with that guy, anyway? Why *is* he such a freak?"

She sighed. There was no way she could explain Drago's perversity to a level-headed guy like Dillon. "Trust me. You wouldn't understand. There's a whole lot of things going on with him, I guess you could say he has his demons," she said, shrugging. Well, it was true, if being a vampire wasn't a demon all of its own, then she didn't know quite what was. Yawning, she rubbed at her eyes. What was the matter with her? Why did she feel so tired, so weak? And her head felt so strange —

"Hey, you okay, sweetheart?" Dillon caught her under her arms as her legs started to buckle from under her, his strong arms holding her upright. Her mind felt so hazy. Why was she feeling so peculiar? The low-hanging full moon caught her eye just then, as it dipped down into the pines, reminding her of the moon the night Lyra had come for her, the night her life had changed forever.

"Are you all right?" Dillon was looking into her eyes, a concerned expression on his face. He had such beautiful eyes, but why couldn't she remember what she was supposed to remember? The moon... She knew it was trying to tell her something significant somehow.

"I'm fine," she tried to say, but she could tell the words hadn't come out right from the confused look on Dillon's face.

"You need to sit down somewhere," he said firmly, looking around. She attempted to protest but weariness stopped the words coming out. *Why am I so damn exhausted?*

Dillon took off his leather jacket from around her shoulders, throwing it to the ground, still keeping his grip on her as he lowered her gently to the floor so that her back was resting against the glass of the school's front door.

"Sit here for a moment, I'll go look for another way in. That lock doesn't look like it'll give easily," he urged her, and she nodded weakly in acquiescence.

What the hell is going on? She listened to the sound of his footsteps crunching over the gravel as her eyelids began to close. Her mind was a whirl of strange thoughts. Her eyes felt so heavy, and even the pines seemed to mock her, their fronds waving eerily, even though there was no breeze in the still night air.

Lyra's face swam before her as sleep began to overtake her. Lyra of the fiery eyes, Lyra who had taken her mortal soul and changed her life forever. She felt herself begin to drift off.

Her eyes snapped open. *That* was it. That was why she felt this way. Lyra's warning rang in her ears as the realization coursed through her, and she groaned aloud, cursing herself for her own stupidity.

"You've been gifted with an immortal strength, but you must remember to feed. If you don't remember to feed, you'll get sick and your strength will weaken."

She remembered the intense look in the vampire's striking eyes as Lyra had issued the warning. She'd not truly understood the words then, but she certainly knew the meaning of them now. How could she have been so stupid? She was sick because she hadn't fed a drop in well over a week. With every ounce of strength she possessed, she raised her wrist, pushing back the sleeve of the borrowed leather jacket to glance at the dial of her watch.

Vain would be closing its doors in an hour. They likely wouldn't be able to make it back there in time, and even if they could, there was no way she would be able to give Dillon the slip tonight in order to pick out a suitable victim. Feeding was going to have to wait until tomorrow night. She was just going to have to get it together somehow.

"Lola?" Dillon's voice. Weakly, she looked up to see him approaching, the gravel crunching beneath his battered brown Timberland boots. He smiled as she looked up at him, raking a hand through his mussed brown hair in a self-conscious manner. Even in her weakened state, she still felt butterflies just looking at his handsome face.

"I've found a way in around the back. Are you strong enough to stand or you want to stay here? I can go check the place out alone if you like." He looked at her with concern.

"No, no, I'm feeling a bit brighter now. I think it's because I forgot to eat. I'll come." She made to get to her feet and he put his hand on her arm to stop her.

"You sure? You look awful pale."

She had to stifle down a snigger of amusement at the irony of his last comment. She'd always been fair complexioned but ever since she'd been turned, her pallor had taken on a practically bloodless appearance. And when she didn't feed, the situation only got worse — just one of the many physical changes she'd had to endure. *And yet more confirmation I'm a freak who doesn't deserve a nice guy like Dillon.*

"I'm sure I'll be fine," she insisted, taking the hand he offered her to haul herself up to her feet and closing her eyes as he planted a gentle kiss on the end of her nose. The way he held her made her feel so safe, like he would never let her go, no matter what.

"Let's go then." He released his grip on her, starting forward into the night, and she followed, falling into step with him as they made their way to the school's back entrance.

"Here," he said, gesturing to an open door. "It wasn't locked."

"Really?" She shot him a questioning look. Something didn't feel quite right. The door to the school had been firmly locked up for a decade.

"Dunno if it was just an oversight or if someone else got here before we did. Either way, guess we're about to find out," he said, shrugging.

He reached forward to hold the door open for her and she walked inside. Dillon followed her, closing the door behind them with a soft click. She looked around, her eyes sweeping over the unfamiliar shapes looming out at them from the semidarkness. The corridor they were in was fairly narrow with multiple doors leading off to the right into what she guessed were classrooms. She crinkled up her nose. The place smelled musty, like it had lain empty for a long while.

"Let's check the rooms along here first as a precaution," she said, looking at Dillon. He nodded his approval. Slowly, she started to move along the passage, her hand closing upon the handle of the first door.

"Here, take this."

She reached up to catch the flashlight Dillon had tossed at her.

"Thanks. Where did you get this from?"

"Figured we might need some supplies, so I grabbed two of 'em when we stopped off at mine." He grinned, holding up an identical flashlight.

"Ever the practical rancher," she joked, pushing her way into the shadowy depths of an empty classroom. She shone the light around, illuminating the darkness. Dillon came up behind her, his body pressed tightly against her. She could tell he was semi hard and she felt a swell of arousal stir inside her.

"Don't think there's any sign of anything in here," he murmured into her ear, the rough scratch of his beard brushing against her lobe and causing a delicious shiver to run down her spine.

"Uh, yeah, we should go check another room," she said, holding on to the doorframe momentarily as a wave of dizziness replaced the pleasurable sensation she'd been enjoying only moments before. *Boy, it sure as hell is going to be a challenge to get through tonight.*

"You all right?" Jeez, he really didn't miss a trick, did he?

"Yeah, I'm fine," she lied, gritting her teeth and forcing herself to press on as the two of them dove deeper into the blackened corridor.

Forty minutes later and they had checked every single classroom on the ground floor without finding a sniff of anything that could give them a clue where Drago had taken Jim. Her body was starting to ache with the effort, and the familiar hollow feeling in her stomach was causing wave upon wave of nausea to rise within her.

"Well, there's no Jim on this floor. Shall we try the basement now?" She turned to Dillon with a sigh.

"Yeah, we can get to it down the staircase at the end there." He nodded, pointing to the far end of the corridor where the staircase that wound its way through the bowels of the school curled its way down. Tiptoeing gingerly behind Dillon's steady tread, she descended the steps, peering over his shoulder and shining the flashlight to illuminate the path in front of them.

"Eeww, is that mold?" She wrinkled up her nose at the dank smell flooding her nostrils.

"Yep, sure is, looks like this place hasn't been maintained for years."

The pair of them were standing in what looked like another corridor, surrounded by two doorways on either side and an open archway that she presumed led into the maintenance area in front of them. The doorways looked like cupboards where the school caretaker might have kept supplies, or perhaps one of them was a former staff room for the groundskeepers and maintenance staff who had looked after the school in its heyday.

A sudden scratching noise made her wheel back, startled, and she clutched at Dillon's arm to steady herself.

"What was that?" She froze, looking around, her eyes scanning the darkness for potential threats.

"Dunno, probably just a rat. There's gotta be a ton of 'em down here," he said, attempting to reassure her.

Somewhat mollified, she nodded, though her senses were now sharply alerted to the possibility of danger. The basement was certainly creepy, with its dank, mold-stained walls, and leery shadows, it wouldn't have looked out of place in a B-movie horror film. Then again, in her present state, neither would she.

"Let's check these rooms out first," she replied, crossing to the left hand door and placing her hand on the door handle. She gave it a swift tug. The door didn't budge.

"Here, let me try it." Dillon crossed the passage in a step, tugging on the door, but the handle still refused to allow them access.

"Maybe we can work it open," he said, reaching into his leather jacket for a screwdriver.

"Wow, you really did come prepared."

"Guess my pa taught me well."

"You must really miss him."

"Yeah, when I get to thinking about it." He winched the door with force, the creaky old oak yielding somewhat to the pressure. Squaring his shoulders, he shoulder barged the door, the screwdriver still held firmly in place between the jambs.

"I miss my parents too. Gets harder on birthdays and Christ—" She stopped abruptly as the door splintered open and Dillon staggered forward, thrown off balance by the force he'd exerted. The beam of the flashlight she held illuminated the gloomy depths of what looked to be an abandoned store cupboard. Mops, paint cans, and part of an old industrial vacuum cleaner were stacked somewhat haphazardly around the inside shelving.

"Well, there's no Jim in here," she said, shrugging at Dillon.

"Not unless Drago's disguised him as a piece of household cleaning equipment," he said, smirking. He looked over the cupboards contents.

"Check the other rooms?" As she spoke, a low, heavy thud echoed somewhere in the basement's recess and she jumped, her eyes wide with fear as she looked at Dillon.

"*That* was no rat."

He said nothing but she saw the familiar clench of his jaw as he shook his head.

"Think it came from under the archway. Probably just a loose tile, this place is old. Stay in here and lemme go check it out," he instructed, easing himself past her as he walked out into the blackness of the passageway.

She hesitated, standing there in the shadows as his footsteps echoed into the darkness. What if the noise hadn't been a loose tile? What if it had been one of Drago's goons? She couldn't just wait here while Dillon walked into who knew what. Clasping the flashlight firmly, she keep the beam low as she maneuvered her way past the mounds of cleaning stuff to the doorway.

Peeking out, she looked left then right, sweeping the flashlight around as she checked the passageway. Nothing looked suspicious, so moving soundlessly, she crossed the hallway to the door on the right, trying the handle. Unlike the first door, this one gave fairly easily, creaking open with a loud sigh. Inwardly, she cringed, hoping that if there was anyone around, they hadn't heard it.

Walking inside, she aimed the flashlight around, realizing the room she'd entered was somewhat larger than a storage cupboard. It was about the size of a classroom — or maybe a staff area — and several tables and chairs were scattered around haphazardly.

She stopped. There was the noise again, a soft thudding sound, like a knock, and it sounded like it was coming from somewhere within the room. She strained her ears to listen as she moved farther inside. Yes, there it was, a funny knocking noise, and a muffled sound, like someone moaning?

Hesitantly she moved toward where her ears told her the noise was originating from, keeping the beam of the solid rubber-handled flashlight trained in front of her and trying to move as silently as she could. She could make out what appeared to be another doorway, set into the far left hand corner of the room. Perhaps it led to some kind of canteen or kitchen area?

She stopped just outside the door, biting her lip nervously as she pressed her ear to it, trying to steel herself to face whatever lay on the other side.

"Mmmph!" The tone was insistent behind the door. It *was* moaning. She had to act. Someone might be hurt in there. *Could it be Jim?* Pushing down on the handle, she tried the door. The metal handle felt slightly resistant, like it had rusted over years of neglect and was in need of a good oiling, but it gave beneath her touch, the door swinging open suddenly.

Her breathing rose unevenly in her chest, her heart pounding with tension as she swept the light around what look liked the inside of a very spacious stock cupboard. A stash of old teabags was piled on a shelf to her immediate left, and to her right, at her feet, stood a drum of what she assumed was some kind of cooking oil.

"Mmmph!" There it was again, much louder this time. The torch flickered around the room over haphazardly stacked shelves decorated with random grocery products, all of the faded packets and boxes now long past their sell by date. She couldn't make out anything that could pinpoint the source of the noise. Where the hell was it coming from?

Just then the torch's beam flickered over something that caught her eye. What the hell was that? It looked like— She stopped abruptly as she realized.

There was no mistaking what glistened back at her from the depths of the cupboard. A pair of eyes. Human eyes. Trembling, she pushed forward, trying to hold the torch's beam steady in order to discern the eye's owner. As the beam swept over the familiar face, relief coursed through her.

In the darkness, wrists and ankles bound by rope cuffs, a piece of silver duct tape obscuring his mouth, was Jim. *Thank God.* They needed to untie him and get out of here as soon as possible, before Marie blabbed and Drago's henchmen got here to try to prevent them from leaving. Or worse still, if they'd found Drago and he was on the loose again. *Where the hell is Dillon?*

"It's okay," she said, bending down and patting Jim on the arm. Poor guy, he looked scared half to death. Whoever it was that had done this to him, and she had a fair idea who it was, they had obviously put the fear of God into him.

The flashlight flickered over his head and shoulders, illuminating the bare skin of his neck. She felt a roar of hunger rise up within her as her eyes took in the naked expanse of flesh. Virgin flesh, with warm blood running through the veins beneath it. She stood there a second, her tongue passing over her lips as the saliva pooled in her mouth. Maybe she could just take a little bit?

What the hell are you thinking, you freak? Biting the only witness who can clear the name of the man you're supposed to love? Have you no self-control? As if you haven't caused enough trouble already.

Snapping herself out of it, she forced herself to focus back on the situation at hand. It must have been apparent she was eyeing Jim up a little oddly because he was now looking at her warily from his position on the cupboard floor.

"It's okay, I was just thinking how we're gonna get you out of here safely," she assured him, and he nodded gratefully, his eyes trusting once again as he looked up at her. Which only served to make her feel like even more of a scumbag for thinking about biting him.

"Hey, this might hurt just a bit," she whispered, as her nails scrambled for the edge of the duct tape obscuring the lower half of his face. Ripping the tape back, she quickly clamped her other hand over his mouth to prevent him from uttering whatever profanity came out first.

"You have to be quiet. There could be someone else here," she warned him, and eyes wide, he nodded, obeying her.

"Is Dillon here?" The look on his face was grave as his nervous eyes sought out her own.

She nodded.

"Then you have to find him and we need to get out of here. There's no time. They'll be back soon to check on me."

"Who's they?"

"Who do you think?"

"Drago's men?"

"Exactly. Hey have you got anything you can use to cut this damn rope with? It's killer."

She looked around the roomy cupboard, her eyes searching for a suitable implement, but all she could see was the boxes and packets of dust-covered groceries.

"There's nothing here and it'd take me an age to try to unpick those knots. Lemme go check in the other room. I'll be right back."

After closing the cupboard door softly, she picked her way as silently as she could through the staff area then eased out through the door that led to the passageway until she was standing in the mold-covered hallway once more.

She stood there a moment listening, though there was nothing to hear but the silence of the night echoing in her ears. Where had Dillon got to? Maybe she should take a look in the maintenance section? She felt a surge of nausea ripple through her, and her head reeled momentarily as she struggled to find her balance.

She inhaled deeply as she held on to the damp brick wall. She really had to get it together. Jim was relying on her. She couldn't flake out now. Especially not when this whole mess was all her damn fault in the first place.

Moving slowly, and using all her strength to push herself upright, she began to ease her way around the passageway toward the arch that led to the maintenance area. She had about two more steps to take when she felt the hand on her shoulder. Instinctively, she wheeled around trying to see who it was, holding the flashlight up defensively to protect her head.

The blow caught her with force on the side of her face, making her stagger backward. The attacker came toward her again with a heavy grunt, the bulk and height of him telling her that it was indeed a him, and a him that was going to get the better of her one hundred twenty–pound frame if she didn't act fast.

Bringing her right leg up, she used every piece of strength she had in her to plant a kick square in his chest right as he lunged for her, the force of her effort making him reel back in surprise as his hands clutched behind him for the wall.

"You little bitch," he cursed, lunging toward her again.

As he moved for her, she swung her right arm at him with a yell, distracting him momentarily as she brought the heavy flashlight down on his skull with a solid crack. Stunned, he seemed to stand there for a second or two, rubbing at his head, before finally, toppling backward, he crashed to the floor. *Phew, job done, for now.*

Even though she was severely winded, this was no time to rest on her laurels. She had to move fast to alert Dillon. Whoever this guy was, he wouldn't be out for long, and he probably hadn't come alone.

Collecting herself, she moved through the archway, panting as she struggled to get her breath back. Her whole body was shaking with the effort she'd just expended and her sweaty palm clutched at the rubber flashlight gratefully. The innocuous-looking tool had probably just saved her life.

Edging in to the large boiler room, she heard a scuffling of footsteps. There was a faint light coming from the end of the room but her eyes couldn't make anything more out in the darkness. From the sound of the scuffling, she reckoned there was more than one person down there but she couldn't be absolutely sure.

"Put the gun down, man." Dillon's voice pierced through the darkness. Gun? Her body broke out in a cold sweat and her heart began to pound uncontrollably. A bullet wouldn't kill her but Dillon wasn't immortal. He wouldn't have the same immunity.

"Where is she?" The other voice was gruff and unfamiliar.

"I dunno who you're talking about," Dillon said, his tone stubborn.

"You know exactly who I mean. The bitch. Tell me where she is or I'll put a bullet in your head."

Her. Whoever it was was talking about *her*. And it sounded like he had a loaded gun which was likely pointed straight at Dillon. She had to do something.

Keeping the flashlight switched off, she crept soundlessly through the darkness, her only guide the voices coming from the end of the room.

"I mean it, man, you better start talking or that pretty face of yours is gonna wind up decorating the tiles in here." The room seemed to stretch on forever as she stalked her way toward them. Dammit, where were they?

"She's not here. She didn't come with me," Dillon lied, obviously stalling for time. She could tell by the angry tone in his assailant's voice that he wasn't going to able to hold out very much longer.

As she got nearer, she could see the voices were coming from behind a large, industrial metal boiler that stuck out of the wall at the back of the high-ceilinged room. Moving to one side, she tucked herself against the wall as she inched her way forward.

Smack. She heard the sound of a heavy object hitting flesh and she automatically winced.

"Why the hell did you do that for?" Dillon's voice, he sounded angry.

She tried not to picture the bruise that sound would have likely produced. Feeling her way along the edge of the wall, she edged closer until she felt the tips of her fingers connect with the back of the boiler casing.

"Shut it. I know the bitch is here. Is she upstairs waiting for you or am I gonna have to finish you off and go look for her myself? 'Cos if you don't tell me where she is, I'll do a whole lot more than pistol whip you, pretty boy," the stranger's voice threatened.

She held her breath as she peered around the edge of the large metal boiler. In the darkness she saw the tall, broad-shouldered shape, the gun protruding from his right hand as he pointed it straight at Dillon.

"One more chance. You tell me where she is or you're toast, bro." The tall shape cocked the trigger as her heart caught in her throat. *Now.*

"I'm right here, fucker," she yelled, lunging forward as she launched a drop kick at the arm holding the gun, her elbow connecting sharply with the bone of man's skull.

"What the — ?"

She heard him yell as the weapon clattered to the floor, spinning noisily away into the shadowy darkness. Dillon was on him in a beat, pinning his arms behind him and pushing him onto his front on the ground.

"That'll teach you for pointing a gun at me, *bro*," Dillon spat as the hapless guy lay neutered, his arms firmly locked behind his back by Dillon's grip. "Guess you saved my ass this time, eh?" Dillon grinned, his teeth flashing white in the darkness.

"All in a day's work," she bantered back, hoping her voice wasn't betraying how sick she really felt. She was so lightheaded it was weird. It was as if she were about to pass out or something.

"You all right?" He took in her rather disheveled-looking appearance with a puzzled frown.

"Yeah, I'm fine, there was another guy here, though, he tried to attack me but I fought him off. Last I saw of him he was unconscious in the passageway. Oh and I found Jim, tied up in a cupboard."

"Jeez, someone's been busy in my absence," he said, shaking his head.

"Uh, yeah, you could say that."

"Think you can unfasten my belt while I hold his hands? I wanna tie this joker up so he can't do any more damage."

"Sure, I can help ya unbuckle, cowboy." She winked, moving behind the guy and tucking the flashlight under her chin as she reached for Dillon's buckle. Deftly her fingers worked to undo the leather, freeing the length of it from the denim belt loops, as Dillon continued to firmly armlock his assailant.

"Here." She thrust the belt forward. He took it in one hand, his face a grimace as he worked quickly to bind the man's wrists tightly.

"That'll teach you to wave a loaded weapon around and to use bad language in front of a lady," Dillon warned him, shoving him forward roughly. "Now let's go find the other one. He's gonna get the same treatment."

She nodded as she bent down to retrieve the pistol that had been knocked out of Dillon's assailant's grip in the struggle. The weapon felt reassuringly heavy in her hand but she knew it wouldn't help much against Drago and the rest of his crew. Most of them had been turned already and a bullet would be no more than a flesh wound.

As she opened the chamber, she stopped in slight surprise. Silver bullets? But of course Drago would want to ensure no one escaped, including her. *And silver's just about the only thing that can kill a freak like you.* Yep, the myths about vampires might be corny but she knew too well that truth was sometimes stranger than fiction. The whole vampires don't have reflections thing was definitely bogus, but one of those babies through the left ventricle and she wouldn't need to feed, ever again — or breathe, for that matter.

She shivered involuntarily, turning to head back to the room's entrance, holding the flashlight out in front of them to illuminate their path.

"Was Jim all right?" He turned to her.

"Yeah, he seemed a little shaken but he's alive. Now we just have to get him out of here and we've got ourselves a witness." *And hopefully Dillon won't have a jail cell to look forward to in his future.*

"You're something, you know that? A really special woman." He shot her an admiring glance. Oh, she was special all right. He didn't know the half of it. Still she knew he had meant it as a compliment and the words made her glow.

"Nah, I'm just plain ole, ordinary me," she said, shrugging as they walked through the arch to reenter the passageway.

"Trust me. There's nothing ordinary about you."

God, he had to stop looking at her like that. The intensity of his gaze was making her feel uncomfortably flustered in the most pleasant way possible. If he carried on, she was going to get aroused all over again and then they'd never get out of here.

"Uh, I left him out cold over there," she said, trying to distract him as she shone the flashlight in the far right hand corner of the passageway.

"I don't see anything." He wrinkled his brow, squinting into the darkness. Following his gaze, her eyes alighted upon…empty air. What the hell?

"Sure you left him there?"

"Positive. He was unconscious. He must have come around. We have to go check on Jim," she said, her voice fraught with urgency as she turned to make her way back to the staff room.

"Hey, wait up. He could still be around. Let me go in front of you. Which door is it?" Pointing to the door that sat to the left of the cleaning cupboard, she allowed him to lead the way through, holding her breath as they picked their way through the darkness.

"Straight ahead. The cupboard I found him in is over there in the corner." Stopping outside it, she swung open the door, looking through the blackness as she shone the torch inside. There was nothing but empty air where Jim should have been. Panicked she swung around, looking at Dillon helplessly.

"I left him here. The other guy must have come back for him. He can't have gotten too far. We have to try to find them before they disappear." Her mouth felt dry and there was a roaring noise in her eardrums. Dillon nodded, his expression grave.

"Let's go. Hopefully we can head them off before they get outside."

Turning around, she began to sprint toward the staircase, Dillon hot on her heels behind her. Dammit, why had she been stupid enough to leave Jim alone? If anything happened to him, she would never forgive herself.

The stairs loomed up ahead as her stomach gave an uncontrollable lurch and she clutched at the wall to steady herself. *Pull yourself together, Lola. This is your mess. Now you have to clean it up.* Hauling herself forward, she climbed the stairs hurriedly, taking the steps two at a time. Her legs were trembling so hard they felt like they were made of jelly, but she knew she couldn't slow down. A minute too late could mean the difference between finding Jim alive or dead.

Reaching the top, she looked about her but there was no sign of anyone in the deserted passageway.

"Where are they?" Panicked, she turned back to Dillon.

"They can't have got too far. Let's head to the front doors. We can see if they're making their way through the grounds," he said, scowling.

Nodding, she began to follow him, as once again he led the way. The blood thumped loudly in her ears as she willed her aching body to keep moving.

Reaching the doors, she squinted through the glass, shining the flashlight through the panes to illuminate the darkened lawn. Nothing again.

"They must have gone out the back way," Dillon yelled, wheeling around as he sprinted down the passage toward the back doors. She took a deep breath before forcing herself to follow him, her vision becoming blurry. There was no way she was going to make it tonight if she didn't feed, but *that* wasn't going to be a possibility any time soon.

Vain would be long shut by now, and they still had Jim to find. She squeezed her eyes shut momentarily, remembering the way the flashlight had flickered over the bare skin of Jim's neck.

Stop thinking like the monster you really are. Isn't it bad enough the guy you love could go to jail for life because of you?

Not because of her. Because of Drago.

If Drago hadn't killed the guy, then none of this would be happening.

But if you hadn't needed to suck Dave's blood, then Drago would never had had the chance to help you walk him to the park.

And she wouldn't have had to fend off his advances and Dillon wouldn't have had to come to her rescue. If, if, if. No use thinking like that now. That wasn't going to help Jim.

She came up short behind Dillon as he stopped outside the back entrance, the beam of her flashlight joining his as they combed the weed-strewn lawn.

"There. I see something moving," she said, pointing excitedly to the far left hand corner of the lawn. Dillon peered through the glass as they both tried to discern what the moving shape was.

"It's them," he yelled, swinging the door open and racing through it. She tried to run too but found she could only manage a sort of lopsided lollop as shapes swam before her eyes and the ground lurched beneath her as if she were seasick. Summoning every ounce of her strength, she willed herself to pick up the pace, her feet staggering through the tumbleweeds as Dillon gained ground on the two blurry shapes up ahead. Boy, he could run fast. She'd always thought herself to be something of a sprinter, but this was something else. She'd never seen anyone move so quick before.

"What the hell!" She heard the man yell out as Dillon surprised him, knocking him on the side of the head with a well-timed punch and causing him to release his prisoner who fell to the ground, covering himself protectively, obviously unsure who this new assailant was.

"Jim," she yelled, waving at him, his eyes lighting up in relief as he saw her. She walked closer. Dillon and the guy were on the ground, a bundle of limbs grappling and swinging in the mud of the school field.

She saw through blurry eyes that Dillon easily seemed to be getting the better of the man. He was climbing on top of him now, pinning him down, punching him in the face — once, twice, three times — until the man suddenly stopped struggling.

"Hey, Lola, are you okay?" Jim's voice swam into her consciousness. Her vision lurched but she forced herself to nod.

"I'm fine. Don't worry about me." Her body couldn't give out on her now. She felt herself stagger, her legs unable to hold the weight of her body upright anymore. Jim put out his arm to catch her and she fell heavily against him, her head hitting his arm as he held her upright.

"Whoa there, steady now," he said, smiling down at her. The moonlight dipped low through the trees, highlighting the bare skin of his throat, the flush of the hemoglobin that flowed beneath temptingly visible. Her nostrils flared. She could practically taste his blood in her mouth already. Somewhere in the background she could just about see Dillon getting to his feet. Just one little bit, one small taste, that wouldn't be so bad, would it?

Leaning forward, she stood on tiptoe as she inched nearer to his neck, the saliva pooling in her mouth as she prepared to sink her teeth into that warm flesh. Oh, how good it was going to taste as his vein opened up and warm blood gushed down the back of her hungry throat. Nearer she edged until she was mere millimeters away. She was totally in the zone now. There was no way she could turn back. Her pulse hammered loudly as the hunger for blood overtook all her senses.

She opened her mouth, her lips curling back as she prepared to puncture Jim's flesh. The hand made contact with her shoulder firmly, causing her to spin around.

"You okay, sweetheart?" Dillon stood in front of her, looking concerned.

"Uh, yeah, I'm just a little beat, Jim caught me as I was about to hit the deck," she murmured weakly. It felt as though the ground were about to give way beneath her feet. Something was very, very wrong.

"Yeah, she needs to rest," Jim chipped in, but his words seemed to come out peculiarly muffled, as if the volume was turned down on them somehow. The air seemed stifling and she couldn't seem to get enough oxygen in her lungs. Silver trails flashed before her eyes as the roaring in her ears grew to deafening proportions. She could see Dillon's mouth moving but she couldn't hear any sound come out. She put out her hand for Jim again to steady herself. She felt awfully lightheaded, perhaps she should sit down on the ground and rest a while?

Struggling to breathe, she tried to force herself to stay upright. She felt her legs giving up the fight from under her. The rushing in her ears seemed to be the only sound in the world as her vision grew darker. Then nothing, nothing at all except darkness. The blackness finally overtook her.

Chapter Ten

When she opened her eyes, the first thing she saw was the unfamiliar ceiling. The concentric rings seemed to blur slightly before her still sleep hazy eyes, and foggily she rubbed at them with the backs of her hands. What had happened, and more importantly, where was she?

"Here...drink this." Dillon thrust the brown glass bottle under her nose and she looked at the dark liquid inside suspiciously.

"What is it?"

"You're sick. This will make you feel better."

"No, it won't help me. I just need to rest," she protested, shaking her head. He didn't understand what she needed. No one could understand. *No one except a freak like you.*

"Just try it. Promise it'll make you feel better."

Oh well, what was the harm. It couldn't exactly make her feel any worse, could it? Taking a deep breath, she knocked it back. The liquid was cold—colder than anything she had ever tasted before, in fact—but the consistency of it felt oddly familiar somehow. Gulping the contents down swiftly, she drained the bottle before handing him back the empty container.

"Here."

"You drank it all?" He looked at her sternly.

"Mhhmm. Yes, Sir." She bobbed her head, a tiny smirk playing over the corners of her mouth. The way he was speaking to her right now made her want to provoke him into punishing her.

He grinned, visibly relaxing as he saw she'd recovered sufficiently enough to crack jokes.

"Good. You had me worried there, you know. So was I right? Feeling better yet?" It was odd but now she thought about it she *was* feeling a bit better, her limbs felt a little lighter somehow, and the awful aching nausea had seemed to have gone away.

"Yeah, I do actually. What the hell's in that stuff?"

"Ah, just call it my magic cure-all. It's never failed me before."

She stared at him disbelievingly, shaking her head slowly. As if he were not already perfect enough, he'd actually managed to make her feel better when she hadn't fed for well over a week. How was that even possible?

"What happened?" She looked up into his brown eyes, searching their depths for an answer. He moved toward her, reaching out to cup her face.

"You blacked out on the playing field. I brought you back here in the coupe and watched you until you came round." The memories came flooding back to her then—Jim's neck warm and flushed with blood so temptingly close, her mouth opening to sink her teeth into that inviting flesh. She hoped Dillon hadn't seen that. Embarrassed, she shot him a nervous glance but his brown eyes merely smiled back at her with concerned kindness.

"Wow, my hero *again*. Guess we really do have to keep you out of jail. I'd be a mess without you eh?"

"Oh, you only want me for my ability to save your ass, huh?" The corners of his eyes crinkled up in the irresistible way they did whenever he found something amusing.

"Well, of course you have your other uses too." She allowed her eyes to drop to his muscular biceps, a frisson of excitement rippling through her as she remembered how they had made love in the lake house cabin.

"Oh yeah?" He traced the outline of her collarbone, his other hand still cupping her face. She could smell the musky scent of him, and the way he was standing over her with his crotch practically at eye level was unbelievably arousing.

"Mmhmm," she said, reaching up to snake her hand under the plain gray T-shirt he was wearing. Her fingertips made contact with the hard taut flesh of his abdomen, causing him to elicit a groan as she stroked him. God, this man was sexy. Those abs were to die for.

"Damnit, you drive me crazy," he growled as she bent her head to plant a kiss on the newly revealed flesh of his stomach.

"How crazy?" She moved to unbuckle his fly, and she looked up at him under half-hooded lids, a wicked smile curving over her lips. Groaning, he hooked his thick fingers in her hair, forcing her head closer to his crotch as her tongue extended to taste the hard, throbbing cock protruding out from the fly of his white boxers.

Taking it in one hand, she gripped it firmly at the base, the heat between her legs unbearable as she bent to it, encircling the fleshy head with her tongue before opening her mouth slowly to form a perfect O around the bulbous tip.

"Oh God," he groaned as his cock slid into her mouth.

The salty taste of him aroused her further as slowly she began to massage him to ecstasy. She felt his hands entwine in her hair as he pulled her to him, the pure thrill of pleasure at his touch making her shiver with anticipation as desire dripped between her legs.

Pulling away she broke for air, smiling up at him teasingly. His brown eyes flashed with lust as she squatted below him on the soft-carpeted floor. Licking her lips, she moved to take him into her mouth again but he stopped her with a throaty growl, catching her wrists with one hand and holding them.

"Sick of all the teasing yet?"

She giggled, squirming beneath his grip as he held her there. He shook his head in mock disgruntlement but his eyes were smiling.

"Do you know what happens to wicked teases?"

"Oh? What happens to them?"

"They get punished. And now I'm afraid you're going to have to take your punishment for being such a naughty girl."

The words and the confident way he spoke them sent an illicit thrill through her. With other guys *she* was the one who was in control of the situation but with Dillon she felt like anything could happen.

"*Moi*, Sir?" She bit her lower lip, looking down at the floor from under the long sweep of her eyelashes, knowing full well the effect she was having on him.

"Oh, you bad girl," he groaned, pushing her backward against the sofa, still holding her wrists with one hand as he forced them up above her head. He pushed up the black tank she wore, exposing the swollen pinkness of her aroused nipples, and gently he kissed and sucked at them. The pleasurable feeling of his lips upon her skin heightened her arousal to ferocious levels of intensity.

"Oh," she breathed, arching her back as the rough scratch of his stubble grazed the cool expanse of her skin, sending her nerve endings into a frenzy of sensation as his mouth tormented her.

"Don't move or I'll stop. No squirming around and no moaning."

The intense look in his eyes told her he wasn't joking.

Nodding, she bit her lip in acquiescence as she tried to comply with the request, mentally willing her body to keep still as his mouth moved ever lower, until his lips caressed her navel. The proximity of him was causing her body to break out in a fine layer of sheeny perspiration and her heart was in her throat with excitement. She could see his swollen cock throbbed with want for her, and she longed for him to take her right there and then, though she dared not say a word.

"There's a good girl," he said, his voice soothing as he unbuttoned her jeans. She so *wanted* to be his good girl, her body was aching to obey him, to give him whatever he desired, for it was there she knew her own pleasure was to be found.

"I'm going to release your wrists. But I want you to keep still while I take off your jeans," he commanded, his voice a low husky growl.

He tugged at the waistband of the denim she wore, easing her jeans down over her hips until the soft, creamy silk of her panties was exposed to his hungry eyes.

"Now close your eyes and hold your wrists above your head. Part those deliciously sexy thighs. I'm going to leave the room to fetch something. When I come back, I want you waiting in that position for me."

He bent to cup her face, his calloused palm massaging the softness of her cheek as he tucked himself back into his pants with his other hand. Internally she gave a groan, as that gorgeous cock was hidden from view once more, but she nodded obediently to acknowledge him even though her mind was racing with curiosity.

"I'll wait for you," she said breathlessly, parting her thighs as he had asked and trying not to make *too* obvious the effect he was having on all of her senses.

"Very good girl. Now close your eyes."

She obeyed him and felt his hands momentarily brush over her stiff areola before a cool rush of air told her he'd left the room. Damn, just when she'd thought he couldn't get any hotter, he did just that. This man knew how to play her body like it was an instrument, but what was even more arousing was the fact that he seemed to know how to read her deepest desires too.

Desires even *she* hadn't known had been lying there dormant. Trying to still her breathing, she lay there spread-eagled on the couch as she waited for him to return. What was he doing?

She knew she wouldn't have to wait long to find out as the heavy tread of his footsteps on the plush carpet informed her of his return.

"Good girl." His rich sexy voice purred with satisfaction as he stood over her, and confusingly, she felt both embarrassed and excited at how exposed she was to him lying there like that.

"May I open my eyes now?" She heard him laugh, a resonant sound full of so much warmth it seemed to fill the room. It made her feel safe and peculiarly expectant all at the same time. She had never wanted to entrust her body so completely to any man before.

"Not just yet," he replied, and she felt the kiss of rope being wound around her wrists as he worked to bind her. She felt her pulse quicken with excitement at what he was doing, she'd never experienced being tied up until he had introduced her to it, and now she couldn't seem to get enough of it.

"*Now* you can open your eyes," he instructed, and she did as he told her, allowing her eyelashes to flutter open as she met his gaze. Twinkly brown eyes met her own violet ones, and she gave a shiver as she saw herself reflected in his pupils, spread-eagled and almost naked, totally willing to give her body up to him.

"What are you going to do?" She gasped the words but he merely grinned at her, placing a finger to her mouth to shush her before claiming her lips with his own, his tongue probing the wetness of her mouth as the hardness of him pressed against her, causing the thin material of her panties to become soaked with arousal.

She found herself breathing harder as he snaked his fingers down her naked sides to caress her inner thighs, causing exquisite rivers of sensation to ripple through the silky smooth sensitive flesh.

"Jesus, you're so beautiful," he said, shaking his head disbelievingly as he gazed down at her. His fingertips brushed over the silk of her panties, stroking lightly over her abdomen, and causing her to arch her back and thrust at him in sheer want for more of his touch.

Slowly he trailed his fingertips down again, dipping and swirling enticingly as they explored her, and eliciting a moan of frustration as they slipped into the space between her waistband and the gentle swell of her stomach.

"Oh," she gasped out loud, as his fingers gently grazed the soft mound of hair there. "Please don't, stop!"

He dipped lower still, causing her body to twist in torment as he sought out the epicenter of her pleasure.

"Stop? Really?" He grinned down at her, his eyebrow raised.

No, she didn't want him to stop at all, why had she said that?

"I can't take it. It's too much," she moaned, her body arching up to meet his touch again as between her legs the fire grew, threatening to consume her. If he insisted on carrying on touching her like that, she knew she was going to end up begging him to take her right there and then.

Smiling, he bent his head to the silk of her panties, planting a gentle kiss on the skimpy material that so tantalizingly concealed the sensitive nub of her swollen and aroused clitoris.

"Don't," she gasped, but he merely looked at her and shook his head.

"I didn't say you could move yet," he said, his voice thick with desire. "Now we have to see what your punishment will be." Using his strong hands to part her thighs wide, he tugged her silken underwear down using his mouth.

"Oh, please," she groaned, as the coolness of the air caressed her flesh. Greedily he drank her in, staring down at her boldly.

"Please what?"

"Don't tease like that. I can't bear it," she said, feeling her cheeks blush as she looked up at him.

"Oh, you want me to stop teasing you, huh? Uh-uh, I know you can beg me for release better than that." The meaning of his words was crystal clear. The blush became a hot stain as she realized what he would have her do.

"Show me," he urged her as she parted her thighs for him, her eyes locking his as mentally she invited him to appraise her, willing and open to him. Never in her whole life had she been this vulnerable to any man before, never had she wanted to be.

"Please," she breathed, as he hastily tore away the cream silk panties from her flesh. Brazenly, she parted her thighs wide as his hands reached for her body, unable to hold back in their quest for her any longer.

He urgently sought her heat with his tongue as he bent his head to her, and she shuddered as the rough sensation of his ministrations sent tingles of pleasure throughout her body.

"God, I could taste you forever," he murmured, his tongue ripe with her juices, his head still half-buried between her thighs. The warmth of his broad, solid chest and shoulders propping her thighs apart was causing her desire to heighten further as she reveled in the masculine solidity of his body.

"Oh God, don't stop," she begged, twisting beneath him as her body undulated in pleasure. She needed this man to possess her completely, to control her body, to have her carry out his every wish, for she knew the secret of her pleasure lay there somewhere, deep in the heart of her submission to him.

"Say how much you want me to shove my hard cock up you then. Tell me how much you need it inside you," he urged her, separating her pink folds to expose all of her to his view. She realized with a hot rush that there was nothing left to be hidden from him.

"Please, I need it so much," she begged, her own words forcing her to drip with arousal, as roughly he thrust first one digit then a second inside her softness. He reached to loosen himself from his pants once more.

She watched from beneath half-closed eyes as he levered his shaft free, the thick veins decorating the stiff length making her whole body quiver with anticipation.

"Jesus, take me." She was unable to hold back any longer. To her frustration he merely smiled as he shook his head.

"Uh-uh. Not just yet," he said, thrusting his hand out and indicating she should take it in one of her bound ones. Obediently she did so, and he eased her to her feet, her legs still quivering beneath her with desire as he caressed the small of her exposed back.

"Come with me." He motioned for her to walk forward. Confused, she turned back to him.

"Where are we going?"

"My bedroom. There's a mirror there. I want you to see your face when you realize what I'm going to do to you."

They walked through the doorway of the spacious, white-painted room, her legs trembling with anticipation, his hand still at her back as gently he guided her to a fluffy white rug that lay in front of the long looking glass fronting the double doors of his closet.

"Here," he indicated, coming up behind her close and encircling her waist as she stared at their reflection in the mirror's pane.

"I want you to see the expression in your eyes as my cock goes in you," he murmured into her throat. The words sent a shiver of excitement along the back of her neck, causing the little wisps of hair there to stand to attention.

Slowly, gently, he guided her down onto the soft rug beneath their feet, his mouth planting a trail of kisses down her neck as he forced her forward on to her knees.

She looked at her reflection. She looked wanton, wild, hair askew and rumpled, her wrists held bound in front of her and her lips swollen with urgent kisses.

"Oh," she gasped out, as she felt his thigh force her legs to part. "Oh," she cried again as he wound his hands around the long, dark strands of her silky hair. He tugged her head back gently and forced her to arch her back while the swollen length of him teased at her entrance, the bulbous head of his cock pushing up against her soaking folds.

"How much do you want it?" His voice was soft, yet she heard the urgency and she felt herself blush again. The room was in semidarkness, the only light the bright fluorescent bulb filtering through to the room from the hallway outside.

"Please," she moaned, arching her back at him, not caring now how desperate she must seem.

"Oh, you bad, hungry girl," he growled, the hot thickness of him straining against her, as finally, he slid inside her, seeming to fill every part of her as he took her.

"Yes." She squirmed beneath him as he rode her, her cheek squashed against the soft white fur of the rug beneath them as urgently she ground herself against him, desperate for more.

"Look," he said, with a growl, his hands twisting in her hair as he forced her to look at the lewd display she was making in the mirror. "Look at how you fucking beg for it."

The words and the way he spoke them sent her way past the point of mere arousal, and her whole body tensed up as she contracted around the hot ridges of his shaft, pleasure tearing through her.

"Oh God," she moaned, her body exploding with sensation as her legs buckled underneath her.

She could see Dillon's jaw clenched with focus in the mirror as he rode her hard, though his eyes gave away the unbridled pleasure he was feeling. That wild look of his, coupled with the fact that her wrists were still bound with rope, made her feel as if she were existing in that moment for pure pleasure alone, and only served to heighten her orgasm as it she went over the edge.

"Good girl. That's it," he said, as she writhed under him, every fiber of her sensitive to even the slightest movement as he thrust into her.

"Now I'm gonna fuck you in the ass," he growled as she struggled to regain control her breathing, his hands encircling her waist again as he lifted her up off her knees, pulling her back against him as he lay back on the rug's soft pile.

Wait, what did he just say? She'd had her fair share of sexual encounters and considered herself to be pretty wild in bed but she'd never done *that* with any guy. Could she — would she — let him take her like that?

He pushed her down with a growl and she felt his cock withdraw from her, her body almost instantaneously craving the loss of him. He spread the curve of her ass wide, her cheeks flushing with shame as she was bared to him utterly, and suddenly the fat head was nudging, pushing into that hot, tight place where sensations were new and strange.

For a moment the pain was almost unbearable and she felt as if her spine might split open, a sheen of sweat breaking out down her back as her fingernails clawed at the carpet.

"No, oh God, *please*, take it out," she panted, breathing hard as her body strained to accept his thick cock, the tight ring of muscle expanding to accommodate him and causing agonizing spasms through her whole body.

"Good girl. Just relax and take me," he murmured, his hand soothing on her back as he stopped thrusting momentarily, allowing her body to catch pace with itself and acclimatize to this peculiar new sensation.

Slowly he began to fuck her again, moving his hips forward and inching in, and suddenly the painful sensation morphed into another kind of feeling, a friction that was not pleasant entirely but not unpleasant either, as if her whole body were being filled by him, stroked from the inside out.

"Oh fuck, so hot... You're so hot," he moaned, obviously enjoying what he was doing to her, his thrusts picking up pace, his cock throbbing inside the tight space that enclosed it. He reached between her legs, plucking and twisting her clit and causing her to squirm and push back on his cock as he buried it deeper into her. His fingers slid into her wetness again as his cock pushed deeper into her ass, making her call out loud into the night as a white-hot heat began to smolder in the deepest core of her.

"Oh, oh," she cried out as the friction of him rubbing up against her suddenly turned to unbearable pleasure, creating a shower of needle-like sparks inside her body, each one of them alighting her senses to jump and dance madly.

"Now look in the mirror see how good you look on your knees with your wrists bound and my cock in you like that?"

She lifted her head again, looking at the picture they made in the mirror, wanton and lewd, him mounting her, his thick cock buried deep in her high, raised ass, her face flushed and desperate.

"You like it now, don't you? My cock in you like this?"

She didn't answer him. She couldn't answer him, even though she wanted to. She couldn't admit *that*.

"Well?" He tugged on her hair, forcing her to look at herself again as he thrust inside her, deeper, harder, before pulling back and thrusting again. The sight of him fucking her that way, like a wanton slut on her knees for the mounting, made her want to come almost instantaneously.

Scowling at her silence, he made as if to withdraw from her, releasing his grip on her hair.

"No, please… I do, I need it," she said, begging.

"I'm going to have you everywhere, anytime I damn well want to. I'm going to access your body and do anything I want to you *whenever* I please to. You understand?"

He spoke the words, still forcing her to look at herself in the mirror, and she was glad the only light was that that filtered through the open door from the hallway for despite her bloodless complexion, she was sure she was a bright beet red by now.

"I… Yes, I understand," she stammered, only to be rewarded by a hard thrust that made her breasts slap against each other and her lips part as she gasped out loud. If anyone had ever dared suggest they were going to do as they pleased to her body before, she would have slapped them right around the face. With Dillon she just found herself hoping he made good on his promise.

"I'm gonna use your body like the dirty little slut you are. My own personal slut."

"Your slut," she whispered, even as her cheeks burned at the words. *Yes, your slut. Oh, God, please.*

"And no damn panties unless I say you can wear them. Short skirts only. I want you available to me anytime I want to take you. Do you hear?" He punctuated the question with a hard thrust, making her groan with pleasure.

Control. He had control of her, control she willingly handed to him—needed, wanted him to take. Maybe because she was so independent, maybe because she was so used to being in charge that this new feeling of submission, of trusting him with her power was so satiating. She *wanted* him to tell her what to do, and she trusted him to order her around. It wasn't demeaning in the slightest. It was liberating, the most exciting and exhilarating sensation she'd ever experienced.

"Yes," she squeaked as she felt his hips bucking as his hand stilled her back, forcing her down, his cock pistoning in and out of her ass, not being gentle now, just greedily taking her—taking what he wanted and making her body drip with pleasure at being used in such a way.

"Now you gonna beg for me to come in your ass like a real good girl?"

"Yes," she cried out again, her body unable to hold back at the words and his treatment of her as her legs shook and her stomach tensed up. "Oh, oh, come in me please," she moaned as the cock continued to saw back and forth, not stopping—not ever stopping—feeling harder and more swollen than ever, so hard. She called out the words again, over and over, again and again into the night, until she felt the hot spurt of him and heard his heavy grunt of pleasure as he released himself deep inside her.

"Goddamn it," he grunted, thrusting himself in again, his cock pumping the last of his pleasure as she scratched at the rug's fur. Gripping her hips with his hands he rode — until his primal cry into the night communicated he was spent.

After, she stayed like that, just rocking, with him still inside her as she milked the very last drop from him and he moaned her name into the silence of the night over and over. Only when he was finally satiated did they allow themselves to collapse back onto the softness of the rug, his hands pulling her close to him, cradling her against his chest, tight against him.

"Wow, you're certainly full of surprises." She grinned as they both lay there panting and sweating, her body nestled against the comforting solidness of his.

"Guess I'm more than just a pretty face, huh?"

"Mmhmm, you're damn good dirty talker too. I think you'd better untie me, though," she said, giggling and turning round to face him as she indicated her still bound wrists.

"I might. I do like you like that, though," he said, the sparkle in his eyes telling her he was wasn't joking. Her heart gave a funny little jump as he gently held her wrists steady, working to unpick the knot.

Don't get in too deep, Lola. You know it can't last. You two are from two different worlds.

As soon as he discovered her secret, he'd probably never want to see her again but for now she didn't care. She felt so blissfully happy lying there in the darkness with him she could almost pretend to herself that whatever came their way, they would endure it, together. After all Dillon had secrets too didn't he?

'Trust me. One day I'll tell you what my story is, but now's not the right time, Lola.'

Well, maybe now *was* the right time? As her wrists sprang free from the rope, she eased her way off his chest, engineering her body so she was lying on her side on the rug. Turning to face him, she maneuvered her knees into the hollow between his chest and abdomen and looked up at him, a smile curving over her lips.

"Hey, sexy," he said, smiling back at her.

"Why, hello, Sir." She poked out her tongue. He grinned.

"You know, when I saw you hit the deck standing next to Jim like that, I realized I've never been so damn worried about someone in my entire life," he said, his expression suddenly serious.

Jim. Panic surged through her as she recalled the lengths Drago and his crew had gone to try to prevent him from testifying.

"Hey, it's all right. He's okay," he said, noticing her stricken expression.

"Where is he?"

"I brought him with us here then I called Lydia to come pick him up. She's taken him to a safe house. Friend of a friend. We're to go see them tomorrow evening."

"You think he's still gonna testify after all of this?"

He nodded his head.

"Really?"

"Especially after all this. I think now he's seen the lengths Drago will go to, he realizes that he really has no other choice unless he wants to leave Burley Falls for good. I just wish he'd never gotten himself involved in any of this on my account. I feel like it's all my fault," he said, shaking his head ruefully.

"Hey, it's not your fault." She placed a hand on his arm, attempting to placate him.

"But it *is*. If I hadn't gotten myself arrested, Jim would never have been dragged into this. I just screw up people's lives. You'd be better off staying away from me too."

She couldn't stand him blaming himself like this, not when it was all *her* fault. She felt worse than a fraud.

"No! It wasn't your fault. If anything, this mess is all *my* fault. If I hadn't needed to —"

She stopped, clamping a hand to her lips. The words had almost tumbled out of her mouth automatically.

"I'm sorry," she choked, trying hard to hold back the tears.

"Hey, it's okay, sweetheart. I know, all right? I know." He rubbed the small of her back in comforting circles.

He knew? How could he know?

"We're the same, you and I. Except you're the better half of me."

"Huh, wha…what do you mean?" Confused she looked at him through blurry, tear-stained eyes.

"I mean I love you no matter what," he said, his eyes smiling as he spoke, reaching to gently caress her cheekbone.

The tender gesture was enough to tip her over, and the tears fell heavily now. He enveloped her protectively in his arms as she clung to his broad chest like a drowning thing. His strong hands patted her back comfortingly as she sobbed into the cotton of his T-shirt.

She knew that right now it didn't matter now what he knew or what he didn't know about her. All that mattered was they were here, together, right now, and in this moment she had never felt so safe.

Chapter Eleven

The next day Lola woke with a start, her body automatically tensing up in panic as she glanced at her watch's illuminated dial and saw the time was four forty-five p.m. The pair of them hadn't fallen asleep until the small hours and now it was nearly evening — thankfully. But although the sun would shortly be fading, at this time of the afternoon it would still be low in the sky, which meant she was still at risk.

How could she have been so stupid as to put herself in jeopardy like that? Never since she had been turned had she spent the night away from her own bed and it scared her to think the depth of her feeling for Dillon had caused her to jettison her sensibilities so casually.

Luckily the wooden blinds decorating the windows were firmly closed, and whatever light might be outside was currently prevented from filtering through to where they lay, huddled up together on the king-size bed.

As her brain recalled what had happened the night before, her stomach tightened and an unbearable ache of yearning pulsed in her groin. Being with Dillon was so excitingly unpredictable she truly couldn't guess what he would do next or what new erotic adventure he would guide her through. She found herself almost constantly on edge in the most deliciously tormenting way, just waiting to see what he would have her do next.

She wanted, needed, to feel as turned on as she had last night again, to feel like every boundary she ever had was being pushed, because it had felt like she were free. She marveled at his quiet and complete dominance of her, at how easy and natural it felt, at how the secret craving for control had lain in her all the years, unexplored until he had known how exactly to awaken it within her.

Beside her Dillon began to stir, his consciousness surfacing as he tossed and turned, pulling the covers with him.

He looked so adorable, just lying there dozing like that, that she couldn't resist leaning in to plant a kiss on the rough stubble of his cheek. His skin smelled addictive. The hazy musk emanating from it made her want to snuggle into him and stay there forever. Or at least until the sun had retired for the evening.

Nestling back alongside him, she nestled into the warmth of his body, faking a yawn as she forced herself to close her eyes. Maybe if she were lucky, he'd stay sleeping until the sun sank firmly beneath the horizon.

"Hey," he murmured groggily, his arm reaching out to snake around her waist, squeezing her closer. Acting as if she hadn't heard him, she kept her eyes shut and her breathing steady as she pretended to be asleep.

"Hey," he said again, leaning over her. Dammit, he wasn't going to quit.

"Mmmph," she mumbled noncommittally, hoping he'd take the hint she was still napping.

"Lola," he said, placing his hand upon her shoulder and shaking her gently.

"Mmm whassamatter," she murmured, still hoping to get away with pretending to doze.

"We have to check the time. I told Lydia we'd meet her and Jim at six p.m."

At least it would definitely be dark outside by then. Twisting round to acknowledge him, she made a show of looking at her watch.

"It's almost five. Where are we supposed to be meeting them?"

"They're staying with Lydia's friend across the other side of town. We have to get showered and be ready."

"Uh, okay, but let me just rest a while. I still don't feel so great," she groaned, pulling the covers tighter around her body, in an effort to stall for a few minutes more. The later she could leave it before they had to get out of bed the better. The last thing she wanted was for Dillon to start throwing the curtains open.

"You don't have to hide anything from me you know." His tone was kind but fear clutched at her heart all the same. *What the hell does he mean by that?*

"I'm not hiding anything," she protested, looking at him in mock indignation. He was so hard to read sometimes it was far too difficult to try and ascertain what he was thinking. He swooped in to kiss her lobe lightly, his stubble chaffing her skin and giving her a little frisson of pleasure at the sensation.

"It's all right, I know about your condition."

Her heart plummeted into her stomach as the panic gripped her. "My...my condition?" Her voice came out in a frightened squeak.

"Your photosensitivity. Photodermatosis? My best friend in high school had a sister who suffered with the same thing."

"Uh, how did you know?"

"It was pretty obvious. You live after dark, always keep the curtains closed and when I suggested meeting in the morning, you blew me off — several times — even though you don't currently have a day job. I just put two and two together." He shrugged.

She felt the relief course through her body though she also felt a slight pull of guilt.

"Yeah…I dunno what brought it on but I've suffered from it since I was seventeen. It gets tricky sometimes but I manage it. But you're right. I'm kinda embarrassed about it."

"It must be pretty difficult." His brown eyes looked so sympathetic that she felt even guiltier at deceiving him. But she wasn't exactly lying to him, was she? Just omitting the complete truth. There would be plenty of time for him to know everything later. For now she had to focus on the trial.

"Hey, like I said, I manage," she replied, trying to look nonchalant.

"Do you have complete insensitivity or partial?"

"Complete." It was true. More than five minutes of sunlight and she was in serious trouble.

"What about the trial, though?"

"What do you mean?"

"Well, it's going to be day when it's conducted — not nighttime. So you're not going to be able to be there, are you?"

Her stomach sunk as she realized the truth of his words. He was right. There was no way she could be at the trial. Unless…

"I *could*. It is possible, but only if I wear thick black clothing that completely covers me from head to toe so I can get in and out of the place without burning and blistering up. I won't need to wear it in the trial room.

It's only sunlight I'm sensitive to and there aren't any windows in the courtroom."

"Hey, I don't want you putting yourself in any danger for me," he said, looking into her eyes with concern.

"I won't. I promise I'll make sure I'm covered. It'll be awkward but it can be done. And I wanna come and see Drago's ass put in the frame instead of you." At least she hoped that was the way it was going to go. Anything else really didn't bear contemplation.

"Yep, and now we've got Jim on our side, we've actually got a real chance of seeing that scumbag served his just desserts," Dillon replied, his jaw tightening in temper.

"Hey, don't waste your anger on him."

"Yeah, I shouldn't think about that lowlife or I'll just wind up doing something I really regret," he said, shaking his head.

"And that would never do. Now how about doing something you definitely won't regret with me instead before we get dressed to go meet Lydia?"

He grinned down at her, his eyes twinkling with mischief as his hands reached to pull her closer.

"Oh, you want more of last night's action, huh?"

She blushed at the memory of how shameless she'd been, splayed out underneath him on all fours on the rug, but the complete eroticism of the moment made her body throb with an immediate and powerful excitement at the memory.

"Maybe we could take it a bit easier this morning. I still need to recover a little," she murmured, his breath warm against the bare flesh of her neck as he kissed and nibbled there.

"Hrrrm, do you think you get to decide, though?" he said, grinning and reaching out to tickle her gently in the side. She wriggled, trying to get away from his teasing fingertips, giggling.

"So what happens if I don't do as you say...Sir?" She looked at him a sparkle in her eyes, the smile twitching at her lips.

"Oh, that's when bad girl's get punished," he said, increasing the tickling till she was squirming unbearably from the sensation. Laughing she fell against him as they both sank down beneath the coverlet, bodies pressed against each other, lips locking as their limbs entwined.

* * * *

Once inside Lydia's friend's front room, comfortably settled on a spacious rattan sofa decorated with piles of brightly colored scatter cushions, Lola turned to the elegant blonde woman inquiringly.

"Do you think we have enough evidence to get Dillon off the hook?" She crossed her legs, acutely self-conscious that she wasn't wearing any panties underneath the black satin pencil skirt she wore, just as Dillon had instructed.

Lydia considered the question for a moment, perching on the edge of a rattan armchair positioned opposite the sofa, her shapely legs crossed at the ankles.

"Well, nothing is one hundred percent certain of course, and *a lot* depends on getting a sympathetic judge. But now that Mr. Cavanagh is prepared to come forward, I believe we might."

"And what about Drago? Will he be charged?" She felt Dillon's hand caress her satin-covered thigh as she asked the question and couldn't help but feel a shiver of excitement at his touch. Trying to collect herself, she cleared her throat. She had to stay focused. She couldn't look like a stammering, blushing fool in front of Lydia.

"Unlikely, I'm afraid." Lydia screwed up her nose.

"Why? If Dillon's found to be innocent, then surely they'll want to find the real culprit?"

"You'd think so, wouldn't you? But it doesn't always work that way. And it's much harder to secure a conviction than it is to get a man off a charge, especially when that man is Drago Graythorne."

"That name sure seems to have a lot of currency around here," Dillon interjected, his expression dark.

Lydia nodded.

"It sure does. The Graythornes are probably the most influential family in Burley Falls. They have more clout than pretty much anyone else around here. It'd be a brave judge that would want to go up against Commissioner Graythorne."

"So Drago will be free to come after us again?" The room felt cold as she made the realization, and a shiver of apprehension rippled down her spine.

"Just let him try. I'll be waiting for him," Dillon muttered, anger wreathing his handsome features as he clenched his knuckles.

"Of course there's always the *Chronicle*." Jim spoke, his brown eyes bright as he looked round at the three of them.

"What do you mean?" The question came out as a funny sort of squeak, Dillon's other hand had slipped behind her to caress her back, and his fingers were tantalizingly close to her ass.

Jim shot her an odd look.

"Well, we may not be able to secure a conviction but if I can get my editor to sign this off, the public outcry could well force a retrial anyway."

"You really think that could happen?" His fingers were circling the small of her back, inching down, down, until his hand was cupping her the curve of her buttock. She was sure everyone in the room could see the effect he was having on her.

Jesus, Lola, you gotta keep it together.

"If we can get the story out there, I do, yeah," Jim said, bobbing his head vigorously.

"Ermm, then we need to get it out there. Can you get your editor to sign it off today?"

The fingers were inching closer underneath her. He had to stop. He was making her all kinds of stupid. It was getting harder to form logical sentences, to understand what people were saying.

Please stop. I can't focus. Please stop.

"Nope. Have to wait until after the trial. Legal confidentiality. Otherwise the paper could get sued for trying to influence proceedings."

The fingers continued, her heart beginning to pound as the familiar tingling started between her legs.

"But won...won't the Graythorne family just use their influence to pressure the *Chronicle* not to print the story? If a judge won't convict, why would your editor be brave enough to go against Drago and his fam—" She broke off midsentence as the finger pushed through the silk fabric of her skirt to place a firm pressure right in the center of her ass.

Faking a cough, she steeled herself to meet Jim's eyes. She was sure he knew what Dillon was doing to her. She'd never felt so mortified and so aroused all at the same time. This was crazy.

"Family," she finished, clearing her throat again as if to pretend that were the reason for her pause. She shifted away from Dillon's touch, shooting him a look. She couldn't stand this a moment longer or she was going to lose all control. His handsome face didn't give anything away.

Jim grinned, his eyes twinkling.

"You'd think so, wouldn't you? But journalists are a funny old breed. We'll do anything for a good scoop. And they don't come much better than this. I've known David for years and this is the kind of story he'd bite someone's arm off to get."

"But first we have to prepare for the trial." Lydia cleared her throat politely, cutting back in swiftly, as she leaned forward to pick up a sheaf of papers resting atop the glass-fronted coffee table.

"Now," she said, looking around at the three of them, "as Mr. Chambers' legal representative, I have the right to obtain any evidence submitted to the court by the prosecution in advance. Of course I've exercised that right, and naturally, since he didn't commit the crime, they haven't got anything concrete that can prove he killed Mr. Eversham. So I can tell you now what they will try to do instead is character assassinate him."

"Character assassinate him? But how? Dillon's innocent."

"Doesn't matter." Lydia shook her head firmly, her glossy blonde strands reflecting the light streaming from the crystal lampshade hanging from the room's stucco ceiling.

"They're going to dredge up everything they can. Which is why, Dillon, I need to find out exactly what happened with Arthur Elgorn."

"Wait... Who?" Lola couldn't help but interrupt, her curiosity instinctively bubbling up at the mention of a strange name.

"The man that claims he was attacked by Dillon on the morning after the murder."

She recalled Max telling her about the incident. Of course, in the chaos of everything else that had occurred, she'd completely forgotten about that little event. Or maybe not so little, judging from the worried way Lydia was regarding Dillon.

"I think I remember something about that, yeah," she muttered, feeling slightly unsure of what to say, and opting to retreat into the far easier option of silence instead. She shot a nervous look over at Dillon, who was seated beside her on the rattan sofa.

"So, Dillon?" Lydia raised an eyebrow questioningly.

"I didn't start anything with him." Dillon scowled.

"But you *did* become engaged in a fight with him?"

"He approached me, looking to start some trouble."

"Why was he trying to start trouble with you?"

"I guess he was one of Drago's goons looking to rough me up in revenge for what I did to that little punk."

"So what did happen with Drago exactly? Did you hurt him badly?" Lydia's tone was insistent. Dillon sighed heavily, turning to shoot Lola a glance as he rolled his eyes. She knew this was getting to him and she felt bad about what he was having to go through. After all, it had been *her* honor he'd been defending.

"He just did what was necessary. What any decent guy would have done. Drago was coming on strong to me and Dillon had to get him to back off somehow," she said defiantly, leaping to his defense.

"I understand you have strong feelings about what happened, but remember, I'm trying to help. The prosecution are going to be aggressive with their questions, and I have to make sure I know everything I need to in order to mount an effective defense," Lydia said firmly.

Okay, point taken, fair enough.

"Sorry, I guess I was getting a little heated. I know you're only trying to help," she said, giving the blonde a small, resigned smile.

"All right, so I understand you were defending Lola when you attacked Mr. Graythorne, Dillon, but what I need to know is who you were defending when you attacked Mr. Elgorn? Because both his lawyers and the prosecution will want to know," Lydia said, continuing her line of questioning.

"I told you I didn't attack him. He attacked me. I was just defending myself."

"The only problem is the wound inflicted on Mr. Elgorn is precisely the same kind of wound that caused Mr. Eversham to bleed out," Lydia said.

She saw Jim's eyes nearly pop out of his skull on stalks. What the hell did Lydia mean, *the same kind of wound*?

"Look, I didn't have anything to do with Mr. Whateverhisname is. I didn't touch the dude. And *he* can vouch for that," Dillon said, gesturing to Jim, who looked far too rattled to vouch for anything much at all.

"I understand, but you can see how it will look to the prosecution. Remember, they're going to do everything they can to turn this to their advantage. We have one enormous spanner in our works and the more information you can give me on it, the better," Lydia warned.

"There's nothing else I can tell you. Elgorn came up to me as I was getting out of my car. The dude was obviously hostile, accusing me of trying to cut him up. I tried to calm him down but he wasn't having any of it. Then he lunged for me, so I had to defend myself."

"But why did you need to bite him, puncture his neck? Wouldn't a punch have been far more effective?" Lydia's clear gray eyes were sharp with intrigue. Lola had to admit, the woman had a point. It did look odd. But she knew that no matter what, Dillon would have a plausible explanation for his behavior. He was too honorable not to have a good reason for having done what he did. *Yeah, unlike you. You're the monster, right?*

"Look, I told you. I was just defending myself. The dude wasn't backing down and I was wrestling to get him off me. The bite was just a way to distract him and it sure as hell worked." Dillon met Lydia's gaze boldly.

"Okay. Let me look into this Mr. Elgorn and see what I can find out about him. If the prosecution is going to be ready to use him in order to smear your character, then we have to be ready to smear *his* tomorrow in court," Lydia said, giving a terse smile as she tidied the sheaf of papers.

The question had been burning on her lips and now she had to ask it.

"But won't the proof we have that Drago was there with the victim be enough? I thought you said if we could get the witness to testify, we had a solid case."

"Mmhmm, I did. But I didn't say we were guaranteed to win. In court anything can happen and as I said, a lot depends on the judge that gets assigned to our case on the morning of the trial." The blonde woman's tone was firm.

"You mean there's a chance we might not win, that Dillon could go to jail for this?" The nausea in her stomach was threatening to overwhelm her.

Lydia shot her a sympathetic smile.

"Look, we've got the cell phone evidence and we have Jim's testimony. That counts for a lot, believe me. But you have to remember the prosecution wants to win and they want to win badly. And they aren't going to let Mr. Chambers walk free without one hell of a fight."

* * * *

Sitting on the passenger side of Dillon's green coupe as he steered the car through the lamp-lit streets, she snuck a glance at his handsome profile, noting the expression of concentration on his face. Her mind mused over the possibilities of what might happen at tomorrow's trial as she observed his face, the fear churning her stomach up as mixed feelings of love, anxiety and guilt all intermingled. If he *was* found guilty by some travesty of justice, then how on earth could she live with the knowledge that her actions were responsible for his incarceration?

She couldn't think like that. Her mind simply wouldn't allow itself to consider the possibility of not having him in her life. Though whatever happened, that was certainly going to be a reality, for even if justice was served and Dillon walked free, he would surely run a mile once he found out the truth about her. Leaning back against the coupe's comfortable headrest, she closed her eyes momentarily, taking in a deep lungful of air. She should try to forget about it. For this moment, at least, she could allow her heart to be full of hope—of possibility for what might be tomorrow and all the tomorrows after that.

She lay like that as he drove the car through the rows of two up, two down neo-gothic-style houses dominating Burley's suburban streets, occasionally opening her eyes to take in the view through the vehicle's thin pane of glass, before closing them again. It was on the fourth round of opening them that she realized they were heading in the opposite direction from her apartment, where she'd assumed they'd both be spending one last night together before the trial started tomorrow.

"You're driving the wrong way," she murmured dozily, turning to Dillon.

He didn't respond, a hint of a smile playing over his lips as he continued to drive.

"Hey, what's so funny? Don't you realize you're driving us in the opposite direction to where we need to be going?" She poked him in the side with a fingernail, which caused a wider smile to break out on his face.

"Oh, I know I'm driving that way all right," he said, turning briefly to grin at her before refocusing his attention on the road ahead, the white flash of his perfect teeth causing a pulse of desire to course through her despite her half-asleep state. Lord, he looked so damn irresistible when he smiled that way.

"This road goes down to the riverside?"

"Sure does." He continued to steer the car, shooting a glance at her as she reclined against the vehicle's pale gray leather interior. A flush came to her cheeks as she felt the heat of his gaze. The way he looked at her was always so intense. She felt as if she were naked before him. Nervously she licked her lips, her hands flying self-consciously to her hair to automatically smooth down the long, silky dark strands that had escaped from the high ponytail she'd pulled her hair into that evening.

Slowing the car to a crawl as he navigated the turn leading to the lane that ran down to the riverside, he fixed her with a lazy grin, his eyes laden with intent.

She felt ridiculously underdressed all of a sudden, the thin flimsy silky tank top she was wearing barely seeming to conceal her nipples, which had apparently decided to stand to attention all of a sudden, and the cool breeze that fluttered in through the slit in the window teased the silky material tortuously against her bare flesh.

"Why are you looking at me like that?" She stammered the words out, feeling peculiarly like a self-conscious teenager. This was madness. Why did she feel so nervous and yet excited with apprehension all at the same time?

"I just wanted to remember how beautiful you look right now. If things don't go so well for me tomorrow, I don't know how long it'll be before I see that pretty face of yours again. So I sure as hell want to remember every single detail of you now."

Her heart felt like it was going to stop and she wanted to burst into floods of tears at his words. Somehow, he managed to cut through all of her defenses, make the nice, safe walls she'd so carefully built to guard her emotions come tumbling down. How could they lock him up for a crime he didn't commit? How could life be so unfair?

Stifling her feelings, she smiled, though the tears were threatening to prick at her eyelids.

"Hey, it's all going to be fine, silly," she said, reaching out to affectionately squeeze his forearm though her throat felt thick as she spoke the words.

Nodding silently, he gave a resigned smile as he shrugged.

"Eh, I know. Just you sitting there like that, you looked so damn pretty. It got me to thinking how hard it's gonna be without you if..." He didn't finish the sentence, opting to shrug again instead as he turned the car down the narrow lane leading to the riverside.

"So why *are* we heading to the riverside?"

A mischievous sparkle flashed in his eyes as he grinned.

"Oh, just felt like it. And all that pretty you got is far too good to go to waste."

The appreciative way his eyes raked over her made her shiver with anticipation at what he might have in store for her. Between her legs she could feel her arousal starting to build.

"You were so bad earlier, teasing me in front of everyone like that," she said, shaking her head at him.

"Oh, was I now? But someone didn't remember their instructions, did they?"

"What do you mean?" She looked at him, biting her lower lip.

"You know exactly what I mean. Remember when I told you I was to have access to your body anytime I wanted?"

"But I couldn't focus. I had to talk to people, I…" She trailed off helplessly as he shook his head at her.

"Uh-uh. Doesn't matter. I said anytime, and you disobeyed me. So now you have to suffer the consequences of not doing what you're told."

The hairs on the back of her neck stood up at the words, every sense in her body alert and primed with arousal and expectation. She wondered briefly for a second if it was wrong to feel how she felt, to crave what she craved, but surely nothing that felt this erotic, this exciting could be wrong? *Oh God, yes, please, punish me. Punish me.*

Cutting the engine, he pulled the car up short alongside the low-running stile that separated the riverside pathway from the road.

"Here we are. Pretty, ain't it?" He moved closer to her, slipping his arm around her shoulders as they both regarded the view that lay out in front of them. The twinkling lamplight illuminated the water, its surface appearing to shimmer and ripple in front of their eyes as they watched it.

"It *is* beautiful," she said, snuggling against his solid frame and trying to relax and enjoy the view, even though her body was tense with anticipation.

"Yeah, I like to come here to think about things sometimes, when I got stuff on my mind that's troubling me."

"What kind of stuff?" Automatically, she reached out to him, placing a hand on his thigh.

"Stuff that can't be changed." His fingers entwined themselves in her hair as bending forward, he moved in to kiss her, his hand running down her neck and along her shoulder, pulling her closer to him. She reciprocated the urgency of his kiss, feeling her heart beating faster as he worked his fingers under the strap of her silky tank, edging it off her shoulder slowly.

"I've been waiting to have you for hours," he groaned, breaking off momentarily, his eyes wolfish as he looked down at her, his fingers finally succeeding as her tank slipped to reveal the smooth, bare flesh of her shoulder blade.

"Someone might see us here," she protested weakly, as hungrily he moved toward her again, the look in his eyes predatory as the desire flared in them.

"Someone might."

"That turns you on, doesn't it? The thought of someone seeing you fuck me?"

"It does." His voice was heavy with lust. Her brain was full of thoughts, should she be offended, why wasn't she offended?

He took her face between his palms, covering her mouth with kisses, and she found herself arching into him, her body responding as if on autopilot to his caress. He wandered down to brush her stiff areola, causing her to moan out with lust as he teased her with knowing fingers, playing her exquisitely, as if she were a violin and he the virtuoso. Then, abruptly, he stopped, pulling back again to regard her, an expression she couldn't quite read etched into his handsome features.

"What is it?" She gasped the words, all too aware of how her uneven breathing gave away the effect he had had on her.

"You see that stile in front of the car?" He gestured to the low wooden fence behind which ran the towpath that lined the riverbank.

"Yes. But I don't understand?" She tilted her head questioningly.

"I want you to do exactly as I ask. Now are you going to be a good girl for me?"

"Yes," she breathed, the anticipation at what he might command of her threatening to consume her. The way he'd spoken those words sent rivers of delicious expectancy coursing down her spine.

"Good girl. Now take your clothes off. Then hold out your arms."

"What? Why?"

"Just do as I say."

She nodded, her hands scrambling to help him undress her, her body arching this way and that to assist him in maneuvering the satin pencil skirt over her hips.

His eyes took her naked form in greedily as she sat there perched in the passenger seat, her legs tucked under her.

"Now, close your eyes and put your arms out straight at the sides."

Obediently she did as he asked. She heard him reach over the seat onto the back of the car, heard a clank of metal, waited, holding her breath.

She felt something hard and long that felt like a metal pole at her back, running across her shoulder blades. Then the click of a metal cuff as one of her wrists were fastened to it, then another click to secure the other, until she was forced to hold her arms outward by the contraption. *What on earth was it?*

"Okay, you can open your eyes now."

"What is this?" She blinked, looking at him.

"It's a yoke. It forces you to hold your arms outward like that and prevents you from moving them."

"Where did you get it from?"

"Oh, I have a few toys I like to use sometimes." The look on his face was darkly exciting.

"Toys?"

"Oh yes. You'll get to play with them all eventually. Maybe I'll even find some new ones."

Oh," she squeaked, unsure of what to say but totally aroused at the possibility of what he was suggesting anyway.

"Now then I want you to get out of the car slowly. I'll help you to your feet. Don't worry. Then I want you to walk over to that stile I showed you over there. Don't turn around, and when you reach it I want you to bend over and close your eyes again."

"But I can't. I'm naked—" She stopped suddenly as he began to shake his head.

"No questions. No protests. You said you were going to do exactly as I asked."

"Ye...yes," she stammered, feeling a hot rush and feeling the blush rise in her cheeks. He was actually serious. He was going to have her walk totally naked to the stile. Anyone passing, a stray dog walker… Anyone could see her.

I should stop this. Why don't I want to stop this?

He hooked his hands under her armpits, helping to maneuver her body around so she could exit the vehicle, as gingerly, she placed one stiletto heel on the gravel pathway for leverage. Once they had her on her feet, she stood there, panting a little and steeling herself for what she had to do.

"Okay, now walk over to the stile. There's a good girl. No turning around. And when you get there, remember to close your eyes."

She walked the few short paces to the stile, the anticipation rising in her as her legs trembled. *Anyone can see. Anyone can see.*

Bending forward and closing her eyes just like he had said, she waited, her breath in her throat. She took a deep breath as the cool night breeze blew against her skin, causing her already-hardened nipples to stiffen even further as she waited for his next instruction.

She heard the click of the car door and the crunch of his boots on gravel and a bolt of pure excitement made her stomach contract, the adrenaline causing her legs to shake as she stood there. Keeping her eyes firmly closed, she felt the anticipation build as she sensed him nearing her, every cell in her primed for his touch. The crunching noise stopped and she could hear the sound of his breathing as he stood at her back but still she didn't dare turn around.

"You *are* a good little submissive at heart, aren't you?" His tone was rich and lightly mocking yet somehow she didn't feel as if he were patronizing her at all. In fact she felt nothing but pure arousal as she stood there, bent over the little wooden stile, willing him to do something, order her, touch her, anything.

Please fuck me. I need you to fuck me. Over and over again. Fuck me and call me a slut again. Please.

"Yes," she said, bobbing her head in answer and waiting, hoping.

"Let see how wet you are," he growled, sliding a finger between her open thighs.

"I'm not." She squeaked as his fingers turned the delicate flesh one way then the other.

"I think you're fibbing."

"I'm not," she gasped again, his fingers unrelenting as they plucked at her. The feeling between her legs was unbearable. She needed him inside her, ached for him to force her legs apart. She felt his thick fingers push deeper into her and she arched her back, parting her thighs wider automatically to allow him more access.

"Oh, look. Your body tells me a different story. Someone *has* been fibbing."

"No, I haven't. I'm not—"

"Sssh," he said, sliding another thick finger in.

Pressing up against her, he planted a soft kiss on the side of her neck, his arm going protectively across her chest as he drew her closer against him, his other hand probing between her legs.

"So," he said, a hint of amusement in his voice, "you mean you're not turned on at all? Want me to stop, do you?" Her stomach dropped at the words. No, she didn't. She really didn't. That was the last thing she wanted. She wanted him to continue, to make her do all the things her body ached do so badly.

"I…" She floundered. His fingers moved farther up inside her, causing her to squirm at the delicious sensations he was causing.

"You just have to say the word, you know," he growled, nibbling her ear and forcing her to bend farther forward so that her exposed and bare ass was by now fully displayed.

"What word?" Her voice came out as barely a whisper and she fervently hoped her desperation wasn't too transparent.

"No." The consonant was short, crisp, and clear, one little word, just one little word. He stroked the hot silk of her, playing and plucking expertly. Waves of lust flared in the very core of her and it was all she could do not to cry out loud with desire. Soon she would be at the point of no return and it scared her slightly to think of relinquishing all control, even as she craved it.

"I-I…" She fumbled again. *No* was the very last word she wanted to say to him right now.

"So you don't really want me to stop at all, do you?" he said, leaning in and tipping her face around gently by the chin. "In fact, I'd wager, being stripped and restrained and ordered to display yourself where anyone might see is actually turning you on."

She bit her lower lip as he regarded her, her cheeks burning with a curious mix of desire and embarrassment.

"Well?" Clearly he expected an answer. Dumbly, she shook her head at him, unable to meet his eyes.

"Say it." He wasn't going to quit. He was going to make her say it.

"No." Her cheeks must have been scarlet with embarrassment now.

"No what?"

"No, I don't want you to stop."

"And?" He arched an eyebrow.

"And, yes, it's turning me on"

"Good girl," he said, releasing his grip on her chin and slapping her exposed ass lightly. The contact the flat of his broad palm made with the tender flesh of her buttocks caused her to gasp and squirm as the sensation stung the delicate skin. Automatically, she pushed her rear out higher, inadvertently wiggling on the thick fingers wedged firmly inside her as she shifted her position from one foot to the other, attempting to calm the prickling sensation. Disturbingly, she felt unbelievably aroused by the slap, and a part of her half-hoped he would do it again.

"Are you asking for another?" The words were provocative, cutting through the cool, evening air.

"No, I'm not," she protested, closing her eyes as she told the lie. He removed the fingers from their position between her thighs and almost immediately her body felt a hollowness, as it needed him to complete her, needed him to feel alive.

"Oh, I think you are. I think you want me to do it."

"I don't, truly." She twisted round to look at him. He was smirking. She knew he didn't believe her. How could he read her so expertly? How did he know what the darkest parts of her, the parts that had never even been explored before, craved?

"No?" He raised a dark eyebrow again, lifting his hand back as if to strike her buttocks again, the movement causing her body to flinch slightly in anticipation, as she arched her back in expectation.

"No," she breathed, almost imperceptibly, though inside her body every sensation was screaming *yes, yes, yes*.

"Okay then," he said, shrugging slightly, and allowing his hand to fall to his side. Almost immediately she felt disappointed, cheated even. Why had he stopped? She hadn't wanted him to. She had wanted him to do it again. How was he so successful at creating a hunger in her that had her begging him to possess her body, begging him to make her do his bidding?

She was so unbelievably turned on now she knew she was close to abandoning all pretense entirely. The sensation of his palm on her bare exposed flesh had released a dam in her. Somehow she *had* to make him do it again.

"I didn't really mind..." She fumbled, the shame of admittance overwhelming her.

"Oh? Really? So you *do* want some more?" The amused tone again, he knew exactly the effect he was having on her, and what's more, he was thoroughly enjoying it. She detected the musk emanating from his pores. He smelled potently of raw sex. She wanted him to take her roughly over the fence right then and there, despite the fact that if anyone came down the lane, their display would be clearly viewable.

The slap landed on the creamy curve of her right buttock, making her cry out suddenly as the blood flooded to the surface, arousing her nerve endings.

"Oh," she gasped, her legs trembling, her sex by now incredibly slick as the moisture pooled there.

"Like that?"

"Yes."

"And again?"

"Yes." She didn't care anymore. She was beyond shame now, so fierce within her was the craving for more, more of this new and utterly compelling sensation.

The third blow struck her slightly between her parted thighs, causing her to jump with a start. She was soaking wet with desire and she needed him inside her more than she'd ever needed anything before.

"Please," she begged, her breath ragged, not really knowing what she was asking for, merely aware that some primal part of her needed him as surely as she needed lungfuls of air to breathe.

She heard a sound as he rummaged for something, in his jacket perhaps. His hard breathing that told her he was on the edge of arousal.

"What is it you're going to do?" she cried, not knowing or caring what, just needing him to act, to do something to quench the raging need inside her that seemed to emanate from her soaking wet sex.

"This," he said simply, and she heard a peculiar swooshing sound a second before the sensation hit. The lash struck her on the fleshy part of her buttock but the blow stung all the same and she yelped out loud into the night.

"Want me to stop now?"

The stinging sensation was spreading across her buttocks and reaching between her legs, turning from pain into a new and strange kind of pleasure. There was no way in hell she wanted him to stop.

"N-no."

He drew back the lash again, swinging it through the air, the second blow harder than the first and causing her to dance with pain. Her flesh burned with the sting of the lash but the physical sensation of pain almost immediately turned into pleasure and the mental eroticism of the situation was doing things to her brain she hadn't even thought possible.

"What about now?"

"No," she yelled, as he whipped her again, her back arching in anticipation of the blow and craving it, so wet was she by what he was doing to her.

She heard the sound of his fly as he unzipped it, the anticipation causing her legs to burn with arousal. Just how much more could she stand of the exquisite torment he was inflicting on her?

"Say please."

"No, I—" She couldn't believe he was making her beg him to strike her? Desperate and aching with desire as she was, she wouldn't. She couldn't do that. Could she?

"Please, whip me again," she gasped, the words falling out of her mouth as if she had no control over them at all. Who was she kidding? She had long ago relinquished all control to him. Her body longed to be a mere tool for his bidding.

"Next time are you going to disobey my instructions?"

"No," she whimpered, shaking her head.

The blow landed almost between her thighs this time, the lash curling around the tender flesh and making her cry out in pain but still her body craved more, craved him.

Embarrassment churned in her stomach but she parted her thighs, baring her sex to him, the expectation hanging in the air causing her heart to pound uncontrollably. She could sense him behind her, the lash hovering above her, the seconds seeming to turn over slowly, as silently she willed him to strike her flesh again.

"Where now?"

"Between my legs," she moaned. The sound of the whip connecting with her tender flesh cut through the night, a much softer blow this time, but pure sensation rippled through her body all the same, causing a moan of pleasure to emanate from her lips.

"Damn it," he growled, bending over her, the strong muscles of his biceps sandwiching her, his palms hungrily pawing her smooth flesh. The bulbous head of his cock thrust up against her wetness and her heart felt like it was going to jump out of the thin frame of her rib cage with the anticipation of wanting him.

"Oh," she cried out as the fat head of it slid inside her, her legs shaking as they parted to accommodate him. He placed a hand on her back, forcing her forward, gently but firmly, the act and the fact she couldn't see his expression only serving to heighten her desire, the sensations between her legs rippling like molten lava as she melted for him.

"Jesus, I want you." He slid in deeper, the swollen length of him probing the very core of her, their bodies answering the other's call, perhaps sensing this might be the very last chance they would have to do so.

He groaned into her hair as she felt his body contract, her own peak following mere seconds later, and as they erupted together, both yielding to pure sensation. As the red-hot shower of pleasure exploded in her brain, she felt as if somehow they were sensing the very truth of each other. Ever since the fire, she had felt so alone, but now, in this moment, she felt so completely connected it was as if something she had been searching for so very long had finally been found.

"I want to remember having you like this forever," he murmured afterward in to her hair, as they both collapsed, still bent over the stile, him on top of her, breathing heavily and holding her tightly to his chest with one strong arm.

She knew what he meant, for she too wanted the night to never pass, wanted nothing more than to stay in his arms half-slumped over the little wooden fence for an eternity.

Chapter Twelve

The next day she awoke to the screech of her alarm clock, set unfeasibly early so she would have plenty time to get ready before the trial. Tearing herself away from the warmth and comfort of Dillon's arms, she shot one last wistful look at his still-sleeping form before planting her feet on the floor and hauling her ass out of the bed.

Her body ached with the pleasures of the night before, and as she twisted her head to examine her ass, she noted with horror the purple welts that were evidence of what she had let him do to her.

I shouldn't want this. So why does it feel so right?

Oh God, what would she do if he lost the trial? Now she'd found him, how on earth could she bear to be without him? She felt slightly guilty about the selfishness of the thought. After all, it was Dillon who was potentially facing the loss of his freedom. Shaking herself out of it, she eased her sore and stiff across the bedroom to her closet, flinging open the white-painted wooden doors.

She looked over the clothes neatly hanging from the rail, up over the shelves where sweaters and swathes of material were neatly stacked, stashed for future use. She'd always had something of an obsession for gorgeous fabric, though she rarely went out shopping. After all, in a relatively small town like Burley, shops and department stores that carried fabric spools were hardly likely to stay open much past sunset.

But she'd picked up the yards of midnight blue luxuriant taffeta when browsing the street market that came to town twice a year, the brightly lit and colored stalls lining the streets of the Falls until almost midnight. She'd not thought about what she'd use it for when she'd purchased it. She'd simply been unable to resist the spools of deep blue fabric as it hung, draped so artfully from the stall's display, but now it would certainly come in handy.

Ahhh, there it was. She plucked the pile of soft material from the middle shelf where it lay, neatly sandwiched between yards of folded black velvet and a soft gray cashmere sweater.

She shook out the folds of fabric, holding it up against her and admiring how the color accentuated her pale complexion. Not that it would be doing much complementing today. Its job was to keep her covered, after all.

She reached above her head to the shelf where she kept the hats she sometimes liked to wear. Plucking down a blue one so dark it was almost a perfect match for the taffeta, she placed the floppy-brimmed headwear on top of the pile of fabric she clutched to her.

Scooping up the spools of material hanging down from her arms, she made her way out of the room, hurrying down the stairs to the little sewing machine she kept stashed in the cupboard under the kitchen sink.

She glanced at her wristwatch and saw she had approximately one hour before she had to wake Dillon. It'd been a long time since she'd made anything at all but she knew she was still good for it. Her fingers would just have to work double time if she wanted to make sure not an inch of sunlight made contact with her flesh for her entrance to the courthouse.

* * * *

They arrived at the courthouse in good time, the green coupe swooping to a halt as Dillon cut the engine. The early-morning sunlight was streaming through the vehicle's windows, the rays cutting sharply through the glass, but today she didn't fear them.

The high-necked black sweater, tight leather pencil skirt, black stockings and long leather gloves plus the black boots, and finally the thick layers of velvet and taffeta she'd carefully sewn around the hat's brim, ensured not an inch of skin would be penetrable by the sun's rays. For extra security she had even donned a pair of black Wayfarers beneath her veil before they'd left her apartment.

Despite the dress code she was forced to wear to protect herself, she wasn't wearing panties, just as he had instructed. She smiled to herself at the irony.

She felt a little warm sitting in the vehicle but that was by far preferable to the inevitable alternative. Unsightly blisters, all over her entire body, plus agonizing pain, and if she didn't manage to get out of the sun fast enough, loss of consciousness, coma and eventually, death.

"Are you okay?" He spoke the words softly, turning to her with a resigned smile, as if to say, well, here we are, guess this is out of our hands now.

She nodded.

"Yeah, I'm all right. Be better when I can take this getup off, though. Wonder what judge will be assigned to our case. Lydia didn't say who it was on the phone this morning?"

"Dunno. Hopefully not one of Commissioner Graythorne's buddies," he said, shrugging, his mouth a grim line. Her heart went out to him. He was acting so casual, but she knew how much the threat of imminent jail time must be affecting him. Reaching across the car, she gave his biceps an affectionate squeeze.

"It'll be okay, you know."

"Yeah, course," he said, still apparently determined to act like the prospect of being incarcerated for the prime years of his life was no big deal to him at all.

"This'll be over before we know it then we'll be laughing about Drago's face as he realized his little plan backfired on him."

"Speak of the devil," Dillon said wryly, indicating out of the window.

Craning her neck to look in the direction he was gesturing in, she saw Drago Graythorne walking into the courthouse, flanked by his usual sulky-looking entourage. Obviously being well connected had helped Drago in his hour of need. His sister must have alerted his cronies to go search for him because the last time she'd seen him, he'd been on his knees in the dusty basement of the cabin with his wrists firmly bound.

"That little punk can't have me beat," Dillon said, shaking his head.

"He won't. I promise," she said, squeezing his arm again. But wouldn't he, really? Drago had some extremely powerful friends, what chance did two relative nobodies have up against the Graythorne juggernaut?

Lydia walked past the window then and Lola waved at her, noting how the lawyer's slim frame was silhouetted neatly in the businesslike gray pencil skirt suit she wore. The blonde woman jumped a little, a startled expression on her face as she spied Lola sitting there, clad head to toe in her inky shroud. Dillon grinned and waved back, reaching over to open the door on the driver's side.

"Good morning, Ms. Lydia," he said, nodding in greeting.

"Morning, Dillon, and err, Lola?" Lydia looked quizzically at Dillon. The grin on his face broadened and he nodded.

"Yeah, don't worry. It's Lola, not some hitman I've hired to take out Drago. She suffers from photosensitivity."

"Oh, I'm sorry." Lydia's eyes were wide with understanding.

"Hey, don't feel bad, I shoulda told you," Lola replied, waving a black gloved hand.

"How long have you...?" Lydia's voice tailed off, as if she were unsure if she had said the wrong thing.

"It's okay, and since I was seventeen. The doctors don't know what brought it on. I've had all the tests. No one seems to have any answers." She shrugged. *Yeah right. I know exactly what brought it on. Lyra.*

"Well, we should all go into court now. The judge will be in her chambers, getting ready to come out," Lydia said, her tone sounding as if she were trying to inject a positive note into the atmosphere.

"Did you say *her*? As in…a female judge?"

Lydia nodded.

"I did and it looks like fairly good news for us actually. Justice Jenny Hogarth, she's got a very good track record, and what's more important, she isn't hand in glove with Commissioner Graythorne."

"That's great news, Lydia. Dillon, isn't that good news?"

No reply. She nudged him with her elbow. He didn't respond, just sitting there staring straight ahead as if he had been hypnotized by something — or someone. Her gaze followed his line of vision, but she couldn't see anything particularly remarkable. The only thing she *could* see was a couple, a dark-haired man and a redheaded woman, about the same age as her and Dillon, walking together arm in arm into the courthouse.

"Dillon?" She nudged him with greater ferocity this time. "Isn't it great about the judge?"

"Uh, what?" he said, looking confused and sitting forward with a start, his focus broken.

"The judge who's going to be presiding over your case. She's not one of Graythorne's cronies. That's good news, right?"

"Oh yeah, I mean…I guess it is," he said, shrugging. He sounded strange, a little defeated somehow, almost like he half expected to lose.

Don't give up now. I need you to fight.

She gave a sigh, shaking her head slightly as she sat back against the coupe's seat cushions.

"Come on. Let's just go in," she said, feeling unsure of just what awaited them inside the imposing red brick courthouse that had overseen every trial held in Burley Falls ever since it had first been built back in the nineteenth century.

* * * *

After waiting outside the courtroom for the judge to prepare for fifteen agonizing minutes, they finally heard the call over the PA system announcing Judge Hogarth was ready.

"Would everyone please enter Courtroom A as Trial One is about to commence," the harsh male voice boomed out over the loudspeaker.

Lola looked at Dillon, trying to gauge his mood, but the expression on his face seemed completely devoid of all emotion.

"Hey, we're up next," she whispered, gently tugging at his arm.

He sighed, taking a breath as though he were steeling himself and she reached up on tiptoe to plant a kiss on his cheek. His bare skin felt so good against her lips she was glad beyond belief she didn't have to wear the thick, stifling veil inside the building. As soon as she was safely inside, she'd thrown it off with gusto, glad to be free of the heavy material.

"Okay, let's go," he said, flatly, his eyes looking unfocused as they stared at nothing in particular. She felt the worry coil tight within her stomach, and silently, she repeated the words that'd been running through her mind all day. *Please let everything go okay. Please let the judge be sympathetic, please.*

"Hey," she said, standing on tiptoe again and reaching up to turn his face so that he had no choice but to look at her directly. He softened as he gazed at her, an affectionate smile curving over his lips.

"It's going to be fine," she murmured, bringing her lips closer to his and closing her eyes to enjoy the sensation, as around them everyone scurried into the courtroom. He began to respond to her, his tongue probing her mouth as if he wanted to claim her right then and there. Surprised by his sudden passion, she felt the arousal stir almost automatically between her thighs.

He broke off the kiss, looking at her fiercely.

"I love you," he whispered, his dark eyes filled with hunger as they searched her own.

Though she thrilled at his words, she found she was unable to respond, although her body longed to, yearned to. How could she lead him on further when he didn't know who he was professing to love? When he had fallen in love with a girl who hid the dark heart of a monster? She remembered the warning words Lyra had uttered just before she had departed.

'Remember, love is not for creatures like us, Lola. We cannot afford to have emotions, lest they lead us to betray ourselves.'

She gave a shiver, trying to squeeze the thought out of her mind.

"You know I'm yours completely," she said simply, opting not to say any more, and he nodded at that as they turned to enter the courtroom, walking hand in hand through the wooden doors of Courtroom A.

* * * *

"Dillon Chambers, defendant, Chambers versus Graythorne, please come to the witness stand," Judge Hogarth said in her clear, matter-of-fact voice, the thin, horn-rimmed eyeglasses she wore looking precariously poised halfway down her slender nose.

"You're up," Lola whispered, giving Dillon's arm an affectionate squeeze, and he nodded, standing up from the hard wooden bench they both perched on and smoothing down his crumpled suit. As he made his way to the witness stand, she sent a silent prayer out to nobody in particular. *Please let everything go well.*

The prosecution lawyer moved predatorily to the witness stand, adjusting the thick sheaf of papers that he clasped between his clawlike fingers and clearing his throat. Judge Hogarth turned to where Dillon stood behind the wooden lectern.

"Are you ready to proceed, Mr. Chambers?" she asked, her gray eyes kind despite her rather imposing bewigged and black-robed exterior. Dillon nodded cursorily and the judge turned back to regard the prosecution lawyer.

"You may proceed, Mr....Venali." She nodded, faltering momentarily as she glanced down at the paperwork on her desk. Venali bobbed his silver-streaked head, walking a few steps closer until his slender six-foot frame was within touching distance of the lectern.

"Mr. Chambers, do you recall your whereabouts on the night of February the twenty-first?" The lawyer spoke plainly, but his voice didn't hide the fact he clearly meant business.

"Yes, sir, I do." Dillon nodded.

"And what exactly *were* you doing on that night, Mr. Chambers?" The question was directed at Dillon but Venali's eyes were fixed on some distance in the midpoint, as if he'd already rehearsed the situation and was primed for what was coming next.

"I spent the night with my girlfriend, sir."

"Your girlfriend. That would be Miss Lola Devereaux. Am I correct in assuming?"

"You are, sir." Dillon bobbed his head.

"And where did you meet Miss Devereaux that night, Mr. Chambers?"

"I met up with her in the club."

"Club Vain? Where Mr. Eversham had visited earlier?" The man's body language was becoming animated. Dillon hesitated a beat then bobbed his dark head again.

"Yeah, but I never saw him there." Dillon paused as Venali raised his hand in objection.

"I didn't ask you whether you saw him. Please try only to answer the questions asked of you, Mr. Chambers."

Dillon nodded sulkily, biting his lower lip and scowling out at Venali from under his dark eyebrows.

"So you met up with Miss Devereaux in the nightclub?"

"Yes, sir."

"And you both spent some time together there? You danced together, talked and enjoyed each other's company?"

"Yes, sir." Dillon appeared to be slightly confused at the man's line of questioning.

Keep it together. Don't fall apart now. All you have to do is tell him what really happened.

"Then Miss Devereaux made her excuses and left you on your own, didn't she?"

"No, it wasn't like that. She was sick. She needed to get some fresh air," Dillon protested.

"Are you sure, Mr. Chambers? You're quite sure Miss Devereaux didn't leave you stranded in the middle of the dance floor so she could enjoy the company of another man? The same man who happened to turn up four hours later in a nearby park dead?"

There was an audible gasp from the courtroom at the obvious implication behind the words. *Keep it together.* She snuck a look at Dillon, the look of anger he wore was plainly etched into his handsome features.

"Look, it didn't happen that way. She didn't leave me stranded for that guy. She went to get some fresh air because she was sick and he must have followed her out there."

"Judge Hogarth, I would like to call another witness to the stand, please?"

Lola gave a little shudder from her position on the cold, hard bench, shooting a worried glance over at Lydia. The blonde woman's face was clearly strained. It was obvious she too was unsure of exactly what direction Venali was taking.

The judge bobbed her bewigged head.

"You may summon your witness, Mr. Venali. Mr. Chambers, please step down from the stand for the moment."

Dillon nodded, turning to make his way down from the box. As he sat back down beside her, she shot him what she hoped was an encouraging smile, but the look on his face was a black one. The lawyer had obviously gotten under his skin. She was just thankful he seemed to be keeping it together so far.

She slipped her hand into his, giving it a demonstrative squeeze as she flicked a glance over at Venali. The gray-haired lawyer wore a smug expression on his face, as if he knew he had something significant up his sleeve, and her heart began to thump with anxiety.

"I'd like to call Miss Michelle Breyan to the stand please, ma'am," the lawyer said with practiced ease, as if he were a circus ringmaster introducing the next act for the audiences' entertainment.

"Very well. Miss Breyan, please make your way to the stand," Judge Hogarth said matter-of-factly, her beady eyes flicking quickly over the assembled courtroom as she tried to discern the source of Venali's next witness.

Lola found herself looking around for the potential witness too, though no one in the courtroom seemed to be getting up. Just then, there was a rustling noise at the back, and a rather curvaceous-looking brunette, clad in a white, figure-hugging, two-piece ensemble stood up. A flash of recognition flickered through Lola's mind as her brain attempted to recall the girl's slightly familiar face.

Where had she seen her before? She peered closer as the girl walked past her, her eyes taking in the brunette locks, the heart-shaped face, the silk suit clinging to those eye-popping curves.

Then it dawned on her. Ms. No-Clothes. Of course, *she'd* been the scantily clad brunette attempting to flirt with Dillon the same night Lola had first met him at Club Vain.

Why on earth had Venali called *her* as a witness?

Venali looked up at the girl as she took the stand, a greasy smile creasing over his sharp features as his steely gray eyes flicked over her.

"Miss Breyan, could you please tell us where you were on the night of February twenty-first?"

The girl thought for the briefest of seconds before nodding her head, her shiny brown ringlets bouncing at the action.

"I went to my friend's house. We got ready to go out. Then we headed out to Club Vain."

Venali nodded thoughtfully. "I see. And approximately what time did you arrive at the club?"

The girl's eyes flicked from left to right as she tried to recall. "We left Freya's around eight-forty-five to walk there—"

"Your friend Freya, I take it she lives close to the club?"

"Just around the corner. We would have got to Vain by nine."

Venali nodded dismissively. "I see. And while you were at the nightclub, do you recall seeing the man who was just previously on the witness stand there?"

The girl's eyes narrowed slightly as she bit her lower lip. "Yeah, I did. We spoke for a while before he went off with someone else," she said, her lip jutting out defiantly. The memory obviously displeased her somewhat.

"And who did he go off with?" The lawyer tilted his head to the side, the gleam in his eyes apparent.

"I didn't know who she was at the time but I've seen her picture in the newspapers since so now I know her name."

"And what is her name?"

"Lola Devereaux."

"So you saw Mr. Chambers go off somewhere with Miss Devereaux at the club, but did you see him again after that?"

"Yes, I did. I saw him twice after that — once on the dance floor dancing with *her*, then I saw her leave him on his own right in the middle of the club. I wondered if he'd said something to displease her because he looked upset, like they'd had an argument or something."

A low murmur rippled around the courtroom.

No, no, no. Lola felt her stomach drop as if she were in an elevator beginning to descend rapidly.

The expression on Venali's face was one of pure victory as he turned to regard the jury.

"Ladies and gentlemen, you heard Miss Breyan's testimony recalling her observing Mr. Chambers, alone and distressed on the dance floor, *after* he had spoken with Miss Devereaux. A statement that appears to somewhat contradict what Mr. Chambers just told us."

Lola shot Lydia a horrified look, but she needn't have worried. The blonde woman was already getting to her feet, gesturing to Judge Hogarth frantically.

"Objection, Your Honor. What the prosecution is implying can't be proven. The witness's testimony doesn't prove Mr. Chamber's state of mind at the time," Lydia said, the set of her mouth determined as she regarded the judge.

"Objection upheld, Ms. Balmain. Would the jury please disregard the statement Mr. Venali just made to this court?"

Too lat. They've already heard it now. But at least the judge had made the point.

Venali shrugged, looking as if he didn't regard Judge Hogarth's decision to be of any great importance.

"Very well, Your Honor. I'd like to recall Mr. Chambers to the stand, please," he said, turning back to the judge.

She nodded for him to proceed, gesturing to where Dillon sat, sandwiched between Lola and Lydia. Lola felt his body tense up beside her and snaked her hand to his well-muscled thigh, giving it a pat through the dark cloth of his suit.

"You'll be okay," she whispered encouragingly, as once again he stood up to take his position at the stand.

Venali shuffled the papers he was clasping before looking up to regard Dillon.

"Mr. Chambers, may I ask, what *was* your state of mind after Miss Devereaux abandoned you on the dance floor?" The question was obviously intended to irk. *Don't let him get to you. Please don't let him get under your skin.*

"I was fine and she didn't leave me abandoned. I told you already, she said she was sick and left me to go to the bathroom." Dillon's face was wreathed in a dark scowl.

"But you didn't believe her, did you, Mr. Chambers? You had your suspicions, didn't you? Understandably perhaps, given Miss Devereaux's somewhat colorful reputation in Burley Falls." The lawyers face was mocking as he taunted Dillon, whose fists were bunched tightly at his sides, the whites of his knuckles bloodless.

"She doesn't have a colorful reputation," he muttered, glaring at Venali.

"Oh? That's not what I've heard but please, do continue. Your state of mind when she left you was?"

"I believed her. Why wouldn't I? We'd only just met. She had no reason to lie to me."

"But you liked her, didn't you? You liked her a lot. And you don't deal with rejection very well at all, do you?"

"What's that supposed to mean?" A confused buzz ran round the courtroom.

"Oh, I think you know exactly what I mean, Mr. Chambers. Now if you will please step down from the stand, I wish to call another witness. Your Honor, may I please summon Mrs. Katy Brandon to the stand?"

"Yes, go ahead, Mr. Venali."

Venali grinned, flashing white teeth as he turned back to face the courtroom. There was a shuffling sound toward the right-hand side of the room as a petite redhead got to her feet and began threading her way past the people seated along the narrow aisles. The girl Dillon had been staring at, the redhead she had seen walking hand in hand with the dark-haired guy outside? What the hell did she have to do with any of this?

Dillon slid back into the seat beside Lola with a heavy plop. She flashed him an encouraging smile but he didn't turn around, staring fixedly ahead instead, eyes firmly on the witness stand, his usually erect shoulders slumped.

"Mrs. Brandon, would you please tell the courtroom how you came to know Mr. Chambers?" Venali said, his thin lips curling in a grotesque smile as he smugly addressed the stand.

Katy Brandon cleared her throat, flicking a glance nervously around the assembled courtroom.

"We dated, for a long time actually. We were engaged to be married."

A hushed murmur of excitement began to build in the small courtroom as people started to whisper. *What?*

"How long were you engaged for, Mrs. Brandon?"

"Two years. We were due to be married August last year back in our hometown a month after we... I...broke off the engagement," she said, swallowing nervously.

"And why did you break off the engagement?"

"Because something happened that scared me." The implication hung in the air and the murmuring fell silent as the entire courtroom seemed to stop in anticipation.

"Was that something Mr. Chambers did, Mrs. Brandon?" Venali raised his eyebrows as he waited for the answer, the delight barely concealed on his swarthy features.

Katy bit her lower lip, chewing it nervously and looking around the room, as if trying to psyche herself up to answer the question. The entire courtroom held its collective breath as an eternity seemed to pass.

"Yes, it was," she said, nodding resignedly. *What?* Lola sat forward in her seat.

"What was it Mr. Chambers did that scared you so much?"

"He tried to attack someone." There was a loud gasp from the people in the courtroom.

"Did he hit you?"

"No." Katy shook her head vehemently. "No, he didn't hit me. He hit Robbie."

"And Robbie is who exactly?"

"Robbie's my husband now. We got married this February." Katy gulped nervously, her hand flying to her slender throat to massage it.

"Why did he attack Robbie? Did he provoke Mr. Chambers in any way?"

"No... Well, perhaps a little but it wasn't intentional. It was—" She stopped, as her cheeks flushed with embarrassment.

"Do go on, Mrs. Brandon."

"Dillon caught Robbie and I together when he came home from work early. Robbie was kissing me in the kitchen."

"So he walked in on the two of you?"

Katy nodded, her cheeks a bright scarlet.

"Yes, but I didn't think he would be home for hours. And Dillon and I had been spending so much time apart because we were both working so hard and Robbie and I seemed to be growing closer. We both worked in the same office. On that day he walked me home after work so I just invited him in for a coffee. I never expected what happened between us to happen, but it did."

"I understand perfectly, Mrs. Brandon. These things happen and I'm sure neither you nor Mr. Brandon intended to hurt anyone's feelings."

Katy looked uncomfortable as she shifted her position from foot to foot.

"No…we didn't. But Dillon didn't take it that way at all. He flew at Robbie. I was screaming at him to get off. I thought he was going to kill him."

The blood began to pound in Lola's ears as an unbearable tightness began to squeeze her temples. Her cheeks blazed as she tried to keep focused on Katy Brandon's words, amid the by-now frenzied clamor of the courtroom. She attempted to meet Dillon's eyes but he just continued to sit there motionless, as if he were somehow separate from the madness erupting around the rest of the room, almost like he was somewhere else entirely.

The judge banged her gavel on the heavy wooden desk in an effort to get the crowd to hush.

"Order, order in the courtroom," she instructed in her thin, reedy nasal tones, as Venali held up a hand to acknowledge his gratitude.

"Thank you, Your Honor." He approached the witness stand once more.

"Mrs. Brandon, please would you tell the courthouse what happened next?"

"I was pulling Dillon by the shirt collar, trying to get him off Robbie. Robbie was under him. He couldn't get away. He's strong, you know, but Dillon's stronger. I had to…"

She paused again.

"Yes, Mrs. Brandon?"

"I had to get a metal skillet and hit Dillon hard over the head with it to make him come to his damn senses."

"You had to hit Mr. Chambers with a skillet to try and get him to stop attacking Mr. Brandon?"

"Yes. Then he just keep shouting at me, saying I was making him crazy and pushing me back against the sofa." The girl's voice broke with genuine emotion as she recalled the moment.

"It's all right if you need to take a moment before you continue, Mrs. Brandon," Venali said, his voice silken with mock concern.

The redhead sniffled, trying to retain her composure.

"It's okay. I'm all right to go on. So I started to really freak out, screaming, begging him to get off me. He was like a wild man, and that look in his eyes… It was like he wasn't human.

"I shoved him off me hard, then he just stopped suddenly. It was as if he was himself again. He just got off me then he kept apologizing, but by then I was so freaked out I didn't want him anywhere near me. I just kept screaming at him to get out and eventually he just left."

Venali stroked his chin thoughtfully. "And when did you next see Mr. Chambers again? Did he try and contact you?"

"He kept calling but I didn't answer. I didn't want to speak to him."

"Did Mr. Chambers leave you alone after that?"

"Yes, he did," she whispered, looking slightly shamefaced.

"Mrs. Brandon, you may step down from the stand now. Thank you. You've been very helpful," Venali said smoothly. The look on his face was one of a man who knew he held the winning ace up his sleeve.

"You see, ladies and gentlemen of the jury, as Mrs. Brandon has testified, Mr. Chambers has previously shown he has a violent disposition when provoked. The defendant is a jealous, possessive man with a penchant for unpredictable outbursts. Is it really too much of a stretch of the imagination to imagine he could be capable of the murder of the man seen leaving the club with the girl he — "

Judge Hogarth interrupted, banging her gavel loudly.

"Objection, Mr. Venali. You're making extremely assumptive statements. Save the speculation for your closing argument please."

"My apologies, Your Honor. I retract my statement immediately," Venali added, bowing courteously to the judge before turning back to face the jury.

"You may dismiss Mr. Venali's statement," the judge instructed, but one glance at the stunned faces of the twelve men and women sitting at the juror's bench told Lola everything she didn't want to know.

Well, they weren't the only ones taken aback by what Katy Brandon had just told the courtroom. Lola's mind was still reeling at the girl's words. Poor Dillon. It must have been so awful to come home and find the girl you loved kissing another man. Her heart went out to him and she turned her head to where he sat.

As if he sensed her eyes on him, he looked up this time, his brown eyes locking hers. The look on his handsome face was heartbreaking. He looked so lost sitting there, and it was all she could do to prevent herself from leaping up and throwing her arms around him. She would have given almost anything in that moment to protect him from what was happening around them.

Judge Hogarth banged on her desk with the gavel again, breaking the moment between them and turning their attention to the front of the courthouse.

"Silence in the courtroom please," the judge demanded, glaring over the rims of her metal-framed glasses as the fervent whispering slowly fell silent.

"Mr. Venali, do you have any further witnesses to call?"

"I do, ma'am. Would Mr. Elgorn please make his way to the stand?" The lawyer smiled, a rictus grin.

Lola's heart sunk. Katy Brandon's testimony had come as a total surprise but this was the moment she had really been dreading. Once the courtroom heard Arthur Elgorn's testimony, it was surely going to be curtains for Dillon's defense.

A burly-looking, bald-headed man seated one row behind the front stood up and strode over to the witness stand. He squared his shoulders as he took his position facing the packed courtroom, his body language aggressive, accusatory even. The white bandage taped to his neck was blindingly obvious to everyone in the room.

"Mr. Elgorn, thank you for coming today. Could you please tell the court your previous association with Mr. Chambers?" Venali's voice was snakelike as he addressed the man.

"He attacked me last week when I was walking home from work. I'd never met the guy before but he did this." Elgorn glared as his fingers flew to the bandage at his neck.

"What did he do exactly, Mr. Elgorn?"

"He came up to me and started yelling at me—just started whaling on me. Jumped me, then sunk his teeth into my neck. Had to use all my strength to get him off me. That dude's got issues."

"You mean to say he attacked you completely unprovoked when you were walking home from work? Where did this attack take place?"

"Bishop's Way. On the path behind the old church."

"I see. And before this evening you'd never met Mr. Chambers before? You had no prior altercations with him?"

Elgorn darted his eyes shiftily around the courtroom. "Nah, never saw him before."

"Very well, Mr. Elgorn. You may step down. That will be all." Venali nodded, looking pleased as he turned to the juror's bench.

"Ladies and gentlemen, I'd like to show you two photographs. The first is a photograph of the wound inflicted on Mr. Elgorn, submitted to this court as Exhibit A. You should each have a copy of it in your files, but in case you do not, please fix your attentions on this."

Venali walked over to where a projector stood by the side of the witness stand, slipping a photograph out from between the sheaves of paper he clutched, and placing it on top of the machine. He flicked a switch, causing the machine to whirr into life, illuminating the whitewashed wall behind it with the image.

A gasp rippled around the room as the graphic image of the injury flashed up on the wall. *Oh God, please no.* As if Elgorn's testimony hadn't been bad enough already.

"As you can see, ladies and gentlemen, this is no mere flesh wound we see pictured here. As the operating surgeon who had to put Mr. Elgorn's neck together has gone on record to state that this was a severe puncture inflicted with the intent to wound."

Lola gulped at the words as she forced her eyes to take in the gory image. She had to admit. It didn't look too savory. It looked like half of Elgorn's neck was hanging off. Was Dillon really capable of doing *that*?

Venali wasn't finished, continuing his appeal to the jury.

"All this done to a man whom Mr. Chambers had never previously met and to whom he had no prior association. Can you imagine what this man might be capable of given a little more motivation?"

She mentally closed her ears, unable to hear any more. Venali's claims, wild as she knew they likely were, sounded way too convincing for her to feel comfortable. Silently she willed him to stop but the lawyer was relentless with his onslaught.

"As we've all heard tonight, from both Mr. Elgorn and Mrs. Brandon's testimonies, Mr. Chambers has a rather different side to his nature than perhaps he would like exposed today. In closing I'd ask to you consider the evidence, evidence that proves categorically that Mr. Chambers is a violent, possessive man with an extremely jealous streak.

"Evidence that shows even when unprovoked he can be irrationally violent, lashing out at an innocent man and causing horrific injuries." The lawyer paused for dramatic effect before delivering his final blow.

"Is it not possible this same man could be guilty of killing the deceased, who had been seen on the night of his death with Mr. Chambers' girlfriend?"

Lola's stomach sunk at the man's bold closing statement, obviously crafted to cause maximum damage. Dillon seemed to bear no reaction to Venali's words, so she slipped a look at Lydia instead, but the blonde lawyer's head was bent as she frantically scribbled down notes.

She squeezed her eyes shut, hoping fervently Lydia had something up her sleeve to counteract Venali's slurs. Otherwise the next time she saw Dillon, he might be behind bars in a maximum security jail and she really didn't think she could bear the thought of that.

Venali turned to Judge Hogarth's bench, a smugly satisfied smile on his face as he whirled around.

"Your Honor," he said, bobbing his head briefly before taking his leave.

Lydia stood up, flashing Lola the briefest of reassuring smiles, but it didn't do much to relieve the waves of nausea she had in her guts as she watched the slim blonde woman mount the stand.

"Your Honor," Lydia addressed the judge, before acknowledging the twelve assorted men and women sitting on the green baize-covered juror's benches with a bob of her neat blonde head.

"You may call your first witness, Ms. Balmain," Judge Hogarth instructed.

"I'd like to call Arthur Elgorn back to the bench, Your Honor," Lydia said, not skipping a beat.

Elgorn? Really? How was calling Arthur Elgorn, the man that had just defamed Dillon to the whole court, going to help the situation? Lola hoped Lydia knew just what she was doing because it sure as hell didn't make any sense to her.

"Mr. Elgorn," Lydia said, after the man had begrudgingly taken his place at the witness stand for the second time, a scowl wreathing his not particularly attractive features. "Mr. Elgorn, could you please tell the court again where you were when you claim Mr. Chambers launched his unprovoked attack on you?"

"I already told that other lawyer. I was on Bishop's Way on my way home from work."

"On Bishop's Way, you say?"

"Yeah...but I don't see what that's gotta do with anything." Elgorn screwed up his face, shooting a suspicious look at Lydia.

Lydia smiled, nodding. "I understand your confusion. Please bear with my line of questioning. Could you now please tell the court your place of work and occupation?"

Elgorn's scowl deepened. "Vanguards Depot. On Poe Lane. But I still don't see what any of this has to do with that son of a bitch attacking me."

Lydia's smile grew wider, and Lola shot a look at Dillon, trying to scan his face to find out more, but there was nothing to be gleaned from the stern set of that impossibly chiseled jaw.

"And if you could tell the court where you live?"

"What the —"

Lydia held up a hand to interrupt. "Please just tell the court the information, Mr. Elgorn."

Elgorn's scowl was an outright glare as he mumbled the answer resentfully. "Cloverfield Heights. Why are you asking me a load of irrelevant details?"

Lydia wasn't just smiling now. She was positively grinning. *What the hell does she have to be so happy about?*

"It's actually a rather important detail, Mr. Elgorn, because after reviewing the details your lawyer was required to submit to the court, I did some research. And I discovered that Poe Lane, where you claim you were walking from, is not only on the opposite side of town to Bishop's Way, but also in the complete other direction that you would need to walk in order to get to your apartment in Cloverfield Heights. How would you explain that exactly, Mr. Elgorn?"

"So I like to walk? A guy can enjoy some fresh air on the way home from a day's hard labor, can't he?" Elgorn looked like he was about to explode with anger, his upper lip quivering in a snarl as he addressed Lydia.

"Of course, but I don't think it was a day's hard labor you were walking home from, was it? In fact, I spoke to your boss, Mr. Cyrell, and he told me on the Thursday you claimed Mr. Chambers attacked you, you called in that very morning to tell him you were too sick to make it in to work."

Elgorn's complexion was ashen but Lydia wasn't stopping.

"*And* I also spoke to the barman who works behind the bar at the Parson's Basin, which coincidence would have it, *is* located conveniently behind Bishop's Way, isn't it, Mr. Elgorn?"

Elgorn refused to look at her. There was no mistaking the triumphant look on Lydia's face.

"He recognized you from a picture I sent to him and told me you visited his establishment not once, but twice, recently — once on the Thursday evening shortly before you claim Mr. Chambers attacked you, and once the evening before. The barman informed me he saw you meeting with Drago Graythorne, whom he saw place a roll of banknotes into your hand. What exactly was Mr. Graythorne paying you for, Mr. Elgorn? Was it to antagonize Mr. Chambers? To draw him into a fight perhaps?"

"Objection, Your Honor! Ms. Balmain cannot be permitted to continue this slanderous line of questioning." Venali stood up indignantly, the spittle frothing at the edges of his thin lips.

Judge Hogarth paused in the middle of polishing her glasses for a second to consider the objection.

"Objection overruled. But please consider this a warning, Ms. Balmain, and do try to refrain from making unproven allegations when questioning your witness in the future."

"Of course, Your Honor," Lydia murmured as smoothly as cream.

"So, Mr. Elgorn? Do you have anything to say about your visit to the Parson's Basin?"

Elgorn shook his head sullenly. "It's lies. You're trying to smear my character to get that son of a bitch off the hook," Elgorn sneered, looking accusatorily at Lydia.

"Would that be the good character that has previously been convicted of violent bodily harm, a crime so serious a judge saw fit to incarcerate you for ten months in a county jail cell? A crime that left your victim needing seven stitches in his right eye and has left him with permanent partial loss of vision?"

Lola didn't even try to stifle her smile as the gasps of the assembled crowd in the small courthouse confirmed what was patently obvious to anyone who had been listening. Lydia had totally destroyed Arthur Elgorn's credibility. Camp Dillon had definitely won this round. But who would win the war?

* * * *

After that, everything seemed to snowball in Camp Dillon's favor. Lydia called Jim to the stand and his testimony and the photographs he'd taken of Drago and the dead man made the whole courtroom erupt once again in outraged gasps.

Even better, what Jim had to tell the court seemed to seriously displease Camp Graythorne. Drago had to be escorted from the courtroom by security after repeatedly ignoring Judge Hogarth's warnings not to interrupt proceedings.

As she sat waiting for Lydia to make her closing argument to the jury, Lola knew all they could do now was be patient and hope. She pressed against Dillon's solid frame and was somewhat comforted when his strong hand reached out to cover her thigh.

Lydia turned to address the jury.

"Ladies and gentlemen, the images I've previously shown and that you all have a copy of in your files place Drago Graythorne with the deceased shortly before his estimated time of death. While they cannot prove definitive guilt—and I would like to stress Mr. Graythorne is *not* the one on trial here—they must surely remove Dillon Chambers as the most likely suspect.

"Testimony from Mr. Cavanagh, as well as previous officially recorded complaints from staff members at the *Burley Chronicle,* have all alluded to Drago Graythorne's propensity to violence and harassment when he doesn't get his way. And while Mr. Chambers' own track record may appear less than perfect, I ask you this.

"Could it not just be possible that a man with powerful friends and powerful connections, seen in the locale with the victim just prior to his death, with good reason to hold a grudge against Mr. Chambers, could have committed this crime?

"And if that is possible, then, ladies and gentlemen, you cannot surely, in all good conscience find Mr. Chambers guilty of this most appalling crime."

Chapter Thirteen

They had filed out of the courtroom and were dispersing into their separate groups, splintering off to reconvene while the jury retired to consider the evidence presented to them. Lola clutched Dillon's hand tightly as he led the way through the maze of corridors in the nineteenth-century courthouse building.

She felt safe with him, so completely protected she never wanted to have to let go of his hand. *But you'll have to, won't you, when he finds out just what you are?*

"In here." Dillon indicated to the open door of a small, windowless waiting room, where a pile of magazines sat atop a low wooden, blue-painted table in the center of the room and several orange plastic chairs were lined up in a row along the wall.

She stepped in and he followed, closing the door behind them with a soft click. Finally the two of them could be alone again.

"Are you okay?" She placed the bag she was carrying on the floor and reached up to him. He'd been so hard to read ever since the trial had started, so distant and far away, and it scared her to see him this way.

"Yeah, just want all this mess to be over, one way or another. But guess I'm gonna get that wish when the jury gives their verdict."

God, could he really be taken away from her in just a few short hours? Could that prospect be possible? She hoped with all her heart not.

"Hey, don't worry. Whatever happens, I'm gonna be just fine," he said, noting her concern. Pulling her head against his chest, he smoothed her hair as his hard frame braced hers.

The smell and feel of his proximity was immediately arousing, and despite the anxiety she felt, she allowed herself to be pulled closer to him as his strong arms encircled her.

By the feel of his hardness pressing against her thigh, her sudden arousal appeared to be reciprocated. His mouth skimmed the top of her head with lazy kisses as his fingers traced a path down her spine, making her shiver with pleasure.

Squeezing her eyelids shut, she pressed even closer to him, enjoying the moment, and forgetting all about the world outside and the twelve men and women sitting in the juror's room.

"I want you to know that I meant what I said outside." His warm voice cut through her erotic reverie.

"Huh?"

"When I said I loved you. I meant it. No matter what happens. I just want you to know that. I need you to know me."

Hot tears stung at her lashes and she blinked them back, swallowing hard.

"I...don't know what to say." A tear fought its way out of its mascara-lashed cage and rolled down her face. Embarrassed she'd allowed herself to be so weak, she reached up to swipe it away quickly with the back of her hand.

He caught her wrist on the way back down, reaching up to brush her cheek gently, tracing the track the silvery tear had left.

"Don't say anything. I know you can't, for whatever reason. But don't deny me the chance to love you."

If only he knew the pain that had dogged her ever since she was seventeen, if only he knew what it was like to lose your whole family — to become an outcast who had to hide in the shadows.

"You don't know me. If you knew me, you wouldn't love me! Not after what I've done, not after what I've become."

She spat the words out angrily, regretting them almost as soon as she'd spoken. A strangled sob escaped her lips as she stared at him, wordlessly, through helpless eyes. He took her by the shoulders firmly, forcing her to look up into those big brown eyes of his, those eyes that shone with so much tenderness for her. How could she do this to him? How could she hurt him this way?

Better to do it now and get it over with before he finds out anyway. It will only hurt him worse when he finds out what a monster you are.

"I'm not who you think I am. I have to tell you—"

She stopped as his finger hushed her.

"I know. It's okay. I already know." He couldn't know. What was he talking about? He obviously didn't understand what she was trying to say.

"No, listen to me, please. When the accident happened that killed my family, I was rescued. But the only reason I survived was because of what Lyra did to me to save me. She was a…" She took a gulp of air, her chest beginning to heave with the strain of the emotional exertion. This was it. This was the moment. He would never look at her in the same way again. How could she bear it?

"Sweetheart you don't have to do this—"

"No. I *do* have to do this. You should know the truth. I should have died back then. It would have been better for everyone if I had." She turned her head away from him, unable to meet the trusting eyes looking at her with so much love. How could she look at him when what she was about to tell him would destroy him?

"Lola—"

"I know it sounds crazy, but I'm not like you. I'm not human. I'm a—"

His lips pressed against hers with urgency, almost throwing her off balance by the sheer force of passion with which he kissed her. She tried to push him away, her hands hammering at his broad chest, but he held her close, seeking her mouth with his tongue, probing, melding with hers. She found her body responding to him, though her brain still screamed at her to get him to recognize the full horror of what she was trying to tell him.

When he'd finished kissing her, he pulled away with a smile in his eyes as he cupped her face.

"I know what you are. You're just like me. It's part of why I love you so much."

She looked up at him still not quite understanding. *What did he just say?*

"No, I'm *not* like you. That's what I'm trying to tell you. I'm not human at all. I was once but not anymore. I'm a vampire, a bloodsucking monster."

Why wasn't he looking at her like she was crazy? Why wasn't he recoiling from her?

He smiled, reaching up to brush her face with a hand again. "I know, silly. That's what *I'm* trying to tell *you*."

"Wh-hat?"

"I know what you are. How could I not? I told you. You're just like me."

Just like him?

"Please. You have to listen to me. I'm being serious. I know it sounds crazy and I know you probably don't believe me, but—"

"Remember that night when we rescued Jim and you collapsed? Because you needed to feed?"

What? How could he have known that? She stared at him, completely stunned by the words coming out of his mouth. Her eyes struggled to focus on his as she scanned his face for some sign that he was playing with her, that this was some bad idea of a joke.

"I knew because I have the same needs you do. The same hunger. The only difference between us is I've found a way to manage mine."

Found a way? Her head was swimming. What was he talking about?

"When I brought you back to my place and gave you something to drink, you remember how good you felt after?"

She nodded, not blinking, her mouth agape.

"That was synthesized blood substitute, something I've been working on for quite a while."

"Wha-what? But I thought you were an engineer?" Her legs felt weak.

He grinned, raking a hand back through his dark hair and smiling wolfishly. "Well, I *am*, of sorts. A biological engineer. I wanted to wait to tell you the truth about me. I had my suspicions about you but I had to confirm them. Then when I saw the way you were eyeing up Jim's neck, I knew."

"You've known all that time? And you didn't say a single word to me?" She stared at him disbelievingly.

"You have to understand. The project I've been working on is secret. I had to be sure...even with you..."

"So everything I know about you is a lie? That stuff you told me about your father wasn't true?" She felt a strange prickle of hurt in the pit of her stomach.

"No, that *was* true, well partly. My father *is* dead. But it wasn't a cardiac arrest that killed him. He died by a vampire's hand, the same vampire that turned me."

"You're really a...vampire?"

"So it seems." His mouth was a hard line but his eyes were tender with understanding as he looked at her.

"But why Burley? Why did you come to Burley Falls?"

His jaw tightened. "Ever since my father died, I'd been wandering around from state to state, searching for answers for others like me, trying to make some sorta sense of it. At times it didn't even feel real. At other times I'd wished with all my heart I'd died that night instead of my father. I couldn't understand why him and not me. He'd been the only one who'd always been there for me ever since my momma died."

"Yeah, I know how you must've felt," she said, nodding with comprehension.

"It didn't seem real at first, especially because I wasn't cursed with being unable to tolerate sunlight. There didn't seem to be anything that made me different from everyone else."

She nodded again. She'd never really understand exactly why she'd been afflicted that way, beyond Lyra's words to her.

"Yeah, I know. Drago isn't photosensitive either," she said, her thoughts darkening as Drago's arrogant face flashed through her mind.

"Yeah, I know all about that little punk."

"You know Drago's a vamp?"

"Well, I'd heard the whispers. And when he tried to frame me after Mr. Eversham died, that was when I definitely knew."

She shuddered, remembering how weak the man had felt in her own arms as she'd drained him. But he'd been alive when she'd left him, hadn't he? It wasn't her fault, was it?

"Dillon, wait. There's more."

"There is?" He raised an eyebrow.

"Yeah, and you need to hear it. The night we met— the night of the murder—I had to feed. It's why I left you in the club. I had to go and feed."

"And did you?"

She lowered her eyes. "Yeah, on Dave Eversham's neck. That's why he was in the park in the first place. He was too weak to stand when I'd finished with him outside Vain, so I had to ask Drago to help me walk him someplace where he could recover. But he was alive when I left him. I swear it. I didn't know Drago would do what he did." Her violet eyes were pleading as she looked at him, hoping desperately for understanding.

"Hey, look, I know you never meant to hurt anyone. I know you needed to feed. I understand the hunger. I was the same before the project. It's okay," he said, his brown eyes full of compassion.

"You were?"

"Yeah, I know all too well what it's like to be taken over by bloodlust."

"The project? How did you...?"

"One night I found myself holding a twenty-one-year-old girl I'd nearly drained of life in my arms. I knew then I had to do something. I couldn't bear what I'd become. It felt monstrous to be preying on others that way."

She blinked back tears, a lump rising in her throat as he spoke. His words echoed her own feelings so perfectly that they made her want to weep with relief. She'd never really discussed how the curse made her feel with any of the other vampires she'd known before, not even Max. It felt strangely freeing to hear Dillon speak now.

"You synthesized blood so you wouldn't have to feed on others anymore?"

He nodded. "Yeah, but not just so *I* wouldn't have to feed anymore. Unlike real blood, the amount you can produce is endless. I plan to launch a feeding station in Burley. Hunt out and find as many of our kind as I can and convince them to sign up, free of charge, so they'll never have to hurt anyone ever again."

"How do you plan to find them all?"

"I don't know, but I sure have to try. I have to do something to live with this thing, something to make sense of my father's death." He jutted out his jaw, the determination written plainly on his features.

"So you never really told me... Why Burley?"

"Ah, yeah. Well, one night I was drinking in a bar with this dude I met in Wisconsin. His girl used to live in Burley and he told me about the rumors surrounding the place, so I decided to come here to see if they were true."

"You came because you heard there were a lot of us here?"

"Mhmm. Then I found out the rumors *were* true, far more than I'd even hoped. So I decided to stay, make this my base. I set up my lab here and started the project to see if I couldn't create some good out of this damned curse."

His voice trailed off as regret clouded his eyes. She was filled with sudden admiration for him, for thinking about how to make some good out of this thing they both had to live with. Impulsively she threw her arms around his neck, squeezing him tightly to her.

She knew he longed with all his heart for the days when he had been human. She knew the regret he felt, as she herself did. She knew too that for both of them those days would never come again. But maybe, just maybe, together they could make some sense of it all — prevent other people from getting hurt.

"I think it's an awesome project. I want to help you. Let me?" She pulled back to look up at him hopefully.

He nodded slowly and began to massage her back in slow circles, the sensation a soothing rhythm as they stood there, locked into each other. She could feel him stiffen against her and as she pulled back slightly, he reached to cup her jaw, drawing her mouth to his and covering it with a kiss.

She responded with an urgency that was hungrier and more passionate than anything she had ever met him with before. What was happening between them now felt darker somehow, and yet so right — forbidden — yet she knew she'd never felt so free. It was as if now there were no boundaries, no limits at all — as though anything could happen. There was no need to hide who she was anymore.

A brief thought that someone might walk in flashed through her mind, but it just as quickly disappeared as their fingers greedily tore clothing, shirt buttons popping to expose smooth flesh.

He broke from the kiss as if remembering something. "I got something for you," he said.

She looked at him curiously as he slipped a hand into his back pocket, pulling out something, as she craned her neck to try to see what it was. The black leather collar he held in his hands was decorated with a plain and simple O suspended from the midsection. To look at it made her feel peculiar, aroused and excited and yet somehow as if everything was finally completely right. She looked at him and he nodded.

"I want you to wear my collar now. Around your neck. For always. Whatever happens."

She nodded, her eyes wet.

"I will. I'll never take it off," she whispered. He unclasped the fastening on the collar, reaching up to encircle her neck with it, then fastened it. The potent symbolism made her body thrill. She was his, truly his now in every way. *His girl. His slut. His goddess.*

"You're mine now, really mine — mine to fuck, mine to pleasure. You belong to me now," he said, his voice thick with want for her.

"Yours," she repeated, and he moved toward her again, his hands reaching for her as her body offered itself up willingly to him.

He hoisted her leg up, roughly pushing up the leather skirt clinging to her tight curves to expose one black-stockinged thigh. She pried out his heavy cock, exposing it, and with a growl he grabbed her by the hips, crudely thrusting into her, her nails clawing at his bare chest as he entered her.

The rhythm of their bodies was frantic as they fused, and as she met his eyes, she found herself trembling with desire, the dark look of primal lust in his brown orbs only fueling her passion to greater heights as she saw just how much he desired her, knew how much he would always desire her.

"You like it rough, don't you, bad girl?" He thrust his cock inside her deeper.

"Yes," she whispered, thrilling at the words, at the sensation. She loved being his bad girl, loved being collared by him. She wanted him to take total control of her body, to submit to him was a feeling so freeing.

"And you know what bad, cock-hungry girls get, don't you?" Another hard thrust.

"No," she said, half moaning and feigning innocence, hoping he'd show her. His answer was to run his hand along her leg, his palm brushing the place where the stocking top met her thigh.

"Take off your stockings and hand them to me," he ordered, his face unflinching. Obediently she peeled the flimsy denier off, placing them in his outstretched hands.

He grasped both of her wrists deftly in one hand, holding them above her head and using his free hand to bind them together.

"They get fucked hard."

"Oh," she gasped when he pushed her thighs apart again, entering her with force. He gripped the denier in one hand, tugging at the knot he'd made lightly to show her who was boss.

"Now tell me how much you want it," he growled, pushing into her deeper as she bit her lower lip, bright red blood running from it. He bent his head to her lips, licking the bright trickle of blood that ran from them as rhythmically he pushed farther inside her, faster and faster, until the whole world seemed to become a hazy blur all around them.

"I want it. Please, I want it," she cried, gripping his lean, muscular frame and pulling him greedily into her as she opened her thighs wide, wider. She knew he liked her to beg for him and she didn't care now how she might sound. She felt as though she could never get enough of him and she'd do whatever it took to have him take her harder.

His hands roamed over her, hungrily pulling her breasts out from the conical black silk brassiere constraining them and bending his head to nip at the stiff pinkness of her areola, torturing and pleasuring her all at the same time.

"You love my cock, don't you?" he said, pulling back a moment and withdrawing most of the pleasure, leaving just the tip of him inside to pique her sensation and make her body beg for more.

"Yes, oh God, I love your fucking cock," she groaned, pulling him deeper into her again, his hips beginning to move faster, faster and faster as he filled her, her own thighs tightening in anticipation as the pleasure thrilled through her.

As their eyes locked and she exploded with sensation, it was as if they understood each other completely — as if they were one person, one mind, the ecstasy erupting through her consciousness and causing her to moan out loud.

Following her peak with a heavy groan of his own, he swooped down to cover her mouth with urgent, desperate kisses, looping his thick fingers through the metal O of the collar and tugging on it as he too found his release inside her.

Afterward as he held her to him, still panting heavily, she could feel his heart pounding loudly against her own. Never had she felt so completely joined to someone before, never had she felt she belonged to another person so completely.

"I love you," she whispered, the words barely audible, even though the only sound in the room was their breathing.

He started in surprise, pulling back to look at her, a smile lighting up his face as he bent his head to kiss her mouth.

There was no point pretending anymore. How could she? She loved this man, body and mind. She had let him collar her, possess her utterly. Why…had he not touched her very soul? There were no barriers between them now. How could there be? There was nothing that could part them, nothing apart from —

Prison. The fear gripped her like an icy tentacle, causing her body to tense up in panic.

"What's the matter?" Dillon looked at her with concern.

"Nothing. I'm just a little nervous about the verdict. I'm sure it will all be fine," she said, trying to dismiss his inquiry, not wanting to show him the terror she really felt.

"Hey, listen to me," he said, taking her gently by the shoulders. "No matter what happens to me, know that I love you. You're my girl. You wear my collar. You'll always be the only one."

"Nothing's going to happen to you, silly." She tried to make the words sound flippant, hoping they didn't belie the raging panic currently surging through her. How could he go to prison? He wouldn't survive. Blood substitute or no, how would he be able to feed? The thought of his incarceration had been bad enough before, but now it was unbearable. *He'll die. He won't be able to survive.*

He pulled her to him again, hugging her tightly and kissing the top of her head.

"Don't worry, sweetheart. It's all going to be fine."

Will it? I hope so. She closed her eyes and leaned against him, allowing the reassuring words to wash over her as she breathed in his scent deeply, hoping fervently the happiness she hadn't known she could ever feel again wouldn't be ripped away from her once more.

Chapter Fourteen

As they filed back into Courtroom A, she clutched Dillon's hand nervously, shooting a cursory glance at the twelve men and women who would by now have decided his fate, as if she might somehow discern something from the expressions on their faces.

No such luck. The dozen jury members all sat with varying expressions of boredom on their faces, as if they couldn't wait to get out of the stuffy courtroom. As they sat down, she flashed an anxious look at Lydia when the blonde woman took her seat, but the lawyer returned her look with a small, thin smile that didn't exactly make her feel any better.

As Judge Hogarth swept into the room looking more than a little bat-like in her big black, wide-sleeved robes, Lola held her breath, squeezing Dillon's hand and enjoying the comforting breadth of it as it enveloped hers. Heat rose in her cheeks as she remembered the feel of him running his palms over her body just a half hour earlier, the memory of him claiming her causing a ripple of desire to surge deep within her. Closing her eyes momentarily, she tried hard not to wonder if their coupling hadn't been the very last chance they would ever have to be together like that.

"Quiet in the courthouse. Trial Chambers versus Eversham will now recommence," the judge announced in her reedy tones, banging sharply down on the desk with her gavel.

The room fell silent, all eyes — including Lola's own — now trained on the juror's bench. Her heart was thundering so loudly she was sure the whole room could hear it. She fully expected Judge Hogarth to bang her gavel again and order her to be quiet, but the judge merely inclined her graying head to the jury instead.

"Ladies and gentlemen, have you come to a verdict?" the judge inquired, as the head juror, a gray-haired and rather nondescript-looking man, got to his feet.

"Your Honor," he acknowledged, bowing to the judge politely, "we have come to a verdict."

"Very good. Then deliver your verdict to this courtroom, please," the judge replied, smiling thinly.

Lola couldn't help but focus on the piece of paper in his right hand as he spoke, and the thundering in her chest seemed to grow louder, the blood roaring deafeningly in her ears. How could that one small piece of paper hold the key to Dillon's future? To her future?

This is it, the moment of truth. Please don't take him away from me. Please don't take him away.

She closed her eyes. She couldn't bear it anymore. She just couldn't bear it.

"Your Honor," the juror said smoothly, "we have found the defendant Dillon Chambers" — he paused to read and her heart felt like it was momentarily suspended from beating—"not guilty of murder in the first degree."

The clamor in the room was immediate, but she struggled to focus her eyes, the room seeming to blur all around her.

What had the man said? Did he say 'not guilty'? Had she misheard? Her head felt woozy like she might black out and she momentarily felt like she had the night they'd rescued Jim.

"Lola. Lola." The voice penetrated her consciousness, forcing her to focus, and she felt a hand on her shoulder, shaking her gently back into awareness.

"We did it, sweetheart. We did it." Dillon was standing over her, peering down at her excitably, a big grin wreathing his handsome features.

"Wha…what?" She forced herself to focus.

"We won. With Lydia's expert help, of course." Dillon grinned, turning conspiratorially to Lydia, who stood beside him smiling.

Was this real or was she dreaming? She pinched her forearm, unable to believe the nightmare of the past few weeks was really over. Nope, she was awake all right. What they were saying had to be real—

Jim bounded up, interrupting her thoughts.

"Congrats, guys." He grinned, clapping a hand on Dillon's back before turning to Lydia. "Another good job done, Lyds." He nodded.

"So it seems," Lydia replied. "But really this case was a stitch-up from the beginning. It should never have gone to trial but obviously *someone* decided they didn't like you, Dillon…"

Lydia paused, her gaze catching on something in the far distance. Lola turned her head to follow Lydia's gaze, her eyes alighting on the open courtroom door, through which a steady stream of people poured forth. Standing to the left of the door, heads bent in what looked to be like quite the intense exchange, were Venali and Drago Graythorne.

"Yeah, someone with powerful friends," Lola murmured in reply as she watched the two of them.

A small shiver ran down her spine as she thought about the influence the Graythornes had in Burley. She knew Drago would be burning with anger that Dillon had walked free and would be desperate to get his revenge. But she didn't want to think about any of that now. Now she wanted to enjoy the verdict and Dillon's freedom. She wished Max could be here to see Dillon's victory, but the bartender was just as photosensitive as she was and two of them arriving at court all bundled up in black garb might have raised even more eyebrows. She'd have to call him as soon as possible and let him know the news, if he hadn't heard it already on the local radio.

Dusk had just fallen, and she knew she could make her way outside now without fear of getting sick. She also knew that outside the courthouse there were likely throngs of reporters. After all, the case wasn't just big in Burley. The mysterious death had made the national news.

Turning to Dillon, she grabbed his hand, reaching up on tiptoe to plant a kiss on his cheek as she whispered to him, a smile curving over her lips.

"Come on, stud. Time for your fifteen minutes of fame. Ready to face the paparazzi with your collared slut, Sir?"

* * * *

As they exited the red brick courthouse, complete pandemonium erupted. Lola had to bring her hand to her face in an effort to shield her eyes from the blinding flash of the continually snapping cameras. A heavy mob of reporters thronged the steps outside, all of them thrusting microphones forward aggressively, firing questions off rapidly.

"Mr. Chambers, do you feel justice has been served or are you angry you were ever suspected in the first place?" A young redheaded reporter thrust his microphone under Dillon's nose as the two of them ventured forward tentatively, meeting the hungry crowd of journalists and other assorted bystanders head-on.

"Umm, I feel relieved, I guess. I've not got to angry yet, but give it time," Dillon wisecracked, a relaxed smile playing over his face. He looked like a huge load had been taken off him, which, she reasoned, it probably had. After all, facing life imprisonment—possibly even death—couldn't be easy. God knows, it had been hard enough on her.

"Do you feel Drago Graythorne should have been on trial in your place?" A sharp-featured blonde woman with hair so perfectly coiffed it looked as if it wouldn't move in a hurricane pushed forward, fixing Dillon with a determined stare, and completely ignoring Lola's presence.

He glanced at Lola, the look in his eyes unsure. They both knew Drago was guilty as sin but was now really the right time to say so? Just then Lydia pushed through the mob thronging the doors, her blonde bob swinging as she confronted the woman with a professional gaze of cool capability.

"Today let's focus on the fact Mr. Chambers has been found not guilty. Justice has prevailed," Lydia said, stepping in smoothly to rescue the situation as Lola found herself breathing a sigh of relief.

"But will charges be pressed against Drago Graythorne based on Mr. Cavanagh's testimony?" The sharp-featured reporter pressed on, obviously unsatisfied with Lydia's answer.

Lydia pressed her lips together as if she'd tasted something sour.

"I feel assured the culprit will be brought to justice in good time, but this is not that day," Lydia said firmly, turning away from the reporter to face the general throng clamoring for attention around the steps of the courthouse.

"I'll be taking any further questions on behalf of Mr. Chambers," she announced as the media surged forward, everyone apparently keen to put his or her particular question to the defense lawyer so instrumental in this most controversial of cases.

Just then a bright flash of blonde hair caught Lola's eye as someone jostled her, and she heard the gathered media erupt in a fresh display of hysteria.

She turned her head, locking eyes almost immediately with Drago, who seemed to be flanked rather protectively by Venali as the pair of them made their way out of the courtroom. So the two of them *had* been hand in glove after all.

"Don't think this is the end of it, Miss Devereaux," Drago whispered obnoxiously as he brushed past her, a sneer plastered on his haughty face.

Aware of the watching media, she tried to remain perfectly composed, even though inside she felt a raging surge of anger. After all, if it had not been for

Drago, Dillon would never have had to go through any of this.

"Don't you think you've made enough threats, Drago? I'd be more concerned with watching my own back if I were you, especially since we all saw where you were on the night — "

"He's over there!"

She heard the shout and looked about confused as the throngs of reporters parted and two police officers pushed their way through the mob. Muscling their way up the steps to where Drago stood, they grabbed him firmly, securing his arms behind his back with cuffs.

"Drago Graythorne, we're arresting you on suspicion of the murder of Mr. David Eversham. You don't have to say anything but anything you do say may count against you in a court of law."

"You can't do this. Don't you know who my father is? He's the Chief Commissioner. He'll have you all fired." Drago was apoplectic with rage and Lola couldn't help but smile as her eyes met Dillon's in shared mirth at the scene unfolding in front of them.

"Sir, you're under suspicion of murder. Your father could be the damn President. The law's still the law," one of the officers said firmly, pushing Drago forward and gripping him by the shoulders as the two policemen frogmarched him down the steps.

The pair of them stood there watching in amazement as the officers steered Drago out through the din of reporters, guiding him swiftly into the marked police vehicle parked outside the courthouse.

Could this day really get any better? First Dillon's acquittal and now she had the satisfaction of seeing Drago Graythorne unceremoniously handcuffed and hauled off for questioning in front of a crowd of hungry media.

Would justice really prevail? She sure hoped it would. She hadn't liked the sinister tone in Drago's voice and if she knew him well enough, which by now she was sure she did, she knew he wasn't going to just let this matter lie. His pride had been insulted, after all. But this was no time to think about any of that.

Turning to Dillon, she squeezed his hand, leaning in to him.

"Wanna get the hell out of here and show me again what bad girl's deserve? I think I might need a little reminder, Sir."

The grin on his face was instant.

"Oh, I know what you deserve."

"Oh?" She raised an eyebrow.

"Mmhmm. Correction, of course. Restraint. Denial. Plenty of teasin'. Oh, and lots and lots of punishment. And kisses in all the right places," he said, his eyes sparkling with naughtiness.

"Best start on my training straight away then because I plan on being very, very bad indeed," she joked, nuzzling into his side as they moved down the steps together, cameras popping frantically all around them.

There would be time enough to think about Drago and his monstrous ego later. Time enough to save the vampires of Burley Fall's immortal souls. Tonight Dillon and she had some serious celebrating to do, vamp style.

About the Author

I'm a thirty-five-year-old London based author and copywriter who harbors a fascination with vampires, fantasy worlds, and all things B-movie. I'm an erotica enthusiast and a fan of classic rock, with an avid interest in Tudor and medieval history. I've a probably unhealthy addiction to virtual reality, and am a self-confessed *Game of Thrones* geek.

Beck Robertson loves to hear from readers. You can find her contact information, website and author biography at http://www.totallybound.com.